And Other Stories

by Emma Bull and Will Shetterly

Cover photo by R. J. Gibson.

"The Princess Who Kicked Butt" by Will Shetterly. *Cricket* (Feb. 1997) and *A Wizard's Dozen*, ed. by Michael Stearns (Harcourt Brace, 1993).

"Oldthings" by Will Shetterly. *Xanadu 2*, ed. Jane Yolen (Tor Books, 1993).

"Brian and the Aliens" by Will Shetterly. *Bruce Coville's Book of Aliens* (Scholastic, 1994).

"Taken He Cannot Be" by Will Shetterly. *Immortal Unicorn,* ed. Peter S. Beagle and Janet Berliner (HarperPrism, 1995).

"Little Red and the Big Bad" by Will Shetterly. *Swan Sister,* edited by edited by Ellen Datlow and Terri Windling. Simon & Schuster, 2003.

"Secret Identity" by Will Shetterly. *A Starfarer's Dozen*, ed. Michael Stearns (Harcourt, 1995).

"The People Who Owned the Bible" by Will Shetterly. His blog, 2004.

"Kasim's Haj" by Will Shetterly.

"The Thief of Dreams" by Will Shetterly. Endicott Studio web site, 2007.

"Black Rock Blues" by Will Shetterly. *The Coyote Road*, ed. by Ellen Datlow and Terri Windling, published by Viking.

"Dream Catcher" by Will Shetterly. *The Armless Maiden*, edited by Terri Windling. Tor Books, April 1995.

"The Princess and the Lord of Night" by Emma Bull. Harcourt, 1994.

"Man of Action" by Emma Bull.

"The Last of John Ringo" by Emma Bull.

"De la Tierra" by Emma Bull. *The Faery Reel: Tales from the Twilight Realm*, ed. Ellen Datlow & Terri Windling, Viking 2004.

"What Used to Be Good Still Is" by Emma Bull. *Firebirds Rising,* ed. Sharyn November, Firebird 2006.

"Joshua Tree" by Emma Bull. *The Green Man* (Ellen Datlow & Terri Windling, editors), Viking.

"Silver or Gold" by Emma Bull. *After the King: Stories in Honor of J.R.R. Tolkien* (Martin H. Greenberg, editor), Tor.

Table of Contents

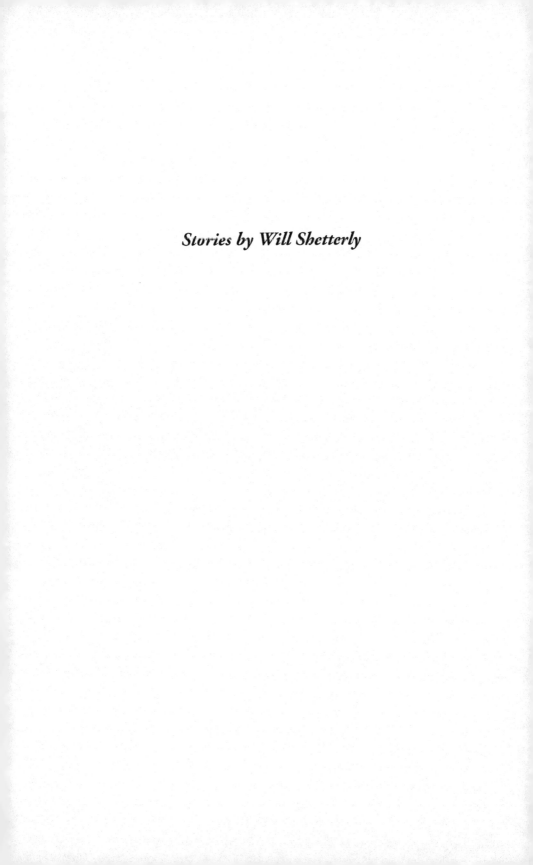

Stories by Will Shetterly

The Princess Who Kicked Butt

Will Shetterly

Once upon a time, there was a land ruled by the King Who Saw Both Sides of Every Question and the Queen Who Cared for Everyone. When their first child was born, the Fairy Who Was Good with Names arrived at the castle in a cloud of smoke and said, "Your daughter shall be known as the Princess Who Kicked Butt."

Before anyone could say another word, the fairy sneezed twice and disappeared. When the smoke had cleared, the king said, "What did the fairy say?"

The queen frowned. "She said, our daughter shall be called, ah, the Princess Who Read Books. I think."

"Hmm," said the king. "I'd rather hoped for the Princess Who Slew Dragons. But reading books is a sign of wisdom, isn't it? It's a fine title."

"I think she'll be happy with it," said the queen.

So the Princess Who Kicked Butt was surrounded with books from her earliest days. She seemed happy to spend her time reading, when she wasn't dancing or riding or running around the kingdom talking with everyone about what they were doing and why.

One day when the princess was older than a girl but younger than a woman, the page hurried into the throne room where the king and queen were playing cards while they waited for some royal duties to do. The princess sat on a nearby windowseat, reading *The Count of Monte Cristo*.

"Your majesties!" the page cried, "the Evil Enchanter of the Eastern Marshes demands to be admitted into your presence!"

"Well, then!" the king said. "Admit him immediately, lest he be angered by the delay."

"At once," said the page.

"Or perhaps," said the king (and the page turned back to face him so quickly that he almost fell over), "we should make the enchanter wait a few minutes, lest he think he can easily sway us to his whims."

"As you wish," said the page.

"Wait, wait," said the king. "Go at once to admit the enchanter. We would not have him think us rude."

"I go," said the page, turning to do so.

"But," said the king (and here the page did trip on the carpet as he turned), "if the enchanter is demanding to be admitted, that's rather rude, isn't it?"

The queen said, "For an evil enchanter, being rude might be the best manners." Then she asked the page, "Have you had enough to eat? If you're dizzy from hunger, we should give you a raise."

"Thank you, Your Majesty," said the page. "I had a raise last week, and I ate an excellent lunch."

The queen nodded. "Be sure you have milk with every meal. Milk builds strong bones."

"I don't think there's anything wrong with his bones, Mama," said the princess, who secretly liked the page.

The king smiled. "If the enchanter's being polite, we should be polite too, and if he's being rude, we'll look better by answering rudeness with civility. Don't dawdle, page. Admit him at once."

"At once," said the page, sprinting for the throne room doors.

"Unless..." The king barely had time to open his mouth before the doors opened again and the page returned. "Your Majesties, I give you the Evil Enchanter of the Eastern Marshes!"

The king smiled at the Evil Enchanter. "Welcome to our castle. Unless you'd rather not be."

"Oh, I'd rather be," said the Evil Enchanter. "Indeed, I feel most welcome to your lands, your people, and your treasure."

"Oh, good," said the king.

"I don't think so, dear," said the queen. "I think he means that he feels welcome to keep our lands, people, and treasure."

"I do," said the Evil Enchanter. "And I shall. My immediate marriage to your daughter followed by Your Majesties' abdication in my favor would be the simplest solution. Oh, and triple the taxes on the people. That would make a fine wedding present."

"Yes, I suppose so," said the king.

4

"Dear!" said the queen.

"—if I intended to permit that," said the king.

"I won't marry him," said the princess, thinking it best to let her father know her position on the matter as soon as possible.

The queen turned to her. "Oh, my poor darling, how cruel of this enchanter! People will suffer, no matter how you choose!"

"It's kind of you to notice," said the Evil Enchanter.

"You're right, my dear," the king told the queen. "We shall decide." He nodded at the princess. "And I say you shall marry this Evil Enchanter, lest he be provoked to further mischief."

"What?" said the princess, the Evil Enchanter, and the page simultaneously.

"But," said the king (and in different ways, the princess, the Evil Enchanter, and the page relaxed), "if we permit this, the enchanter's next demand will surely be even more unforgivable. Therefore, I say you shall not marry him."

"That's your last word?" said the Evil Enchanter.

"It is," said the king.

"Very well." The Evil Enchanter waved his arms once in a broad pass, and he, the king, and the queen disappeared in a cloud of smoke, just as the king said, "Unless—"

The princess and the page stared at the places where the three people had been. "What shall we do, Your Highness?" asked the page.

"Why, I'll rescue them, of course," said the princess.

"I'll accompany you!" cried the page.

The princess said, "Don't be silly. Someone has to run the country while I'm gone." Before the page could reply, the princess strode from the throne room out to the royal stables.

The royal hostler bowed as she said, "I need a horse."

"Of course." He gestured toward a lean midnight black mare. "This is Arrives Yesterday, the fastest horse in the land."

"Won't do," said the princess.

"Of course not," said the royal hostler, stepping to the next stall, which held a broad-shouldered golden stallion. "This is Carries All, the sturdiest horse in the land."

"Won't do," said the princess. She stepped to the next stall, which held a wiry horse with black and white splotches on its gray hide. "And this?"

The hostler swallowed and said, "This is Hates Everything, the angriest horse in the land."

"Perfect," said the princess. And before the hostler could say another word, she saddled Hates Everything and rode out.

The moment they passed through the palace gates, Hates Everything tried every trick that every horse has ever tried to escape from its rider, and then he invented seventeen new tricks, each cleverer than the one before. But the princess held onto Hates Everything's back when he bucked, and she lifted her right leg out of the way when Hates Everything scraped one side against a wall, and she lifted her left leg out of the way when he scraped the other against a tree. She ducked when he ran under a low branch. She jumped off when he flipped head over heels onto his back, and then she jumped right back into the saddle when he stood up again. Finally Hates Everything stood perfectly still in the middle of the road, snorting steam and glaring angrily from side to side.

Two palace guards stood by the gate, watching helplessly. One whispered to the other, "Did the fairy really call her the Princess Who Read Books?"

"Maybe she read a book about riding," said the other guard.

"You're just wasting time," the princess told Hates Everything. "You're not going to get rid of me."

Hates Everything jumped straight up in the air, did a triple somersault, and landed on his feet with the princess still on his back. "You see?" said the princess. "When you carry me to the palace of the Evil Enchanter of the Eastern Marshes, I will set you free."

Hates Everything turned his head to look back at her.

The princess said, "Don't you hate wasting time?"

Hates Everything raced eastward toward the marshes and the palace of the Evil Enchanter.

When they arrived in the Eastern Marshes, a goblin the color of granite stood in front of the Evil Enchanter's gates. He called, "Have you come to marry my master?"

"No," said the princess.

"Then I cannot let you pass," said the goblin. A long sword appeared in his hands.

"Your fly's open," said the princess.

6

"Oh!" said the goblin, dropping the sword and turning away to button up its trousers. Then it turned back. "Wait a minute! I'm a goblin! I don't wear clothes!"

But the princess and Hates Everything had already ridden past the goblin and into the courtyard. "Mama! Papa!" called the princess. "I've come to rescue you!"

The Evil Enchanter appeared in a cloud of smoke. He waved his arms to fan away the fumes, and when he quit coughing, he said, "You've come to rescue no one. Now that you're here, you shall marry me." He waved his arms once, and a priest appeared in a cloud of smoke. After everyone quit coughing, he turned to the priest and said, "Marry me!"

The priest said, "But I don't know you."

"No, no, no!" said the Evil Enchanter. "Marry me to the princess!"

"Oh," said the priest. "That's different."

The princess whispered to Hates Everything, "When we've defeated the enchanter, you'll be free. Don't you hate—"

But Hates Everything had already lunged forward and begun to chase the Evil Enchanter around the courtyard.

"Wait! Stop!" cried the Evil Enchanter. "I can't make a spell if I can't stop to think!"

"That's the idea," said the princess.

"Stop this crazy horse, please!"

"Then free my parents and quit trying to marry me and promise not to bother anyone ever again."

"What!" said the Evil Enchanter in outrage, and then "Ow!" as Hates Everything nipped his buttocks. "It's a deal!"

"On your word of honor as an evil enchanter!"

"Yes! Yes!"

"Very well." The princess leaped down from the saddle. "Hates Everything, you're free to go."

Hates Everything seemed as if he hated having to stop chasing the Evil Enchanter (and he probably did), but he came to the princess and looked at her as if maybe he didn't hate her as much as he hated everything else. The princess removed his saddle and gave him a hug, and he let her do that, even though he clearly hated it. Then he charged away from the enchanter's palace as if he didn't hate anything at all.

The Evil Enchanter said, "You didn't really beat me. The horse beat me."

"Goblin!" The princess yelled, "I'll double your salary if you'll cut off the enchanter's head."

"Good deal!" said the goblin, appearing in the courtyard with its long sword in its hands.

"Wait!" said the Evil Enchanter. "O.K., you beat me fair and square."

"Don't cut off his head," said the princess.

"Darn," said the goblin.

"You can still come and work at our palace," said the princess.

"Good deal," said the goblin.

The Formerly Evil Enchanter waved his arms, and the king, the queen, the goblin, the enchanter, the priest, and the princess all appeared in the throne room where the page was assembling the country's generals to go rescue their missing royal family.

"Papa?" The princess said. "See how well the page managed things while we were gone? Don't you think you should make him a prince and engage him to your daughter?"

"I hadn't—" said the king, but the queen nudged him with her elbow. "Oh, right. That's exactly what I was planning to do. If that's all right with you, young man."

The page smiled shyly, then said, "Yes, Your Majesty, that's very much all right with me."

The Formerly Evil Enchanter said, "What about me?"

The king said, "You can't be engaged to my daughter, too."

The princess said, "That's not what he meant. He meant it gets awfully lonely on the Eastern Marshes." She cupped her hands and yelled, "Fairy Who's Good with Names! Am I really the Princess Who Read Books?"

The fairy appeared in a cloud of smoke. When everyone had quit coughing, she said, "Indeed not! You're the Princess Who Kicked Butt."

"That's more like it," said the princess.

"Oh, my," said the queen.

"Hey," said the Formerly Evil Enchanter to the Fairy Who Was Good with Names. "Nice smoke!"

And then the priest, who still didn't know what was going on but who knew a good opportunity when it presented itself, gave everyone a business card that said, in large print, Marriages Are Our Favorite Business.

And they all lived happily ever after.

Oldthings

Will Shetterly

Jeffy got silver bullets, Jill got a matched pair of big golden crosses, and I got a lousy wooden stake. I sat crosslegged on the floor, looking at this three-foot-long pointed stick, and said, "What's this? A carve-your-own-cane kit?"

Poppa Fred had his sense of humor removed when he was four, I think. He said, "You know what it is, C.T."

Mother Dearest said, "There's a mallet, too."

"Oh, great," I said. When I shifted some wrapping paper, I found a hammer made of polished oak, like the stake.

"Frederick made it himself," Mother Dearest said. "For you."

Poppa Fred looked away like he didn't care.

Jeffy and Jill had collaborated on their presents for everybody: string necklaces with crude wooden crosses set between bulbs of garlic.

"See?" said Jeffy. "It's, like, two-in-one."

"It was my idea," bragged Jill.

"That's great," I said. "You can pick your teeth with the wooden piece, and with that stinky garlic around your neck, you won't have to take a bath ever again."

Jeffy said, "No, C.T., the garlic's s'posed to keep off—" He stopped then 'cause Jill had begun to cry. Mother Dearest hugged her, of course, and made a face at me like I'd said something wrong. Poppa Fred just kept looking away at the window like he could see right through the wooden shutters.

And Grams kept on staring at the fireplace like no one was in the room at all.

I'm not always so grouchy, especially at Krizmiz. It's just that this was the first Krizmiz since Grams's brain went south. I loved her more than anyone, 'cause she'd known so much. Mother Dearest and Poppa

Fred were trying to give us an old-fashioned Krizmiz, but they didn't understand it the way Grams did.

Grams knew the old stories about Krizmiz back before Thingschanged. Then Krizmiz wasn't a day of giving each other secondhand junk or stupid ugly homemade things. Before Thingschanged, Krizmiz was a season of its own. Stores put up decorations three months in advance, and the whole country worked together making wonderful stuff for everyone to buy. And on Krizmiz, everyone in the country got lots and lots of the wonderful stuff, and everyone was happy.

But after Thingschanged, none of the wonderful stuff worked, not the 'lectrical stuff or the mot'rized stuff. People went back to the country, 'cause in the cities, there were riots and fights and folks starving. And it was all made worse 'cause after Thingschanged, the Oldthings returned.

It was a drakla that got Gramper. It would've got us all if Grams hadn't known what to do. There were lots of draklas for a while, men in dark suits and women in soft, shiny dresses, but the worst was when Gramper came back. Grams did what had to be done. She taught us all what to do, before she had her stroke.

Besides draklas, there were witchers, wolf-folk, dusty bandaged people, ghosters, and stiff, slow shufflers with glassy eyes. The safest thing was to stay in at night, so that's what we usually did. If an Oldthing did catch one of us out of doors, we took care of it—the same treatment worked on all of them.

Krizmizeve was a cold, windy night. Jeffy and Jill and I decided to sleep in the living room in front of the fireplace, near Grams. Jeffy and Jill were still mad at me, so they put their blankets on the far side of Grams's cot. It'd been a long day for the twins. They fell asleep almost immediately.

I lay there, watching the fire dying and listening to Grams breathing and wondering if things would ever get better for any of us. I was almost asleep when I heard a clompety sound on the roof like fat eagles had landed. I remembered that draklas and witchers could fly. That woke me up completely. My Krizmiz stake was lying beside me, so I grabbed it and lay there, clutching it in both hands.

And then I felt stupid. We hadn't seen a drakla in two years, or a witcher in near as long. I told myself whatever I heard couldn't be an

Oldthing. And even if it was, all the doors and windows were bolted. Nothing was going to get into our house. I looked at Jeffy and Jill and Grams, and I smiled, thinking I'd have to do something nice for the twins 'cause their stupid garlic crucifixes must've taken a lot of work. And I started to go back to sleep.

The fire was very low, hardly more than cinders, and my eyes were almost closed, but something made me look around again. I prob'ly heard a change in Grams's breathing, but I can't swear to that. I can swear to what happened next, though.

Two heavy black boots oozed out of the fireplace.

I don't know why I didn't scream. Maybe I still didn't believe it. Maybe the Oldthing in the chimney had some power to make people drowzy. I think that was it. I think if I'd been completely asleep, I wouldn't be here to tell this story.

After the black boots came blood-red trousers, and then a matching crimson coat edged with bone-white fur, and finally a bloated, grinning Oldthing stood in front of our fire. It was too fat to have squeezed down our chimney—Jeffy or Jill couldn't have squeezed down that chimney—yet there it was. Its eyes were black beads, and its bloated cheeks were bright red as if it'd fed on something's blood, and in its ash-white beard, its soft mouth twisted into a triumphant leer.

Grams spoke. "Sa? Tah?"

It spun, maybe even more startled than me, and faced her. Grams hadn't talked in months. She sat up in her cot and she smiled madly, and she twitched while she tried to say something to the Oldthing or to the rest of us.

The Oldthing brought a red-gloved finger to its thick lips and grinned. In its other hand, it clutched a sack that'd grown to be as large as the Oldthing itself, maybe larger. It stepped closer toward Grams, still making the gesture for silence. It pointed at Jeffy and Jill, sound asleep, as if Grams should understand.

But I understood then. It didn't matter whether it had something in that sack to deal with us or whether it wanted to stuff us all into the sack to carry us off. Grams had done all she could by speaking. It was up to me now.

I leaped out of bed in my nightdress with my Krizmiz stake ready, and I yelled for all I was worth, "Satan!"

The Lord of Night whirled toward me. Its eyes and its maw gaped in surprise. I plunged the stake towards its heart as it staggered back toward the chimney. The point grazed its chest, but I was too slow. I knew that it'd escape, and return with its servants, and everything would be my fault.

Then it stumbled. Something had struck it in the head. I glanced at the twins's bed, and Jill grinned back One crucifix lay on the floor at the feet of the wounded Oldthing. The other was in Jill's cocked hand, ready to throw.

A shot rang out. The Oldthing stumbled, clutching its leg. I saw Jeffy fumbling to load another silver bullet into his .22, but it didn't matter. He'd given me the time I needed. I hurled myself forward as Grams cried out again.

When Mother Dearest and Poppa Fred came into the room, they saw that they'd given me a fine present. Jill said, "C.T. killed it," and I smiled, shy and proud all at once. Poppa Fred nodded at me. Before he could say anything, we heard a clattering on the roof.

We ran into the yard, all except Grams. A team of antlered deer were launching themselves into the sky, dragging a blood-dark sleigh behind them. Poppa Fred's blast of silver buckshot took out the leader. With it hanging in the traces, the rest were easy targets.

We smoked and ate the stringy little deer, all except the mutated one with a glowing nose. In the Oldthing's sack, we found toys and tools and clothes and all kinds of wonderful things, just perfect for each of us. Since we didn't know who it'd stolen them from, we had to keep them for ourselves.

That would've been the most perfect Krizmiz ever if Grams had lived. We found her in the living room. I find it comforting to know that the last thing she saw was me killing the evilest of the Oldthings.

Before her stroke, Grams had often said that if we survived the bad Oldthings coming back, good Oldthings might follow. I think she was right. Early this spring, when the last of the little deer had been eaten and we were afraid we'd all starve, a giant rabbit with a basket of eggs showed up on our lawn. That gave us meat for a month.

It's a fine new world. I only wish Grams was here to see it.

Brian and the Aliens

Will Shetterly

A boy and his dog were walking in the woods when they saw a space ship land. Two space aliens came out of it. One alien was blue, and one was green, and they were both covered with scales, large red eyes, and long tentacles. Otherwise, there was nothing unusual about them.

The aliens walked into the middle of the clearing and jammed a flag pole into the ground. The flag had strange colors on it that hurt the boy's eyes, and odd lettering that looked like "We got here first. Nyah-nyah."

The boy whispered to his dog, "I'm not scared. You go first."

The dog said, "Rowf! Rowf!"

The boy thought the dog meant, "Yes, you are, you can't fool me." So the boy said, "Am not," and he walked toward the aliens. (What the dog really meant was, "If you'd throw a stick, I'd chew on it until it was soft and slimy, and then I'd bring it back so you could throw it again.")

The blue alien said, "Hello, native person. I am Miglick and this is my partner, Splortch. We have discovered your planet."

"Yep," said the green alien. "We did. It's ours."

"And we name it Miglick Planet," said Miglick.

"Yep," said Splortch. "We do. No, wait! We name it Splortch Planet."

The boy said, "It has a name. It's Earth."

Miglick told Splortch, "Perhaps we should name it for our home. We could call it New Veebilzania."

"Boring!" said Splortch.

"Everybody calls it Earth," said the boy.

"Rowf! Rowf!" said the dog.

Splortch said, "Are these Splortchians trying to tell us something?"

Miglick said, "The little Miglickian said 'Rowf!' I believe that means they'd like to give us all their gold." (What the dog really meant was, "Are these aliens friendly? Do they want to roll in some mud?")

"Um, we don't have any gold to give you," said the boy.

"That's too bad." All of Miglick's eyes squinted. "Then what were you saying, Miglickian?"

"My name's Brian. And I'm a human on Earth. This is Lucky. He's a dog."

"His name's Pry-on," Splortch told Miglick. "He's of the tribe of Splortchians called hummings. This clearing where we landed is called Urp. The littler Splortchian is extremely fortunate. Its tribe are called ducks."

"I know that," said Miglick. "I heard everything the Miglickian said."

"No, you didn't," said Brian. "The entire planet is called Earth. The people who live on it are called humans. My name's Brian, his name's Lucky, and he's a dog. Okay?"

Most of Splortch's eyes squinted in a frown. "Excuse me. If you want to name things, discover your own planet."

"But humans were here first," said Brian.

"Okay," said Miglick. "Whenever we can't think of a better name for something, we'll use the old humming name. Isn't that fair?"

"That's fair," said Splortch, squatting on its tentacles to look at Lucky. "You don't have much to say, do you, fortunate duck?"

Brian said, "Ducks fly. They have wings. Lucky's a dog."

All of Splortch's eyes squinted in a frown. "I understand, Pry-on. I'm not stupid." The alien leaned close to Lucky. "So, where are your wings, fortunate duck?"

Lucky licked Splortch's face.

Miglick said, "I think that means the duck would rather not fly just now, but it is grateful that we discovered Miglick Planet."

Splortch looked at Brian. "You may lick my face, too, Pry-on."

Brian said, "No way!"

Miglick said, "The humming does not think it is worthy to lick your face."

Splortch said, "Ah, modest humming, you are indeed worthy to lick my face."

Brian shook his head. "Excuse me, but I don't want to lick anybody's face."

All of Splortch's eyes opened wide to stare at Brian. "Does that mean you aren't grateful that we discovered your planet?"

"Well," said Brian, "I always knew where it was."

Miglick sighed. "These Miglickians are so unreasonable. And to think I was sorry that they would all have to die."

"Have to what?" said Brian.

"Die," said Splortch. "You breathe oxygen, right?"

"Right," said Brian.

"Okay, then," said Miglick.

"Okay, then, what?" said Brian.

"Okay, then, you'll all die when we replace Earth's oxygen with methane," said Miglick. "Isn't that obvious?"

"Oh, dang," Brian said.

Splortch said, "Veebilzanians breathe methane. We took oxygen-breathing pills when we landed, but they don't last very long. And they taste terrible."

Brian said, "I don't want to seem rude or anything, but why do you have to replace our oxygen with methane?"

Splortch looked at Brian, then shrugged several tentacles and said, "What kind of rest stop would Splortch Planet be if Veebilzanians had to breathe oxygen? Can you imagine being cooped up in a space ship for hours and hours and hours, and finally you come to a planet where you can get out and walk around, and there's no methane to breathe?"

Miglick looked at Splortch. "Inconceivable."

"But Earth isn't a rest stop," said Brian.

"Of course not," said Miglick. "Until we replace the oxygen."

"These Splortchians aren't very smart," said Splortch.

"No," said Miglick. "Well, let's start the methane-making machine."

"Wait!" shouted Brian. "You can't just kill everything on Earth."

"Sure we can." Splortch pointed at a control panel on the side of the space ship. "We just press the red button. That starts the methane-making machine. Presto, Earth's a rest stop, and everyone's happy."

"But what about humans and dogs and everything that's already here?" asked Brian.

Miglick nodded. "The humming's right."

17

Splortch nodded, too. "Well, they won't be happy. They'll be dead."
Splortch extended a tentacle toward the red button.

"Don't do that!" shouted Brian. "It's wrong!"

"It is?" Splortch drew its tentacle back to scratch its head. "It's not
the green button, because that starts—"

"No," said Brian. "It's wrong to kill people."

"Hey, we know that." Miglick reached to press the red button.

"Don't!" shouted Brian. "Humans are people, too!"

"You are?" All of Splortch's eyes opened wide.

Brian nodded.

Splortch said, "Do you speak Veebilzanian?"

"Well, um, no," said Brian.

"Do you worship the great Hoozilgobbler?" said Miglick.

"Um, I don't think so," said Brian.

"You don't have tentacles," said Splortch.

"Well, no," Brian agreed. "But we're still people."

"Hmm," said Miglick. "Do you have space ships that can travel
between the stars?"

"We have space shuttles that can go around the Earth. And humans
went to the moon once."

"Only to your moon?" Miglick laughed. "That's not a space ship.
That's a space raft."

"We're really people," said Brian. "If you got to know us, you'd
see."

Splortch and Miglick glanced at each other. Miglick said, "This
planet would make such a nice rest stop."

"True," said Splortch. "But hummings and ducks might be people."

"Quite right," said Miglick. "We'll have to find out."

"Whew!" said Brian, thinking the aliens would become someone
else's problem now.

"Rowf!" Lucky said. (What Lucky meant was, "Does anyone want
to go home and see if there's any brown glop in my food bowl? If there
is, we can all get down on the floor and eat together.")

Splortch said, "You two Splortchians stand over there. We'd like to
take your image."

"Our picture?" said Brian.

"I guess so," said Splortch.

Brian shrugged and led Lucky under a tree, where he stood looking at Splortch and Miglick, who were standing in front of the space ship. Miglick said, "Perfect," and Brian smiled as the alien pressed a green button on the control panel.

In the next instant, Brian was looking at a boy who looked exactly like himself and a dog who looked exactly like Lucky. The blue alien was standing beside Brian, and the green alien was missing. The tree was behind the boy and the dog, and the space ship was behind Brian and the blue alien.

Brian said, "Hey! What happened?"

The blue alien said, "Rowf! Rowf!"

Brian raised a green tentacle to scratch his head, and then he stared at the tentacle.

The dog said, "Ret's go, Sprortch. And you two hummings, be carefur in our bodies."

"Don't press any buttons while we're gone," said the boy. "You don't want to start the methane machine until we're back."

Brian stared, then shook his tentacles in frustration.

"Rowf!" The blue alien rubbed its head against Brian's tentacles until Brian patted it. "Rowf!"

"Rots o' things smell grr-reat!" said the dog.

"Come on, Miglick," said the boy. "The sooner we prove hummings aren't really people, the sooner we can start the methane-making machine."

"Rokay! See you rater!" The dog ran ahead of the boy to get a good whiff of a dead skunk. "Yo! That's grr-reat!"

"Dang!" Brian stomped his tentacles twice, and then he squatted and told the blue alien beside him, "It's okay, Lucky. We'll fix this. Um, somehow."

Just then, a woman behind him said, "All right, who's making a monster movie?"

Brian turned around. A tall police officer stood at the edge of the clearing with her hand on her holstered pistol.

Brian said, "I'm not a monster, I'm a space traveler. I mean, I'm a kid, and this is my dog. No one's making a movie. Can you help?"

The police officer cocked her head to one side, then called, "Jack, what do you think?"

A fat police officer came out of the woods and walked toward the space ship. He stared at it and said, "I think I don't know what I think, Sarge."

"It's simple," said Brian. "Only I can't explain it. And there's not time to try, 'cause we have to save Earth right away!"

"You're a kid?" The policewoman moved her hand away from her pistol and scratched her head.

"Sure," said Brian. "The aliens switched bodies with us by pushing that green button." He pointed at it with a tentacle.

"This one?" the policeman asked. And he pressed the green button.

•

Meanwhile, the alien who looked like Lucky and the alien who looked like Brian walked out of the woods. A girl called, "Brian!"

"Herro," said the dog.

"No, I think I'm Pry-on," said the boy. He called to the girl, "Who are you, humming from Urp?"

"What's the game?" said the girl.

"There's no game," said the boy. "I'm Splortch. This is Miglick. We're from Veebilzania. We must decide whether we should kill everyone on your planet by turning it into a rest stop for space travelers."

The dog nodded in agreement.

"Okay," said the girl. "I'm Captain Brandi of the Starship Enterprise."

"Glad to meet you, Captain Pran-dee."

The girl said, "I've got your space ship locked in a tractor beam. You have to leave Earth alone, or I'll blow up your ship with my photon torpedoes."

"Oh, oh!" said the dog.

The girl said, "Is Lucky okay?"

The boy said, "Um, we have to go now."

"No way," said the girl. "Or I'll blow up your ship. Besides, Mom said you have to come in for lunch."

The boy said, "These Urp creatures are more clever than we suspected. Maybe they really are people."

"I don' know," said the dog.

20

The girl patted the dog's head. "Poor Lucky. Did you eat something you shouldn't have?"

A woman stepped out of a house and called, "Brian! Brandi! Lunch is ready!"

"Coming, Mom!" The girl grabbed the boy's hand and tugged him toward the woman's house. The dog stared at them, then back at the woods, and then followed the girl and the boy inside.

At the kitchen table, the girl sat in one chair, so the boy sat in another. The dog jumped into a third. The Mom looked at the dog and said, "Down, Lucky!"

"But he's hungry," said the boy.

"He has food." The Mom pointed at Lucky's dish, which was full of brown mush.

"Good!" said the dog as it jumped down.

"Lucky sure sounds strange," said the Mom.

"He can't speak as well as I can," said the boy. "And he can't pick up things in his hands." The boy pointed at his thumb. "I think it's because hummings have this special finger, and ducks don't. Tentacles are far more practical. And far more attractive."

The girl and the Mom laughed. The girl said, "Brian's a space alien. I always knew it."

The boy nodded proudly. "I am Splortch from Veebilzania. That is Miglick, my partner."

"Herro," said the dog, looking up from his dish.

"How do you like the duck food?" asked the boy.

"Good!" said the dog.

The Mom asked, "How'd you train Lucky to bark like that?"

"He di'n't," said the dog.

"I didn't," said the boy. "We learned your language from your television broadcasts."

The Mom put her hand on the boy's forehead. "I think you've been watching too much television, mister. Do you feel all right?"

Before the boy could answer, someone pressed the door buzzer. "I'll get it!" the girl said.

"Oh," said the boy in relief. "That's not the sound of you hummings blowing up our space ship?"

The girl opened the front door, then said, "Mom? It's the police."

21

"No, it's not." A fat policeman walked into the room. "It's me, Brian."

"Rowf," said a tall policewoman, trotting in after the policeman.

"Oh, oh," said the boy.

"Ro, ro," said the dog.

"Mom!" said the policeman, pointing at the boy and the dog. "They're aliens and they want to kill everyone on Earth. We have to stop them!"

As the policewoman ran toward the dog dish, the policeman called, "Lucky! Come back here!" The policewoman barked sadly and returned to the policeman's side.

The Mom looked from the two police officers to the boy and the dog.

"It's me, really!" the policeman said. "The aliens switched bodies with Lucky and me. And when the police showed up, I got put into the policeman's body by mistake."

"That is not true," said the boy. "I'm Pry-on the humming, not Splortch from Veebilzania." He pointed at the dog. "This is a fortunate duck, not my partner Miglick. Send away those hummings in blue clothing and let us stay with you until we decide whether you're really people."

The Mom stared at the boy.

The boy added, "Please?"

"Brian?" the Mom asked the boy. "The joke's over now, understand?"

"It's not a joke!" said the policeman. "If you don't believe me, they'll turn all the oxygen into methane, and everyone will die!"

"Yes, they're playing a joke!" said the boy. "But not me! I'm really Pry-on! Make the joking people go away!"

The Mom said, "This isn't funny, Brian." She turned toward the police officers. "And you two should be ashamed of yourselves, playing some game like this—"

The policewoman whimpered. The policeman said, "Oh, dang."

The girl pointed at the policeman. "Mom, that's Brian."

The woman stared at the boy. "Then who're you?"

"Oh, all right," said the boy, sighing. "I'm Splortch. I traded bodies with Pry-on."

The dog said, "But where are our real bodies?"

"Right here," said someone at the door.

"Hey, great!" said Brandi. "Space aliens!"

The green alien pointed a tentacle at the policewoman, who was hiding behind the policeman. "Just don't let me eat dog food, okay?"

"Don't worry, Sergeant," said the policeman. "Lucky does everything I tell him to. Except when he doesn't."

At that moment, a man in cowboy boots walked in the front door and stared at the two aliens, the two police officers, the two children, the dog, and the Mom.

"Dad!" the policeman yelled, wrapping his arms around the surprised man and giving him a big hug. "You're home early!"

"Uh—" began the Dad.

"Roo's he?" said the dog.

The policewoman started drinking water out of Lucky's water dish.

The boy said, "Please tell Captain Pran-dee not to destroy our space ship. We could put our rest stop on another planet."

"I—" began the Dad.

"Do you live here?" said the blue alien. "Or are you another space alien?"

"Um—" began the Dad.

"Everything's under control," the green alien said. "But your son promised he wouldn't let me drink out of the dog dish, and look at me now." The alien pointed a tentacle at the policewoman, who was happily lapping up water from the dog dish.

"Oh, sorry." The policeman released the very confused Dad and called, "Lucky! Stop that." The policewoman looked up from the dog dish, then ran over and crouched beside the policeman.

The Dad said, "If I go outside and come back in again, will this make sense?"

"I doubt it," said the Mom. "But if it works, I'll try it too."

"We only saw your television broadcasts," said the boy. "We didn't know you were intelligent beings."

"Rat's right," said the dog. "We won't take away your grr-oxygen now."

The girl gave the Dad a hug. "Isn't this great? Everyone's in the wrong bodies, except for us!"

The blue alien said, "Sarge, I sure hope you'll write the report on this case," and then coughed.

The green alien nodded, said, "Maybe we should say we fell asl—" and then coughed, too.

The Dad scratched his head. "This is one of those TV shows where they trick people, right?"

"No time to explain, Dad!" said the policeman, running outside with the policewoman following behind him. "C'mon, everybody!"

"Hey, our bodies!" cried the space aliens, running after the police officers.

"Hey, our bodies!" cried the boy and the dog, running after the aliens.

"Hey, Brian and Lucky!" cried the Dad, running after the boy and the dog.

"Hey, Dad!" cried the girl, running after the Dad.

"Hey, everybody!" cried the Mom, not running after anyone. "Who's going to explain what's going on?"

"Not now, Mom!" said the policeman, stopping for a moment at the edge of the woods. "The aliens said their oxygen pills don't last very long!"

"Rat's right!" said the dog. "Grr-I forgot!"

"What oxygen breathing pills?" said the blue alien.

"I don't like the sound of this," said the green alien, and then it coughed again.

"Hurry!" said the girl, grabbing her Mom's hand to lead her into the woods.

The Dad looked up into the trees as they ran. "They sure hide the video cameras well."

Just as everyone entered the clearing where the space ship stood, the two aliens fell on the ground and began gasping desperately. The dog pressed a purple button on the space ship's control panel, and two small yellow pills popped out. The dog gave them to the aliens. As soon as the aliens popped them into their mouths, they quit coughing.

After Splortch and Miglick used their machine to put everyone back into their proper bodies, Splortch said, "Thank you for not destroying our ship, Captain Pran-dee."

The girl shrugged. "Oh, that's all right."

Splortch said, "And thank you for remembering about the oxygen pills, Pry-on. You saved us from having to live the rest of our lives as hideous freaks. Um, nothing personal."

"I kind of liked being a duck," said Miglick.

"I kind of like being alive," said the policewoman. "You did good, kid."

Brian blushed and shrugged. "That's all right."

Splortch said, "After we build a rest stop on Pluto, you all have to come and visit us."

"That'd be nice," said the Mom.

"And bring some of that good duck food," called Miglick as the space ship's door closed behind him.

"Goodbye!" everyone shouted as the space ship took off. After it disappeared in the sky, the Dad said, "They use very long wires and a really big mirror, right?"

"Let's go finish our lunch," said the Mom.

Brian patted Lucky's head. "Glad to be a dog again?"

Lucky licked Brian's face and said "Rowf! Rowf!" And everyone knew that meant "yes!" (Though it really meant, "You smell that dead skunk? Let's all go roll on it!")

Taken He Cannot Be

Will Shetterly

Things die. This is the lesson that everyone learns. Some do not learn it until the instant before death, but we all learn it. We pass our final exam by dying. Dr. John Henry Holliday earned his diploma from the school of life at a younger age than most. At twenty, he had been told that consumption would kill him in six months, yet at thirty, he still lingered around the campus. He supposed he was a tenured professor of death, which made him laugh, which made him cough, which made him think about the man they had come to meet, and kill.

He rode through the midsummer heat beside his best friend, Wyatt Berry Stapp Earp. They had both grown beards to disguise themselves, and they had dressed like cowboys instead of townsmen. No one who saw them pass at a distance would recognize the dentist-turned-gambler or Tombstone's former deputy sheriff, both wanted in Arizona on charges of murder.

They rode to kill John Ringgold, better known as Johnny Ringo. Wyatt had said that Wells Fargo would pay for Ringo's demise, and Doc had always believed in being paid to do what you would do cheerfully for free. He did not know or care how much Wells Fargo might pay. He was not sure whether Wells Fargo had made an offer, or Wyatt had merely assumed the coach line would show its gratitude for the death of the last leader of the Clanton gang. Doc knew Wyatt had asked him to come kill Johnny Ringo, and that sufficed. Had anyone asked him why he agreed, he would have said he had no prior engagements. The only person who might have asked would have been Big Nose Kate Elder, and she had left him long ago.

•

The brown hills stirred frequently as they rode. The two riders always looked at motion—in a land where bandits waited for their piece of wealth from the booming silver mines, you always looked. They never expected more than sunlight on quartz, or dust in a hot puff of wind, or a lizard darting for food or shelter. Vision was simultaneously more powerful and less trustworthy in this dry land. The eye saw far in the parched atmosphere, but it did not always see truthfully.

The unicorn showed itself on a rise. Doc never thought that it might be a wild horse. Though it was the size of a horse, it did not move like a horse, and he had never seen a horse with such white, shaggy fur, and that long, dark spear of its horn left no doubt, at least not in a person who lived by assessing situations instantly, then acting.

Doc acted by not acting: he did not flinch or blink or gasp or look away in order to look back. If this apparition was his private fantasm, he would not trouble Wyatt with its existence. If it was not, Wyatt would say something.

And Wyatt did. "Doc?"

"Eh?"

"What's that critter?"

"Unicorn."

"Eh."

They rode for another minute or two. The unicorn remained on the ridge. Its head moved slightly to follow them as they passed.

Wyatt said, "What's a unicorn?"

"In Araby they call it cartajan. Means 'lord of the desert.'"

"I can see that."

"'The cruelest is the unicorn, a monster that belloweth horribly, bodied like a horse, footed like an elephant, tailed like a swine, and headed like a stag. His horn sticketh out of the midst of his forehead, of a wonderful brightness about four foot long, so sharp, that whatsoever he pusheth at, he striketh it through easily. He is never caught alive; killed he may be, but taken he cannot be.'"

"Huh. Shakespeare or the Bible?"

"Some old-time Roman named Solinus, translated by some old-time Englishman who might've supped with Master Will and King Jim."

"I ain't never seen no unicorn before."

"Nor yet. That's a mirage. A will o' the wisp. The product of a fevered brain."

"I reckon you're contagious, then."

Doc laughed, then coughed, then said, "Well, ain't no one known to've seen one before. Not for sure. All that's written down is travellers' tales, 'bout things they heard but never saw."

"We're the first to spot one?"

"In centuries. Far as I know."

"What do you think a circus'd pay for a critter like that?"

Doc laughed and coughed again. "Have to catch it first. It being a bastard of the mind, I reckon it'd race as fleet as a thought."

"Faster'n horses?"

"S'posed to be."

"We could corner it in a box canyon, maybe."

"That horn ain't s'posed to be for decoration."

"Animal worth anything dead?"

"Depends on the buyer."

"Could stuff and stand it in a penny arcade. I seen a mermaid once. Looked like a monkey and a fish sewed together, but you got to admit, a sight like that's worth a penny."

"At least." Doc was rarely reluctant to tell anything to Wyatt, but he hesitated before he finally said, "Horn's s'posed to cure most sicknesses." He coughed. "Turn the horn into a drinking cup, and it takes the power out of poison. You can smear its blood on a wound, and the wound'll heal right up. Some say its whole body's magical. You're s'posed to eat its liver for something, but I forget what. There's folks who say it can make you young again, or live forever, or raise the dead."

"Any o' that true?"

Doc shrugged. "Three minutes ago, I would'a' said it was all proof a lie lives longer than a liar. Now I'm not so sure."

"Let's find out." Wyatt drew on the reins. As his horse halted, he dropped to the ground and pulled his rifle from its boot on his saddle.

Doc said, "Ain't neither of us sharpshooters. One miss'd scare it off for good."

Wyatt paused with the rifle butt at his shoulder. "You all right, Doc? Ain't like you to pass on an opportunity set before you."

"I do make some note of the odds, Wyatt. Leastways, when I'm anything like sober."

29

"Mmm. Your old Roman said they could be killed. There a trick to it?"

Doc considered the answers, and thought of Kate, and said, "We ain't got the means."

"Hell." Wyatt spoke with no particular emphasis. "Then there's no reason not to try what we got, is there?"

"No." Doc whipped his short-barrel Colt from its holster and fired in the general direction of the unicorn. It seemed to study him with disappointment while the sound of the shot hung in the hot, clean air. Then it danced aside as Wyatt's shot followed Doc's, and it tossed its mane and its horn in something uncannily like a laugh before it skipped back behind the rise.

"Damn it, Doc, if you'd'a' waited till we could'a' both took aim with rifles—"

"Why, sure, Wyatt. I reckon I could'a' taken me a nap, and once you had ever'thing to your liking, I'd'a' risen well-rested to shoot ever so nicely, and we'd now be arguing whether unicorn liver'd taste best by itself or with a big plate o' beans."

Wyatt stared at him, then said grimly, "With beans," and slid his rifle back into its boot.

Doc laughed and coughed and holstered his Colt. Then he let his surprise show on his face. The unicorn watched them from the next rise. Wyatt swung back onto his horse, looked toward the unicorn, then looked toward Doc, who said, "It sure is pretty."

He did not expect Wyatt to answer that. Wyatt did not surprise him. The unicorn studied them as they rode by. When they had left sight of it, it appeared again on a further ridge that paralleled their ride.

Wyatt said, "If we could lure it in close, we'd plug it for sure."

"Mmm," Doc said, and then, "Maybe we should let Ringo live."

"Eh?"

"Ain't like he was one o' the ones who killed Morg."

"He stood by 'em. He planned it with Curly Bill. He was in on the attack on Virge."

"That ain't proven."

"Is to my satisfaction."

Doc laughed, said, "Hell, Wyatt, we'd have to kill half of Tombstone to get everyone who stood by the Clantons," then coughed.

When he lifted his head again, Wyatt was watching him like the unicorn had, with cool speculation. Doc wiped his mouth with the back of his hand and smiled. Wyatt said, "All right."

"All right, what?"

"All right, Ringo don't need to die. 'Less he insists on it."

"How so?"

Wyatt smiled. "Like I said. Depends on him."

Doc nodded, and they rode on. The sands stayed a steady white-hot glare, and the sky continued to leach moisture from their skin and their lungs. The unicorn accompanied them, always at a distance. Each time it disappeared, they thought it had abandoned them, but it always appeared again at a new, improbable vantage where only the most accurate marksman might take it.

Fred Dodge had said Ringo was on a drunk and camping in a canyon in the Chiricahuas. Both of these things turned out to be true. Near a creek in the shade of a boulder, they found him reading aloud from the Iliad with an empty bottle and a pair of boots beside him. His out-stretched feet were wrapped in strips of light cotton. He looked up as they rode near and switched from Greek to English to say, "Achilles and Patroclus, welcome."

"Hell, you are drunk if you don't recognize us," said Wyatt.

"Who you think you're playing?" said Doc. "Hardly Odysseus. Poor Hector? Brash Paris? The accommodating Panderus, perhaps?"

Ringo lifted his right arm from beside his body to show them his . 45. "Anybody I damn well please. That's a good one, you two whoremasters calling names."

Wyatt said, "Doc, I forget. Why'd you want to warn him?"

"Seemed a fair notion at the time." Doc turned to Ringo. "You began the exchange of pleasantries, my Johnnie-O."

"Oh, all right, all right." Ringo waved the matter away in a broad circle with his Colt, then rose unsteadily to his feet. "So. To what do I owe the honor of this visit?"

Wyatt said, "Wells Fargo wants you dead."

"Wells Fargo?" Ringo drew himself erect and stated, precisely and indignantly, "I am a rustler, not a highwayman."

"It's the price of fame," Doc said. "A few hold-ups, they ask who's like to've masterminded 'em, and your name's sitting at the top of the heap."

31

Ringo blinked. "So why'd you two come in talkin' instead o' shootin'?"

Wyatt said, "Ask Doc."

Doc worked his lips and wondered at the impulse that had brought them under the gunsight of the man they had hunted. He said simply, "There's been a lot o' killin'. Mind if I water my horse?"

Ringo waved again. The weapon in his hand did not seem to be any more significant to him than a teacher's baton. Doc swung down from his horse, and so did Wyatt. Doc said, "I'll take yours," and led both horses toward the creek.

Ringo said, "So, I'm to infer you take no interest in the blood money?"

Wyatt said, "Why would you do that? We're hardly gonna let that money go to waste, not after we crossed back into Arizona."

"Hmm," said Ringo. He brought the barrel of his pistol to scratch his moustache, and Doc, moving toward the creek with his horse, wondered if the cowboy would shoot off his nose. "So, you're not after me, but you are after the reward on me. Am I to lie very still for several days? If you kept a bottle of good whiskey near my coffin, I might manage."

Doc squatted upstream from the horses to splash a handful of water against his face. As he lifted a second handful to drink, he saw the unicorn walking toward him.

Wyatt and Ringo were only a few yards away, talking about money and death. Boulders and brush gave Doc and the unicorn some privacy. The horses noted the creature, but they continued to drink without a sound of fear or greeting.

The unicorn paused on the far side of the creek. It raised its head to taste the air. Its horn could impale or eviscerate buffalo, but if there was any meaning in the lift of the horn, it was a salute.

Wyatt was telling Ringo, "We'd meet in Colorado after they paid us. We'd give you your third, and you could go to Mexico or hell, for all we cared. Everyone'd be happy. You're gettin' a little too well known to keep on in these parts as Ringo, you know."

"How would I trust you?"

Wyatt made a sound like a laugh. "How would we trust you? Our reputation with Wells Fargo will hang on you stayin' dead once we said you was."

"Huh," said Ringo, and then he laughed. "Hell, I ain't been dead before. Why not?"

The unicorn, if it heard the speakers, ignored them. It stepped into the creek. At the splash of its hoof, Ringo said, "What's—"

Doc heard them, but he kept his eyes on the unicorn, suspecting that now, if he looked away, he would never see it again. He thought of Big Nose Kate, and how she had cared for him, and he wondered if she had known any man who could not be said to have failed her.

Wyatt said, "Hell, Johnny, ain't you seen a unicorn before? That there's Carty John, the lord of the desert."

"Well, I never," said Ringo.

Doc heard the two men move closer, and saw the unicorn glance toward them. As it stepped sideways, ready to turn and run, Doc said calmly, "Back off. This is my play."

He heard Wyatt and Ringo withdraw a few feet. The unicorn's gaze returned to Doc's face. He extended his left arm, palm upward to show there was nothing in his hand. The unicorn took the last step, and its breath was warm on Doc's skin. He was afraid he would cough and scare it away, then realized he felt no need to cough.

Wyatt called softly, "Want me to fetch a rope?"

Ringo laughed, "Hell, ain't no need of that."

Wyatt said, "What do you mean?"

Ringo said, "Look at that! It'll follow Doc like a lovesick pup now." He laughed again, even more loudly, and Doc heard the sound of a man slapping his knee in delight as Ringo added, "And you know why?"

Wyatt said, "No. Why?"

Ringo said, "'Cause there's one thing a unicorn'll fall for, and that's —"

Doc heard the pistol shot, then felt the pistol in his right hand. Ringo slumped to his knees and fell forward, hiding the hole in his face and exposing the larger one in the back of his head.

Wyatt went to calm their horses. The unicorn stayed by Doc. It had not spooked at the sound, sight, or smell of death. Doc let the pistol slide back into his holster.

Wyatt said, "Well, it'll be easier to convince Wells Fargo he's dead now."

"Mmm."

Wyatt squatted by Ringo, drew a knife, and cut a piece of scalp from Ringo's hairline. "What you want to do with Carty John there? Start up a unicorn show, or sell him?"

"He won't abide crowds."

Wyatt dropped his hand to the gun at his thigh. "You figure to shoot him then, or should I?"

Both pistols cleared their holsters at the same time. Neither fired. Doc and Wyatt stood still, Wyatt's pistol aimed at Doc's sternum, Doc's pistol aimed more toward Wyatt than anything else.

Time passed, perhaps slowly, perhaps quickly. Wyatt lowered his head, but not his gun, a fraction of an inch in a question. Doc answered by swinging his pistol behind him as he yelled, "Git!" The barrel struck something soft, and he thought it had been easier to send Kate away.

The unicorn did not try to impale him. It spun and ran. As it splashed across the creek and onto the sand, Doc holstered his pistol. He listened to the unicorn's hooves, but he did not turn to watch it go. He stepped forward, then fell coughing to his knees in the creek.

Wyatt took him by the shoulders to lift him and direct him toward the bank. While Doc sat on a boulder in the sun, Wyatt found Ringo's horse, saddled it, rolled Ringo's body in a blanket, then lashed it across the back of the horse. Wyatt said, "You want his boots?"

Doc looked where Ringo had been reading, then shook his head.

Wyatt said, "If they were all that comfortable, he'd'a' been wearing 'em."

Doc said, "I'll take the book."

Wyatt picked up The Iliad, handed it to Doc, then said, "Ready to ride?"

"At a moment's notice," Doc said, and he stood, wondering if that was true. He tucked the book in his saddle bag, then swung himself onto his horse's back. "Where you taking him?"

Wyatt turned his horse back the way they had come. "I got a plan."

"As good as your last one?"

"I 'xpect."

"That's comforting."

"Killing Stilwell and Curly Bill so publicly just created messes for us. I figure to prop Johnny down by the road into town, which ought to get a story goin' that he up and killed his sorry ass hisself."

Doc considered several flaws in the plan, but said nothing. It would be a last joke on the town that had driven them away. He could hear people arguing why Ringo's boots were missing and whether a self-inflicted wound should be ringed with powder burns. It would be less than a joke, or more. It would be a mystery, and therefore it would be like life.

"Sure," Doc said, and coughed.

They left Ringo near a farmhouse and let his horse go free. Wyatt had hung Ringo's cartridge belts upside-down on him, but Doc did not ask whether that was to make it look like Ringo had been extremely drunk, or was another little taunting detail for Sheriff Behan and Tombstone's legal establishment, or was simply a sign that Wyatt's mind was on other things.

When the scene of Ringo's suicide was complete, Wyatt said, "Doc, maybe we ought to split up for a while."

That would be prudent. If anyone decided Ringo had been killed, it would be best if no one could say that two men looking like Wyatt and Doc had been near these parts. Doc nodded.

Wyatt said, "I'll get your share to you."

Doc nodded again.

Wyatt smiled. "Half's better'n thirds, ain't it?"

Doc coughed, then nodded a third time.

"You'll be all right?"

Doc said, "Sure."

"Well. Be seein' you."

He watched Wyatt ride away. A bullet in Wyatt's back would surprise no one, but Doc did not draw his gun. He loved anything that was simple and strong and beautiful. Some things should live forever, and some things should die.

Coughing, he rode on alone.

Little Red and the Big Bad

Will Shetterly

You know I'm giving the straight and deep 'cause it's about a friend of a friend. A few weeks back, just 'cross town, a true sweet chiquita, called Red for her fave red hoodie, gets a 911 from her momma's momma. The Grams is bed-bound with a winter bug, but she's jonesing for Sesame Noodles, Hot and Sour Soup, and Kung Pao Tofu from the local Chineserie—'cept their delivery wheels broke down. So Grams is notioning if Red fetches food, they'll feast together.

Red greenlights that. Veggie Asian chow and the Grams are solid in her top ten. So Red puts on her hoodie, leaves a note for the Moms, and BMXes away.

Now, down by the corner is a fine looking beastie boy who thinks he's the Big Bad, and maybe he is. He sees Red exit the eatery with a humongous bag of munch matter and calls, "Hey, Little Red Hoodie Hottie. Got me a tasty treat?"

Red doesn't slow. She just says, "Not if you're not my Grams, and you're not."

This Big Bad wouldn't be so big or so bad if he quit easy. He smiles and follows Red to her chained-up wheels. While Red juggles dinner and digs for her bike lock key, the Bad says, "Take five? Or all ten?" and holds out both hands.

Red warms to his style and his smile—this beastie boy isn't half as smooth as he thinks he is, but half is twice as smooth as this town's seen. Red hands off the bag, the Bad peeps in, and his stomach makes a five-two Richter. He's thinking he's holding the appetizer, and Red's the main course.

Red mounts her wheels, takes back the bag, gives the Bad a gracias, and pedals off down the main drag, riding slow . She doesn't want to be a sweatpig when she gets to Gram's. The day's as sweet as a sugar donut, but Red's not happy. As she rides, she calls herself a ho for flirting up a corner boy with Grams so sick. Pumping the right pedal is like pins. Pumping the left is like needles.

The sec Red rounds the corner, the Bad's off on a mountain bike, zipping 'cross town, cruising down alleys, cutting through yards, taking every shortcut he knows and making up seven new ones. 'Cause when he peeped in the chow sack, he saw the foodery's little green delivery slip spelling out Grams' name and address.

The Bad gets to Grams' front door while Red's still blocks away. He leans on the buzzer till a weak, weak voice asks, "Who's there?"

The Bad pitches his voice like Red's . "It's me, Grams! It's major munching time!"

Grams laughs and buzzes him in. She's laughing right until she sees the Bad, and then she's not laughing at all.

Red's the gladdest when she gets to Grams' place. Walking up to the door, she pokes her nose in the bag of Chinese tastiness, snorting peppers and garlic as if she were dipping her face in a spicy sauna. She has to smile. What can be wrong when a great dinner's coming?

In Grams' bedroom, the Bad thinks the same as a tap-tap comes at the door. He hops in the Grams' bed, calls, "Hurry in, my sweet surprise!" and pulls the covers up over his nose.

Red walks in the front room, saying, "You shouldn't leave your door open."

The Bad calls from the back, "It's just to let you in, my munchiliciousness."

Red heads down the hall, saying, "Your voice sounds funny."

The Bad calls, "It's just my sore throat getting sorer. It'll be better once I eat, my little main dish!"

Red brakes at the bedroom door. The place looks nice, if nice is a dark, dark cave. On the shadow that she knows is Grams' bed is a shadow that could be Grams. The shadow says, "Now come snuggle your poor, cold Grams," and pulls the bedcovers back to invite Red in.

Red sets down the food, gives the shadow some serious squinteye, and wants to turn on every light in the room.. Then she hears Grams, near to tears, add, "Or don't you love your Grams?"

Red says, "Sure do, Grams," and hops in bed without a doubt in her head. But when the Bad pulls her close, Red's a little spooked. She says, "Your eyes are way bright, Grams."

"'Cause I'm way glad to see you," says the Bad, pulling her closer.

More spooked, Red says, "Your arms are way strong, Grams."

"'Cause I'm way glad to hold you," says the Bad, pulling her closest.

And as spooked as spooked gets, Red says, "And your teeth are way sharp, Grams."

"'Cause I'm way glad to eat you," says the Bad.

Now, I could say that's when a bold cop hears Red scream, runs in faster than the Bad can bite, shoots down the Bad like the cold, cruel creature he is, finds Grams tied up safe in a closet, and Red and Grams and the cop all get the happy ever after.

Or I could say there's no scream, no handy cop, and the Bad has a happy belly glow for days, thanks to Red and her Grams.

Either way, there's uno problemo with my story: If the Bad dies, how do I know how he gets 'cross town? If Red dies, how do I know how she feels biking to Grams'?

Here's what's sure: One dies. One lives to tell the tale. And the one telling the tale is guessing 'bout the other.

Now pick the end you like. But before you do, think on this:

The storyteller's still around. Maybe nearer than you think.

And everyone's got to eat.

Secret Identity

Will Shetterly

Everyone assumed I'd had my masker card for years. Wasn't I the son of the great Galaxian? The Vampire's kid had become the Vampire II; everyone assumed I'd be Galaxian, Jr. or Kid Galaxian or something that clearly announced my heritage. When I flew down the halls of Hero High, people were as likely to call me Galaxian as Alec. I never bothered to correct them. The only reason I hadn't visited the Department of Masquerader Registration to make it official was that there was no rush. No one else would claim Dad's masker name.

I was on my way to Latin when Steeljack called, "Hey, faggot! Yeah, you!" I winced, but I didn't look. He wasn't talking to me. To Steeljack, I was one of the most powerful gamma-level Celestials on the planet. He was a beta-level bully who liked tormenting alphas and Earthers.

Jason Zi'Garis answered, "Oh, S.J., you don't even have to ask. Of course I'll go to the prom with you."

I stopped and looked then, just like everyone else within fifty feet. Half the kids laughed. Half just stared, fearing what would happen next. I was in the second group.

Those who were laughing had good reason. Jason ought to have been scary. He stood eight feet tall. His shoulders were nearly four feet wide. His grandfather had masked in the '50s as the Big Boss Man. At sixteen, Jason was bigger and stronger than his grandfather had ever been.

But Jason was always clowning around. He'd dance down the halls like Fred Astaire when everyone else was rushing businesslike to their next class. He'd take outrageous parts in school plays and wear his costumes to class. Now, with Steeljack furious at him, Jason was affecting a high voice and a swish walk. Who could stay afraid of him?

And no one should have been afraid of Steeljack. He was a skinny kid, two-thirds Jason's height and a quarter Jason's weight. His real name was Larry Si'Valy, but he only answered to his mask name. He was dressed, as usual, in his registered costume, which looked a lot like a Nazi Stormtrooper's uniform.

That costume heightened their differences. Though Jason was dressed inconspicuously—for an eight-foot kid—in jeans, running shoes, and a varsity jacket, he was wearing a black T-shirt with a pink triangle. He had just registered at the DMR as the Pink Puma.

It made the morning news in a big way. There'd always been jokes and rumors about maskers, ever since Dad showed up in tights and a cape in 1938. An Earther woman claimed to have been the Star Woman's lover, but the Star Woman was killed when Russia invaded Hungary in '56. Though a TV movie called Her(o)love had been made, no one knew if that affair really happened. Mr. Sandman had confirmed the rumors about himself when he wrote Out of the Closet and Off with the Mask, but Mr. Sandman was an Earther masker. Jason was the first and only Celestial out of the closet.

I looked up and down the hall for teachers and didn't see any. Steeljack had probably checked before he yelled at Jason.

"Pink Puma." Steeljack sneered. "More like, Pink Pansy."

"Ooh, wish I'd thought of that." Jason smiled as he started to walk around Steeljack. "I'll tell everyone you're the one to ask for gay masker names."

More kids laughed. I didn't. Jason was an alpha whose physical strength strained the limits of human possibility. He could take care of himself in most circumstances. But beta-class abilities had nothing to do with human possibility. Steeljack was a metamorph whose favorite shape was a metal-skinned kid with razor fingertips.

Chris Naiy was down the hall, flirting with Wanda Chan. They both got quiet when Steeljack stepped closer to Jason. Chris and Wanda glanced at me. I looked away fast.

Steeljack said, "You're pathetic, Pink Pooftah. You're disgracing Celestials, and you're disgracing maskers. You make us look like a joke."

"No way, S.J.," said Jason. "You're a self-made man."

Someone snickered. As Steeljack figured it out, his skin became chrome. Someone screamed. Steeljack's fist was flashing toward Jason's head, and Jason was bringing his arm up in a block as he backed away. We all knew Jason's flesh couldn't deflect Steeljack's metal blow.

Then Chris was standing behind Steeljack. A streak the brown of Chris's skin and the red of his jacket and the yellow of his jeans hung in the hall, from the place he had been to the place he stood. His hands were on Steeljack's shoulders, and Steeljack had been wrenched sideways. His punch ended in the air several feet away from Jason.

Chris released Steeljack, letting him lurch forward, off balance. Steeljack spun and glared. Six-inch spikes sprang from his knuckles. Then he saw what had happened.

Chris was a gamma who could timeslip, slowing the world down around him. Chris couldn't hurt Steeljack in his metal form, but Steeljack could never hope to touch Chris. It was worse than a stalemate.

In fifth grade, an older kid on a bicycle had called Chris a nigger. An instant later, the kid was still where he had been, but his bike and his clothes were up in a tree, and the kid was covered from head to toe with chocolate syrup. The kid landed on his butt, then took off running. Everyone called him Sundae for the next three years.

Steeljack shrugged, shifting from metal to flesh. "Hey, I wasn't really going to hit him."

Chris nodded and began to turn away.

"Besides," said Steeljack, "my complaint's with Fagman, not you."

"Yeah, Chris," said Chiller, a cryokinetic whose skin frosted over when he got excited. Right now, his hands and face were blue with a sheen of ice. "Is Jasey-poo your boyfriend?"

Chris stared at Chiller as if that was the lamest thing he had heard. Then he put his arm around Jason's waist. "Why, yes, he is, and I don't care how jealous you get, you chilly-silly dude."

The crowd laughed as Chris and Jason made kissy faces. They laughed more when Wanda sniffed loudly and said, "Oh, Jason, he'll break your heart like he broke mine, that shameless hussy!"

Steeljack flexed his hands. Metal razors rang like chimes. A red-headed girl smiled and called, "Hey, Larry, quit showing off." Blue-hot jets of flame appeared from her fingertips. "Skykids need to be careful. Someone might get hurt accidentally."

Steeljack frowned. "Yeah, right." The razors became skin again.

The bell sounded then, and we all scrambled for our classes. Steeljack and Chiller headed one way, Wanda and the redhead ran another, Jason cartwheeled down the hall toward his room, and Chris and I raced to ours. I flew, but when I arrived, Chris was sitting comfortably in his seat. "What took you?"

I grinned, then lost the grin when Wanda whispered, "Chris wants to know why you didn't do anything. Don't you like Jase?" She was in a room two floors away, but when telepaths whisper in class, they can whisper in any class they want to.

I said, "He shouldn't have gone public if he wasn't ready for the consequences."

"You would've just watched? Steeljerk could've killed—"

"It's none of your business, Wanda."

"Well, gee, sorry I asked." Her mind left mine before I could say anything more.

•

After school, I flew to Geneva. Dad was getting an award from the U.N. for helping with the Balkan crisis. He wanted me there as the heir apparent. I smiled when I was expected to. Mostly, I was ignored. It was boring, but it was fast, and when it was done, Dad and I sprang into the air for that final photo op of Galaxian and son returning to the City of Angels.

We usually flew without talking. The best times with Dad were when we didn't need to speak. I like flying, the wind whipping at my hair and clothes, the Earth rolling beneath me. In the sky, I feel sorry for teleporters. Sure, sometimes you wish you could hop instantly from one place to another, but traveling is always better than arriving.

My thoughts were interrupted as we decelerated over New York. Dad flew close to say, "Earth people seem inconsequential from here, but they're not."

I glanced at him.

He said, "Never forget that. Based on the genetic evidence, they're our ancestors. It doesn't matter whether an Empyrean scout ship picked up a few of them and bred us from those samples, or whether Earth's a lost Empyrean colony that never had enough enhanced stock to breed true. We have obligations to Earthers. At least as many as we have to chimpanzees. Probably more."

I shook my head. "You're such an alien, Dad."

He laughed. "So are you."

"I was born here."

44

"That doesn't make you one of them." We flew on. Then he said, "My greatest regret is that I cannot show you the beauty of deep space."

I shrugged. I had flown to the Moon last summer. The excitement of being all by yourself in a near vacuum gets thin after a few hours. I had finished the trip because I had told my friends I was going, but it had been the most boring week of my life.

On Earth, I've flown among the Andes with condors for company. I've raced tornadoes, then rested at their hearts. I've dived into storm clouds and danced with lightning. I've plunged into the sea to play tag with dolphins. I've watched volcanoes erupt from the ocean floor. I've hunted for human history in sunken ships and lost cities. I've flown among the trees of the rain forests and invited monkeys to leap onto my back. I've followed bats into caves where no climber could ever go and accompanied sightless fish up subterranean rivers that no one but me has ever seen.

Ask me to choose between the life of Earth and the emptiness of space. That one's easy.

Dad said, "When we build another ship, you'll see the galaxy and know that splendor, son. The dance of the stars is slow and stately. You can't imagine that perfection."

"No," I agreed.

I suppose I expected him to hear my sarcasm. He glanced at me. "I try to be true to myself, Alec. You must do the same."

Somewhere over the plains of the Midwest, I said, "You want me to be true to myself by becoming someone I'm not."

His sigh was carried off by the wind. "You have a responsibility to your people. That responsibility is part of who you are. I became Galaxian for many reasons. Only one was to silence rumors of monsters from outer space hiding among ordinary Americans. There's still a need to assure Earthers that we only want to live in peace."

I said, "Three thousand, four hundred, and eighty-one."

"What?"

"That's how many times you've told me Celestials need a wholesome, all-American, apple pie-eating representive, or we'll be feared and persecuted."

He smiled. "I think you placed the decimal too far to the right, but I take your point." I didn't smile. He said, "Being Galaxian is a chance to help Celestials and Earthers both. You'd be surprised how good that makes you feel."

"Yeah. You're a saint, Dad."

I figured I had made another point, though it didn't make me happy. He said, "Fair enough. I enjoy the fame and glory, too. Too much, sometimes. If I'd indulged in fewer of the opportunities that came my way—"

I wondered if he would mention Mom or the affairs or the divorce, but he didn't. Somewhere over the Rockies, I said, "A Celestial I know got his masker card and announced he was gay."

Dad winced. "I heard. I wish he hadn't."

"Why?"

"During the Second World War, the U.S. confined Japanese-Americans in camps. There was also a camp for Celestials. Super-powered homosexuals would be some Earthers' greatest nightmare."

"The kid I know says if you hide, you're admitting you have something to feel guilty about."

Dad looked at me. "We want to live in peace on this planet, Alec. That's all we want. Why make trouble over things that aren't important?"

I nodded. We had reached L.A., and now we hovered high above our house.

He said, "Will you be at the Masqueraders' Ball?"

"I'm the son of the great Galaxian. Of course I'll be there, O great Galaxian."

"We'll speak then. Remember that I love you, son."

I watched as he flew south. He had told Amnesty International that he would spend a few days hunting for political prisoners in Central America.

I whispered, "Bastard." If he was listening, he did not look back.

•

After dinner—a cheese sandwich I made at home—I flew to Wilshire Boulevard, landed in an alley, and walked to our favorite café. No one noticed me until I sat across from a Celestial whose size could not be hidden by custom-made street clothes. Then there were the usual whispers as people wondered if I was also a masker or a movie star or someone famous. After all, I was meeting with the Celestial whose face

46

had been on all the news. The wondering about us died quickly, and no one came to ask for autographs.

Jason said, "I'm glad you came."

I said, "I had to."

The waiter approached. Jason told her, "The usual." She smiled and left.

I said, "If Steeljerk had hit you, I would've killed him."

He laughed. "I know that."

The waiter set a root beer in front of me and a cappuccino in front of Jason, saying, "It'll stunt your growth."

He said, "Promises, promises."

The waiter grinned and left. I said, "She must think we're mighty cute together."

"And why not? We are."

"Well." I blushed. "Look—"

"You don't have to explain."

"Dad would think I'd betrayed our people."

Jason shook his head. "He'd think you'd betrayed his people. He'd be right."

"Gee, thanks. That's sure comforting." I stared at the foam of my root beer.

Jason did his John Wayne. "A man's got to do what a man's got to do." Then he added, "It doesn't change how we feel."

"I'm worried about you going on patrol. You'll be a target—"

He nodded. "A mighty big target. Gaybashers look for easy prey."

"I don't like it."

"So tag along. My route hits the parks and gay neighborhoods. It'll be a walking date."

I shook my head and couldn't look at his face.

He laughed. "Your dad would love the headlines. 'Galaxian's Son Cruises Homosexual Hangouts.'"

I shrugged.

Jason's voice shifted suddenly. He said, "'Gee, Jase, why don't we talk about other things?' 'Sure, Alec; what do you want to talk about?' 'How about your beautiful eyes, Jase, you big gorgeous hunk of a man, you?'"

I wanted to say he did a lousy imitation of me, but I heard myself laugh instead. We talked about school and friends and how the world

47

should be changed. Then he went on patrol, and I flew back to do some homework.

The eleven o'clock news showed him strolling through the streets in costume while people cheered. An ancient Hispanic woman said she thought he was wonderful. A guy who looked like he had an ulcer said he thought Jason was disgusting. A young guy said, "White maskers, black maskers, human maskers, skyguy maskers, straight maskers, gay maskers. They're all egomaniacs in tights. Who cares?" That's one form of acceptance.

I wanted to be with Jason. Then I thought about Dad and the harrassment I'd get at school, and I decided I'd done the right thing.

•

I woke on the sofa. Something needed my attention. I had the phone to my ear before I understood what was happening. Jason's mom said, "Alec? Pamela Zi'Garis." Her voice was quietly formal, which seemed odd; I'd had dinner at their house, and she'd been as loud and happy as her son. "Jason asked me to call. First, you should know that he's going to be fine, and second—" She inhaled suddenly, then said, "He'd like to see you. Visiting hours—"

"Where is he?" I asked.

"Kennedy Clinic, Room Seven-thirteen. Visiting hours—"

"Thanks." I hung up the phone.

Two minutes later, I set my bare feet onto the hospital roof near the helicopter landing pad, found an open door, flew down the stairwell to the seventh floor, scanned the hallway for watchers, and flew into Jason's room.

He was asleep, breathing raggedly. Two beds had been pushed together to hold him. Two sheets had been draped over him. In the dim light, his skin was blue. His head was bandaged. One leg and one arm were in casts.

Shortly before dawn, a nurse looked in. "Who're—"

I put my finger to my lips, then followed her into the hall. "Did they catch them?"

"Catch who?"

"Whoever did this. Were they caught?"

"They usually aren't. How'd you get in?"

"I flew."

48

She frowned, studied my face, then nodded. "He'll be fine. Go home, get some sleep, come back after school, okay? That's when visiting hours officially begin."

"Can you tell me what happened?"

"I can tell you what the clues suggest, but they don't make sense."

"Okay."

"Someone hit him in the face with a ball of slush that froze over his eyes. Then someone took a metal club and beat him until he collapsed."

I nodded, thanked her, and flew away.

•

Steeljack and Chiller sauntered into the schoolyard about ten minutes before the first bell. They quit sauntering when I landed on the sidewalk in front of them. Surprise touched their faces for only an instant, but I could hear their hearts continue to race like drums in a bad jungle movie. Kids passing by looked at us, then gave us plenty of room.

I said, "Why'd you do it?"

"Do what?" said Chiller.

"Come on," Steeljack told him. "Young Galaxian thinks we did something we didn't."

"Yes, you did." Wanda's telepathic whisper vibrated in all of our skulls. She stepped out onto the front steps so Steeljack and Chiller could see her.

Chiller's hand began to frost over. "Says who?"

"Says you," said Wanda. "Loud and clear."

"Forget it," said Steeljack. "Mind reading's not admissible in court."

"Who said anything about court?" Chris appeared beside me. For an instant, a shimmer of brown and blue ran up the sidewalk to show where he'd been, then dissipated.

Steeljack stepped backward. "Oh, yeah, right. Gang up on us."

I said, "You set a fine example." Then I said, "Relax. Jase won't press charges. He didn't see anyone's face. He didn't hear anyone's voice. He couldn't make anything stick. It worked just like you planned."

Steeljack and Chiller glanced at each other. Steeljack smiled a little, and the soundtrack of their heartbeats slowed.

I said, "Legal charges aren't Jase's style. He says if you'll get counseling, he'll forget the whole thing."

49

"Dream on." A cloud of cold air shot from Chiller's throat as he laughed.

Chris said, "Be kind of rough, coming to school and never knowing if your clothes were about to disappear. If you might suddenly have the worst haircut you'd ever seen. If you might find yourself wearing a clown nose and diapers."

Chiller stared. "You wouldn't."

Steeljack said, "Wouldn't dare." His hand became a spiked ball on a steel chain that he began to whirl at his side. "Declare war, and someone's getting hurt."

"You already declared war," I said. "Someone's already hurt. But you're right. If we continue like this, things'll only get worse."

Steeljack grinned.

I said, "So maybe I should fly you to the top of Kilimanjaro or Mount Everest. Got a pref?"

Steeljack sneered. "I'd get back. One way or another."

"Yeah," I said. "So maybe I should drop you in the middle of the ocean."

"Hah," said Steeljack. His hand became a knife that he pointed at me. I stared at it. He returned his hand to flesh, but continued to point at me. "You pacifist pussies don't scare me."

"Pacifist pussies," Chiller repeated with pleased respect.

"It's a problem," I admitted. "Wanda?"

"Meow." She strolled down the steps, waving to Chiller and Steeljack like a cat stretching its claws. "People like you must've gone through some horrible things to turn out like you did."

Steeljack touched his chest with both hands. "Oh, no. Poor little misunderstood me." He and Chiller snickered. Steeljack said, "Keep your pity."

"Pity? Nah. No pity here." Wanda smiled. "A telepath following you around, digging into your thoughts, could learn a lot. Things that everyone would know. Things that'd be waiting around school for you, written on blackboards and in washrooms. Think about it."

Chiller swallowed. "That's blackmail."

Chris nodded. "Give the man a prize."

Steeljack said, "I thought telepaths could only read surface thoughts."

Wanda smiled. "Want to test that?"

Steeljack looked at each of us. After a moment, he shook his head.

Chris said, "By this afternoon, we want to hear you've met with a counselor and confessed. Got it?"

Chiller shivered. Steeljack said quietly, "Okay." They began to walk by.

I said, "Oh, something you should know." I pulled a masker ID out of my jacket. "Guess who registered today?" I held the card out so they could see my photo, my name and address, and the name typed in as my masquerader ID. Steeljack and Chiller looked at it, then at me, and walked away shaking their heads.

Chris said, "You think therapy will do them any good?"

Wanda stared at him. "Who cares? They'll *hate* it."

•

Jason grinned when he saw me hovering outside his hospital window, pressing my masker card against the glass. In my skull, I heard Wanda's whisper. "He says you didn't need to skip school to tell him. He heard it on the radio, Gaylaxian."

"That's not why I skipped school."

I stayed by the window. Wanda said, "I wish I could give you two some privacy. But then you couldn't communicate."

I said, "Yes, we can." I blew Jason a kiss, and then I did a triple back-flip in the air. I didn't need to hear his laugh to know how it sounded.

The People Who Owned the Bible

Will Shetterly

It was time for another Mickey Mouse Copyright Extension to keep Disney's star property out of the public domain. Somebody's nephew had a bright idea. Instead of telling Congress to add the standard twenty years to the length of copyright, why not go for the big time? Extend copyright by 500 years.

Somebody's niece added a smarter reason: A 500 year extension would let Disney track down Shakespeare's heirs and buy all rights to the Bard. No matter how much the heirs wanted, the deal would pay for itself in no time. Every school that ever wanted to perform or study Shakespeare would have to send a check to Disney. Every newspaper or magazine or radio show that wanted to quote the Bard would have to send one, too. So Disney asked, and Congress gave, and the World Intellectual Property Organization followed Congress's example. Disney paid off Shakespeare's heirs, then used the Shakespeare profits to buy all rights from the heirs of Dumas, Dickens, Twain, Mary Shelley, Jane Austen, Bram Stoker and more. Once most of the films in every other studio's library were subject to Disney's copyright, they went bankrupt or became divisions of Disney.

And everyone was content, except for the storytellers who had to buy a Disney license or prove that their work owed nothing to the last 500 years of literature.

Then Jimmy Joe Jenkins's DNA proved he was the primary descendent of the translators of the King James Version of the Bible. At first, Jimmy was satisfied with ten percent of the price of every KJV sold and 10 percent of every collection plate passed by any church that used the KJV. But when some churches switched to newer translations, Jimmy sicced his lawyers on all translations based on the KJV. That got him a cut of every Bible and every Christian service in English. Some translators claimed their work was based on older versions and should

53

therefore be exempt, but none of them could afford to fight Jimmy in court.

So the churches grumbled and paid Jimmy his tithe, except for the Mormons, Christian Scientists, Seventh Day Adventists, Quakers, and Unitarian Universalists. Jimmy said their teachings hurt the commercial value of his property and refused to let them use the Bible. All of those groups dissolved, except for the Unitarian Universalists, who didn't notice a change.

Then Jimmy took out all of the parts of the Bible that criticized rich people. Most of the surviving major churches didn't notice that. But they did complain when Jimmy changed the traditional translations of Yusuf and Miryam to Jimmy Joe and Lulabelle, the name of his pretty new wife.

But when his Lulabelle ran off with a Bible salesman, Jimmy retired to one of his mansions and refused to let anyone print any more Bibles or use the Bible in any way that raised money.

The surviving churches sent delegates to Disney, begging them to get Congress to shorten the copyright period to put the KJV back in the public domain. But Disney had picked up the rights to a Restoration revenge tragedy that looked like a great vehicle for Britney Spears, so they made a counteroffer.

Congress extended copyright for an additional two thousand years, and the WIPO followed their example. Jimmy had to pay every dollar he had made to the Catholic Church, because the KJV was based on St. Jerome's Vulgate version. In order to use the Bible, all Protestants became Catholic. Disney bought the copyrights and trademarks for Robin Hood, King Arthur, and the Arabian Nights.

And everyone was content, except for the storytellers who had to buy a Disney license or prove that their work owed nothing to the last two thousand years of myth and folklore.

Then Spike Greenbaum's DNA proved she was the primary descendent of Jesus or his brother James. Spike agreed to let Catholics use their Bible after the Pope married her to her girlfriend. Then she said that since Catholic priests could be married or celibate for the first thousand years, and then had to be celibate for the next thousand, all priests should be married to at least one other person. And since Jesus had told his followers to sell their goods and give their money to the poor, every expensive thing owned by the Church had to be given up for AIDS research.

Catholics grumbled, but they took some satisfaction when the courts ruled that the Qur'an was a derivative work, and Spike would not let Saudi Arabia use it until they ruled that women could drive cars and men could not.

The Pope briefly considered recreating the church of Mithra, which would let his people keep worshipping on Sundays and celebrating a virgin birth on December 25th. But his wives pointed out that Rome's Mithra Cult fell within the current period of copyright, and the primary heir was a charter member of NAMBLA who was preparing legal action against Spike for the rights to the Bible. So the Catholics sent delegates to Disney, begging them to shorten the copyright period to put Jesus's words in the public domain.

But Disney had just picked up the rights to the Satyricon, which looked like a great vehicle for Ashton Kutcher, so they made a counteroffer.

Congress extended copyright an additional twenty-five hundred years. Spike Greenbaum owed every dollar she had made to Israel, because St. Jerome's translation was based on Hebrew sacred texts. To use the Bible, all Catholics became Jewish, and Disney bought the rights to the Iliad and the Odyssey.

And everyone was content, except for the storytellers who had to buy a Disney license or prove that their work did not owe anything to any story that had ever been part of human civilization.

Then Kurosh Jadali's DNA proved he was the primary descendent of Zarathushtra, whose teachings about monotheism had been adopted by the Jews during the Babylonian Captivity. Kurosh said that since Zoroaster had taught religious tolerance, he would be glad to let the Jews use their sacred texts. In return, he only wanted a thousand Euros for each Torah that was published and three-fourths of any money that flowed through a synagogue. When the rabbis grumbled, Kurosh asked if they were communists who didn't respect intellectual property.

So all of the branches of Judaism sent delegates to Disney, begging them to roll back the period of copyright so that Zarathushtra's teachings would be in the public domain. But Disney had picked up the rights to the Epic of Gilgamesh, which looked like a great vehicle for Jim Carrey, so they made a counteroffer.

Congress extended copyright for an additional hundred thousand years. Kurosh Jadali had to give all his money to the United Nations, since everyone's DNA proved they were the descendants of the first people to tell stories about gods. Disney bought the rights to a story that had been painted on a wall about some people with some animals that they thought would be a great vehicle for Mel Gibson.

And everyone was content, except for the storytellers who had to buy a Disney license or prove that their work did not owe anything to any story that had characters doing anything.

Until one day a woman came into the Disney offices and said thanks to the extension of the period of copyright law, patent law had been extended, too. And since her DNA proved that she was the primary descendent of the first person who cast shadows on a wall and told stories about them, she would like to speak to the C.E.O. about every movie and television show that Disney had thought it owned.

Kasim's Haj

Will Shetterly

Years ago, I read a version of this story online. The writer guessed it might be from the 1001 Nights, but it doesn't feel like a story Scheherazade would tell.

•

Haroun al-Rashid, caliph of Baghdad, dreamt that he was at the gates of paradise and heard a voice: "What would you like to know, Haroun al-Rashid?"

He wanted to know if he would enter paradise when he died, but it seemed rude to ask for himself. Since he had just made his pilgrimage to Mecca, he asked, "Which of the pilgrims who made the Haj this year will enter paradise?"

"Only one."

"And who is that most favored and deserving one?"

"Kasim of Ismail Street."

The caliph woke. He disguised himself as a man of modest means and went into his city. The hour was early. No one stirred. When he came to Ismail Street, only one window in a tiny shop had its shutters open. By the light of a small lamp, an old man in old clothes was sewing a new sole onto an old shoe. Haroun al-Rashid asked, "Do you know where I would go to find Kasim of Ismail Street?"

The shoemaker said, "Oh, my friend, I am very sorry that I cannot tell you where to go to find a man by that name."

Haroun al-Rashid sighed in disappointment.

The shoemaker added, "The only man I know by that name you have already found."

Haroun al-Rashid stared at him. How could this be? The shoemaker was too old to make the Haj alone and too poor to make the Haj with helpers. Haroun al-Rashid asked, "Did you make the Haj this year?"

"No," said the shoemaker. "I have not had that honor."

"I am sorry to have troubled you," said Haroun al-Rashid, wondering how his dream had sent him so wrong.

"I planned to make the Haj this year," the shoemaker said. "I saved a penny every week for forty years to make the Haj. And I thought I had saved enough coins at last."

"But you hadn't?" Haroun al-Rashid asked.

"Oh, I had," said the shoemaker. "But on the coldest day of winter, my wife said she would like to eat camel meat. We had not eaten anything but water and rice for several weeks, and she was pregnant."

"So you bought so much camel meat you couldn't make the Haj?" Haroun al-Rashid asked.

"Oh, no," said the shoemaker. "I told my wife we could not afford meat. But then our house began filling with the smell of camel stew. The smell came from our neighbor's house. We could not escape it."

"And then you went to buy meat?" asked Haroun al-Rashid.

"Oh, no," said the shoemaker. "My wife said she would die if she did not have a taste of camel stew. She asked me to go to the neighbors and beg them for one bite."

"But instead you went to buy meat of your own?" asked Haroun al-Rashid.

"Oh, no," said the shoemaker. "I went to my neighbor and said that my pregnant wife had not eaten meat in weeks and could he spare a bite for her? He began to cry. He said, 'My friend, you do not smell camel stew. We have not had any food in our house for weeks. To keep my children from starving, I went into the market and bought an old donkey skin for a penny that we are boiling for soup. I am sorry that I have no camel stew for your wife. May God grant her wish soon.' So I went back to my home and dug up the coins I had saved for the Haj and gave them to my neighbor." The shoemaker shrugged. "God willing, someday I might make the Haj."

Haroun al-Rashid nodded. "God willing, someday I might make the Haj, too."

The Thief of Dreams

Will Shetterly

A tiger dreamed of gazelles running free across the plains. Then the tiger woke, its dream gone. It saw a gazelle and leaped upon it to make the gazelle its breakfast.

A serpent dreamed of a city overgrown by the jungle. Its walls were strong, and its wells were full of cool, clear water. A child came. The serpent told it, "I guard this city for you and your people. Take it, grow strong, and help others."

Then the serpent woke, its dream gone. A child passed nearby, walking toward the city. The serpent sank its fangs into the child's ankle.

A king dreamed of a leader who lived like her people in a simple home with simple food and helped them build schools and hospitals.

Then the king woke, his dream gone. A servant brought his breakfast on a tray of gold. As his ministers advised him to raise the taxes to keep the army strong, he told them, "I had a dream. It's gone now."

"It was stolen," said the servant.

Everyone looked at her, but the king only said, "By whom?"

"The Thief of Dreams," said the servant.

"I must catch this thief to get back my dream," said the king. "I will post a reward. I will send out my troops. I will have my wisest counselors learn who steals dreams."

The servant said, "Only you will know your dream. You must seek it yourself."

So the king, alone and on foot, set out on his quest.

On the plain, a tiger leaped upon him. As its jaws closed around his throat, the king cried, "Tell me, before you kill me, did you steal my dream?"

The tiger said, "No. But I have had a dream stolen."

"Our dreams were taken by the Thief of Dreams," said the king. "Let's seek the thief together."

"Agreed," said the tiger, so they set out side by side.

In the jungle, a serpent struck at the king. As its fangs touched his skin, the king cried, "Tell me, before you kill me, did you steal my dream?"

The serpent said, "No. But I have had a dream stolen."

"I have also had a dream stolen," said the tiger at the king's side.

"Our dreams were taken by the Thief of Dreams," said the king. "Let's seek the thief together."

So the king, the tiger, and the serpent searched the world.

Years passed, and the tiger died.

More years passed, and the serpent died.

Even more years passed. The king, old and ill, met a stranger. After telling his story, the king said, "The tiger, the serpent, and I wasted our lives pursuing the Thief of Dreams. What did we leave behind?"

The stranger said, "In the plains, the gazelles run free. In the jungle, a child found a city with strong walls and good wells that has been brought alive again. And in your land, the people made your servant their leader. She helped them build hospitals and schools."

The king knew the stranger then. "You stole our dreams!"

The stranger touched the king's hand and, as the king died, said, "No. I gave them."

Black Rock Blues

Will Shetterly

1

He's running above the sun-splashed ocean, leaping from cloud to rainbow and back again, grinning because no one can catch him, when someone walks up beside him, smiles in the smuggest way, and says, "Wakey-wakey."

He says, "G'way," and pulls the sleeping bag over his head.

The smug walker is a beautiful young woman with skin the color of the deepest sea and hair the color of the darkest night. She's naked. Street would like that if her smile wasn't so annoying. She says, "Time to wake up, trickster."

He sits up fast, thinking something's terribly wrong if he has a visitor in his hideaway, but at least the smug walker from his dream will be gone.

Only she's not. She's in his room. Or, to be precise, she's in a storage room at the back of the Dupree Building that's full of cartons of Hi-John's Good Luck Lawn and Garden Spray. She's wearing a blood-red jacket and purple jeans and low gray boots, and her head has been shaved and her skin is only as dark as a plum, but her smile is at least as annoying in reality as it was in the dream. She looks remarkably familiar for someone he's never seen. Maybe it's just that her smile reminds him of someone, but he can't remember who. He wants to say something clever. What falls from his lips is, "Hunh?"

Her smile gets even more annoying. "Yes. You were always loveliest in the morning."

He blinks three times. She refuses to disappear like the dream, so he says, "Wha— Who're you?"

She shakes her head. "Now, that'd be telling, wouldn't it?"

He wants to get out of his sleeping bag because he doesn't like looking up at her. But when he found this room, he arranged the cardboard boxes so six formed a bed and two made a table and four made a chair with a back and a footstool. His clothes are on top of the remaining stacks across the room. "What do you want?"

"And that'd be telling, too."

He frowns, then sees that this poor girl is trying to play the player. He grins and stretches. "What'd you call me?"

Her smile falters. She says, "All right. You get one. Trickster."

His grin is so wide he has to crank it down for fear of hurting his face. "Well, now and then, I s'pose." He points at his clothes. "I'm putting those on." He points at the door. "A lady would wait outside."

She points at the window. "While a two-bit grifter takes the back door? My thought is not."

He stands and tries not to shiver as he walks across the cold concrete floor. "O ye of little trust."

She taps the side of her head. "O me of much smart."

He tugs on gray silk boxers, but leaves his socks off because there's no way to put them on without the annoying girl seeing the holes in the heels. "They call me Street."

"Unless they're looking for a light-fingered fool or a punk to run a cheap-ass scam. Then they ask for Trickster."

"And when they ask for you?"

She hesitates, then shrugs and says, "Oh."

"Mystery woman."

She smiles. "That, too."

"Oh!" He has to laugh. "They call you O!"

"Now I've given you two."

He nods. "O'Riley. Odegaard. Oprah. Eau Claire. Open Sesame. Oh, what a pain."

O shakes her head. "Wasting time, T."

Street frowns as he buttons up a black guayabara. "So, O, how'd you find—" Her smile makes him hear himself, and he gets the grin back to say in time with her, "That'd be telling, wouldn't it?" He puts one leg into his tan chinos. "You didn't tell the cops—"

"Of course not."

He pauses with the chinos half on. "You're all right, O. Y'know, if you snuck in hoping for some quality time with a fine young fellow like myself—"

"I told Bossman Sevenday."

With one leg halfway into the chinos, Street looks at her instead of what he's doing and falls, landing hard on his hands. "What the—" As she laughs, he pushes himself up, jerks up his pants, and glares at her. "Why would you—"

"Things've been too easy, T. You need some spice in your life."

He yanks his belt tight, grabs a turquoise silk jacket, and steps into dark red loafers. "What'd I ever do to you?"

She smiles cooly.

He gives her a mocking smile in return and says, "That'd be telling, wouldn't it?"

O nods. "They'll be here in two minutes. We better take the fire esc —"

Street frowns. "We?"

Which is when the storage room door swings in as if it was kicked by a mule. The mule is a huge man so tall that he has to duck when he steps inside. His T-shirt says, "Looking for someone to hurt."

O says, "They would be early."

Street wrenches open the storage room window. "Come on! If—"

A little man in a dark red suit drops onto the fire escape with a friendly smile and a large pistol. "Tut, tut, my tricksy. A gent pays his bills afore making his departure. And it's true you'll be making the big departure soon, but Bossman Sevenday'll have what's his first, now, won't he?"

2

Mr. Big and Mr. Small don't offer answers, so Street doesn't ask questions. They drive from the Dupree Building in Flashtown to the country homes of Hillside while Big and Small sing Tin Pan Alley songs in perfect harmony. O follows the black limousine in a small silver roadster with the top down. Street thinks she must be working with his captors, but he can't figure out why she was acting more like audience than actor, and he doesn't like thinking about her. So he joins Big and Small on the choruses, and he smiles as they wince whenever he goes off key.

They pass many walled homes before Mr. Big turns toward a high gate like gleaming ivory. It swings back at their approach. The limousine rolls over a long white cobblestone driveway and stops beside a bone-white mansion. Small leaps out to open Street's door, saying, "If you'd be so kind, my tricksy." Street feels safer staying where he is, until Small nods at Big and adds, "The kindness is for my compatriot. He must clean the car if a guest is reluctant to leave it."

Big grins sheepishly, and Street leaps out.

O parks her roadster beside the limousine and walks over to them. For the drive, she added racing goggles and a white scarf. She pushes the goggles up on her forehead. Street thinks she's the finest thing he's ever seen, then wishes he hadn't thought that.

"On with the show!" O calls, waving the others toward the back of the mansion.

Street asks, "Do I get paid?"

Big says in a very gentle voice, "Oh, you should hope you don't, Mr. Trickster."

O leads, and Big and Small follow, and Street sees no choice but to be escorted around the mansion. In the back, a man lounges by an enormous pool, drinking a pina colada. He wears a black top hat, smoky round glasses, a black Hawaiian shirt printed with silver skulls, gray pinstriped surfer shorts, and black flip-flops. He looks up and laughs. "Trickster! O! So very good to see you!"

Street, knowing who this must be, says, "And I couldn't imagine anyone better to see me, Mr. Bossman Sevenday, sir. I'm just afraid there's a teensy misunderstanding—"

"A misunderstanding?" says Bossman Sevenday. "When Trickster is involved? Oh, no. How could that be?"

As Bossman Sevenday and Big laugh heartily, Small whispers, "He's not happy, my tricksy. You should make him happy."

Street desperately wants to do precisely that, and has no idea how. He looks at the swimming pool, an elongated hexagon, then looks closer. It's the shape of a coffin.

Bossman Sevenday laughs harder and says, "You like my pool, Trickster? You may swim in it anytime. Some people like it so much, they go in and never want to leave."

Street swallows and says, "I love your pool, Mr. Bossman Sevenday, sir. But I was thinking how happy I would be if I could do something

64

for you. Whatever you liked. All you'd have to do is tell me what you wanted, and I'd be on my way to do that this very second, Mr. Bossman Sevenday, sir."

Bossman Sevenday stops laughing and says, "The rock."

"The rock?" Street says.

Bossman Sevenday nods.

"That's it?" says Street.

Bossman Sevenday nods again.

Street looks at O. She says, "He wants the rock."

Street says, "Of course he wants the rock! I'll go get it now." He begins to back out of the yard. "Mr. Bossman Sevenday, sir, I'm very, very grateful for the chance to get you a rock. I mean, the rock."

Bossman Sevenday begins laughing again. "Of course you are, Trickster. You have twenty-four hours."

Street says, "I might need a little—"

Bossman Sevenday frowns.

Street says quickly, "—less time than that. You never know. Twenty-four hours, that's plenty. You'll have it in a day, at the very latest."

"Good Trickster," says Bossman Sevenday. And, as he laughs and Street backs away, the flesh from Bossman Sevenday's face drips like candle wax from his skull.

Street trips and leaps up and runs. Bossman Sevenday's laughter follows him around the bone-white mansion and down the cobblestone drive. The cobblestones sound hollow like drums beneath Street's feet. As he reaches the front gate, he thinks the cobblestones are skulls and imagines people buried together, packed as tightly as cigarettes. He leaps onto the gleaming ivory gate to climb it, but it swings inward. He drops from it, runs into the road, then hears a car racing down the driveway.

3

The silver roadster pulls up beside him. O says, "Faster if you ride with me."

Street doesn't slow down. "No," he puffs. "Way."

O says, "I'm not about to take you back. Not without the rock. If you want to get away from here—"

65

Street jumps over the side of the roadster and buckles himself into the passenger seat. "Go!" O puts the speedometer exactly at the posted speed limit. Street says, "Faster!"

O says, "If a cop stops us, we'll go a lot slower."

Street nods. "Right. Good thinking. I'm cool with that." But Street breathes fast and sweats profusely. He knows he doesn't smell like he's cool with anything. He says, "Back there. Did you see anything odd?"

"Odd?": O grins. "Nope."

The melting face must've been a freak of the sunlight. The cobblestones must've only sounded hollow. Street says, "Me, neither. Just wanted to show the Bossman I'm dedicated to finding his rock."

O says, "I think he knows that."

"Except I don't know what it is," Street admits. "Or who took it. Or why he expects me to find it."

O says, "Why doesn't matter as much as the fact he expects it."

"True. You know where it is?"

O shakes her head. "If you were looking for something that people wanted, where would you go?"

Street frowns, then grins.

4

Street leads O through Meandering Market. Today, it's in a freight lot near the docks. His grin is back, because people are nodding and smiling, saying, "Howzit, T-man!" and "Yo, the Streetdog!" and "Tricks baby, lookin' so fine!" The impromptu aisles are thick with people who like bargains and don't care about sales slips. Street usually moves through the Market like a prince, perusing each dealer's wares, looking over clothes, tunes, shows, tech, gems, and all the sweet distracting things of the world. Now he's moving just fast enough not to make anyone wonder why he's moving fast.

The crowd is full of people who want to be seen in their bright colors and careful hair. Picking any of them out would be a challenge, but Street's challenge is greater. He looks where he thinks no one is, in shadows and quiet places. He spots the little brown man at the tent and aluminum trailer called Pele's Cafe. Mouse sits on a stool near the back, nursing a cup of the house java.

Mouse spots Street just as quickly. He sets the coffee cup down, looks around, and Street knows Mouse is doing the math, distance to aisles and number of obstacles and the length of Street's stride and the speed of Mouse's. Then Mouse smiles at Street, telling Street two things: Mouse figures he can't get away, and Mouse would really, really like to get away.

Mouse says, "How ya, Tricks? You and the lady seeking a seat? You can have mine in half a mo, if you fancy."

Street says, "Ah, Mouse! How long has it been?"

Mouse shrugs. "There's just dead time between deals. You looking for a ride? I know someone with a lead on a silver Zephyr, good as new —"

O says, "If it's parked by Dingo's newsstand, you don't."

Mouse says, "Or a bulletproof vest? Only one hole in it."

Street says as if he knows exactly what he's talking about. "I'm after the rock."

Mouse's eyes don't change at all, meaning he's much more guilty than if he looked scared. Mouse says, "The actor? Plymouth? The Hope Diamond? Not my speed, Tricks. You know me. Sweet and small, nothing memorable. I so hate trouble."

Street says, "Mouse, you got to know yourself. Take me, for example. I am a very smooth liar."

O snorts, but if it might have turned into a laugh, she stifles it when Street glances at her.

He tells Mouse, "You're a smooth facilitator. Someone wants to sell and someone wants to buy, no one's better than you at making it happen. But you're not a smooth liar. No shame there. Perfection in all things is a gift given to few of us."

"Very few," O agrees. "Very, very few." Street glances at her again. She says, "So very few—"

Street tells her, "Should I need your help, you'll know because I'll have ripped out my tongue and used it to hang myself to spare me from asking you."

O says, "Ooh! Looking forward to that!"

Street puts a hand on Mouse's shoulder to keep him from sidling away. "So. The rock."

Mouse says, "Haven't seen it."

Street says, "And if you had, what would you have seen?"

Mouse shrugs. "A black rock. I don't know. I just hear what you do."

"And if you were looking for the black rock, where would you go?"

"You got me confused with the library reference desk, Tricks."

"Fair enough. Should I receive anything of value, you take ten percent."

Mouse shrugs. "But I don't know anything."

Street nods.

Mouse says, "And I take fifteen."

Street nods again.

Mouse says, "Mama Sky."

O's mouth opens as if she's going to say her nickname, but she closes it.

Mouse says, "See you in better times," and slips away, a faint shadow that dissolves in the surging sea of Market shoppers.

5

As the Zephyr speeds up Sunset, Street says, "You got to admit that went well."

O keeps her eyes on the road. "True. If there's one thing you know, it's how to deal with scumbags."

Street glares at her, but she's not looking, so he laughs. "Got us a name, didn't I?"

"A name's not the rock."

"Anyone else get this far?"

O says grudgingly, "No."

Street laughs.

O says, "How're you going to find Mama Sky?"

Street smiles. "I'm not."

O glances at him as a truck comes around the corner. O takes the shoulder of the road, spraying dirt, then swings back onto the road, and says, perfectly calmly, "You're not."

Street shakes his head. "Saw your face when Mouse said the name. You know her."

"True."

"I'm thinking we're heading there now."

"You're thinking right."

"So. Who is she?"

"My mother." O's voice says it would be a good idea not to ask more questions, which makes Street want to ask a lot more. Then he

68

looks at her face and decides that while she's probably twice as annoying as any annoying person could be, he can wait until she's ready to talk again.

6

O slows at the top of Sunset, then speeds along High Road and parks. For a moment, Street thinks they've stopped at a garden with a view of the city and the ocean. Then he sees they're in front of a small house that's the same blue as the sky. A large woman in a loose house dress of the same blue comes out of the front door to stand perfectly still with a perfectly calm expression. Her skin is as dark as O's. Her white hair billows from her round face like clouds.

Street looks at O and the large woman. The light dims, and he glances up. Heavy clouds are gathering in front of the sun. As the sky darkens, so does the color of the house and the woman's robes.

Street says, "If it's about to rain, it'd sure be nice to go inside or put up the top."

A drop of rain hits him, then another, and water begins to fall more heavily.

O says, "Mother."

Mama Sky says, "Daughter."

O says, "Is this necessary?"

Mama Sky says, "Am I happy?"

O says, "You have the rock."

Mama Sky says, "Why would I have the rock?"

O says, "You never tell me what I want to know."

Mama Sky says, "I always tell you what you need to know."

O says, "How do you know what I need to know?"

Mama Sky says, "Because I'm your mother."

O says, "I don't know why I came here!" and reaches to start the car.

Street catches her hand. "Because of the rock."

"I don't care about the rock!"

Street says, "I wish I could say that." The rain is a cold torrent. He's soaked, like O and the roadster. He gets out, splashing through deep puddles to stand at the bottom of the porch. "Mama Sky, ma'am? I'm —"

She says coldly, "I know who you are."

69

Street says, "Oh. Well, I'm powerful sorry you don't like what you've heard. I hate the notion that a fine looking woman like yourself isn't glad to see me."

Mama Sky squints at him, then laughs. "You are a most foolish young man who thinks that flattery excuses most of his faults."

As the rain slackens, Street says, "When a fine looking woman with a laugh as big as the world thinks a man has faults, he hopes telling her the truth will excuse all of them."

Mama Sky shakes her head. "What my daughter sees in you, I'll never know."

O says, "Mama!"

Mama Sky smiles again, and the rain stops. Street thinks that Mama Sky knows what a young woman might see in him. Then he wonders if that means O sees something in him that isn't as annoying as what he sees in her. He glances at her and only sees annoyance.

Mama Sky says, "You children come in."

The return of bright sunlight feels good on Street's skin, but he says, "Thank you, ma'am," quickly to keep O from saying anything. He grins at O, then heads inside.

The living room is small and comfortable and filled with furniture in every shade of dawn and dusk and clouds and rainbows.

Mama Sky says, "Let me get you some tea," and O says almost as quickly, "We can't stay," and Street says just as quickly, "Tea would be lovely."

O glares at him. Mama Sky beams and goes into the kitchen. Street circles the living room, ignoring O and looking for anything that might be called a black rock. The only things in the room as dark as an overcast midnight are a pillow and a plate stand and the bindings of some books.

Mama Sky returns with a blue tray, a blue teapot, and a blue plate heaped high with macaroons and meringues. Street says, "Allow me," and hurries to help her.

She smiles and shakes her head and sets the tray on a coffee table painted with children flying kites and sailing in boats. "I'm not so helpless." She pours a cup of tea for each of them.

Street's afraid that O will refuse hers, but she accepts it and says quietly, "Thank you, Mother."

Street takes a deep drink. It's green tea with ginger, and he doesn't have to lie when he says, "Delicious!" He crams a meringue into his mouth, swallows, sips tea, crams a macaroon, swallows, sips tea, and then notices the women staring at him.

Mama Sky says, "When did you last eat?"

Street opens his mouth to answer. When he thinks about the past, he remembers playing tricks, sometimes for money, sometimes for fun. He remembers running and hiding because few people have as finely developed a sense of humor as he. He remembers eating and drinking things that had to be consumed quickly because they tasted terrible or he had to get someplace quickly. But he can't remember when he last sat still and ate. "I've been kind of busy today." He eats six more cookies, but more slowly, savoring each bite.

Mama Sky says, "Let me fix you a sandwich."

Street says, "I'd surely love that some other time, but I'm under a deadline. With the emphasis on dead."

Mama Sky frowns. "Whose deadline?"

Street says, "Bossman Sevenday's."

The room darkens. Street thinks it will rain again. Then everything lightens, and Mama Sky says, "You're trying to find this rock for Bossman Sevenday?"

Street says, "Yes, ma'am."

Mama Sky says, "I wouldn't have anything belonging to that, that —" She spits into a flowerpot. "But Ms. Brigitte's a fine lady, and I'd help you for her sake, if I could. But I can't."

O stands. "Dead end, T. Let's go."

Street asks Mama Sky, "Do you ever shop at the Meandering Market?"

Mama Sky says, "Why would I? I have my garden. Visitors bring me things. I have much more than I need."

O says, "See, T? All done here. Let's go."

Street says, "Did anyone bring anything like a rock? Maybe something for your garden?"

Mama Sky says, "No, I assure you, that is not the case."

O says, "Wasting time, T. You got free food. Time to move."

Mama Sky says, "But you know, someone did bring me something last week. That Stormboy." She looks at O. "He's quite proper, and dependable, too." She looks at Street, then laughs. "All kinds of dependable, though. Sometimes dependable fun is best."

O says, "Stormboy isn't dependable fun. He's dependable un-fun."

Mama Sky says, "Maybe I shouldn't have pushed you to take up with him."

"Maybe not," O agrees.

"Trickster's not so bad," Mama Sky says. Then she looks at Street and says, "But I'll count my silver when you leave." Then she laughs.

Street says, "I wouldn't take anything from you, Mama Sky."

Mama Sky says, "You know, I believe you, which proves I have some foolishness in me. But you took something from Bossman Sevenday."

Street shrugs. "I don't like him." Then he frowns. "But I didn't take anything from him."

Mama Sky says, "Why does he want you to find his rock?"

Street says proudly, "Because I can." Then he frowns. "Bossman Sevenday seems to think I'm responsible. But I'd remember—"

O says, "What?"

Street says, "That's mad."

O says, "What is?"

Street says, "I remember everything I did for the last six days. I don't remember a thing before. It's like the world started then."

Mama Sky smiles. "World's much, much older than that, Trickster."

Street shakes his head, then says, "What did Stormboy bring you?"

Mama Sky goes to a shelf covered with little things like white twigs and seashells and porcelain statues of white and black pugs. She picks up a blue cloth bag tied with blue string and says, "Stormboy said this brings luck in love. So long as I don't look in it, there's hope for him to court my O. But if I think he's not the one to encourage, I might as well open it and keep what's in it." Mama Sky looks at O. "And since you're so set on not having him—" She starts to pull the end of the string that's tied around the bag.

Street and O yell together, "No!"

Mama Sky looks at them. "Don't you want to know if it's this black rock?"

Street says, "If I was playing a trick, I'd set up something like that." As the women frown at him, he adds, "Only it'd be a subtler, smarter, and much kinder trick than I'd expect someone like Stormboy to play."

72

O says, "Yours are hardly ever subtle, smart, or kind." Then she adds, "But Stormboy's idea of subtle is a mudslide or a lightning strike." She holds her hand out to Mama Sky. Mama Sky sets the blue bag in O's palm. O traces the shape of the thing in the bag, then nods. "It's the rock."

Street says, "And it's a trick?"

O nods. "Stormboy is an even more despicable weasel than you."

Street grins. "You like someone less than me?"

O says, "Now you only have to move higher in my opinion than everyone else in the world."

Street laughs. "A start is a start."

7

As O drives down Cigarillo Canyon, Street lifts the blue bag off the console. The rock inside is the size of a small chicken egg. It feels familiar in his hand.

O says, "Put it back."

"I was thinking I'd take a little peek."

"You were not."

"Okay, I was thinking I'd pretend to take a little peek to trick some information from you."

"Like?"

"Like what would happen if I took a little peek."

"Why would I know?"

"Because you stopped your mother as fast as I did. Maybe faster."

"Maybe I had the same thought you did."

Street tugs the string to untie the bag.

O says, "No!" and reaches for it.

Street dangles it just beyond her reach. "Here's what I think. I think there's all kinds of things you're not telling."

"As if that's hard to figure out."

"And something stole my memories six days ago. This rock."

O laughs. "A rock takes people's memories. Yeah, right."

"Last, I think if I take the rock out, I'll lose six more days, but you'll lose everything up to this moment. And we'll be equal."

O glances from the road to him. "That'd be a dirty trick."

Street nods. "Yeah." He ties the bag up and sets it back on the console.

73

At the end of Cigarillo, O turns onto Tree Lizard. Street can't read what's going on behind her smooth expression. He thinks that she's her mother's daughter, then wonders why he likes knowing that. He says, "I don't know if it means anything to say you're sorry for something you don't remember, but I am sorry."

O flicks her cool eyes to him, then back to the road. They're driving through Flamingoville, a neighborhood that's nice for nothing special except being nice: bright little houses, friendly shops, good cheap restaurants, sidewalks filled with lazy, happy people.

Street says, "I think I did something stupid, and you tracked me down, and now you're trying to help and punish me at the same time."

"What do you think you did?"

"Since you're too fine for me to have gone chasing someone else, um, I stole the black rock from Bossman Sevenday?"

O nods. "You're such an idiot."

Street hits the glove compartment with the flat of his hand. "Oh, man! I am such an idiot!"

"I told you that."

"I was hoping you'd say someone framed me. I really stole it?"

"They say you were drunk at the Talon with a little box, telling our crowd you were the best thief ever because you could steal the black rock from Bossman Sevenday and put it back before he noticed. And you had the rock to prove it."

"He caught me putting it back?"

O shakes her head. "Everyone laughed and said anything could be in that box. How could you know what you had in it? So you got angry and looked inside—"

"Am I that stupid?"

O nods. "Then you wandered off looking twice as drunk. No one knew what happened after that. So I started asking for the word on Trickster, and I heard about a kid called Street who went by that handle. The rest is history."

Street grins. "So, um, does that mean you and I are—?"

O says, "Were."

Street grins wider. "I may be stupid, but I do have great taste."

"Did you hear the past tense?"

Street keeps grinning. "I still have great taste."

O shakes her head sadly. "I still have terrible taste." Then she finally smiles at him. The wait was worth it

When O turns the smile back to the road, Street says, "What bothers me is why a man would have a rock that makes people forget everything?"

O says, "Who said a man had a rock like that?"

Street swallows. "So, Bossman Sevenday is—?"

O says, "Who would you steal from to prove you're the best thief ever?"

"Not the All One. No way it's the All One. Tell me I'm not that stupid."

O says,"You're not that stupid."

Street stares ahead, and feels his eyes stretching wide, and he wants to scream. He closes his mouth and says quietly, "Death. I'm stupid enough to steal from Death."

O nods. "All the newly dead still have their memories, thanks to you. Bossman says they're making quite the ruckus. He'll be glad to get the rock back."

Street looks at the blue bag. "He's getting it back. He'll be glad." Street laughs. "Nothing to be worried about, then."

O says, "He's Death."

Street says, "Is there someplace else we can go?"

"Where Death can't find you?"

Street tries to swallow again, but his throat is dry. He says in a rough whisper, "Then let's take him the rock."

"Good," says O, and she turns off Memorial into the big ivory gates to Bossman Sevenday's home.

8

As they walk up the white marble steps, the door is opened by an elegant dark woman in a dress as black as the heart of a cave. She says, "You're early."

O says, "Yes, ma'am."

Street says, "You're Ms. Brigitte? I'm—"

"Trickster," says the dark woman. "Indeed, you are. I shall tell my husband—"

Bossman Sevenday's voice booms from deep within the mansion. "Trickster! Oya! So good of you to return so soon!"

Ms. Brigitte steps back, opening the door wide. A pale hall with many closed doors along its sides stretches into murky shadows. Street's focus is on Bossman Sevenday, striding toward them in impeccable evening wear. Even the near end of the long hall is dim. There's a reddish glow to the west, though Street was sure he came into the house from midafternoon.

Ms. Brigitte says, "Business tires me," and leaves the hall, closing a pair of white doors behind her. The air smells of cigarettes and perfume and oranges and peanut butter and all the other smells that Street has ever known, but muted. He hears music and laughter and crying and gasps that are the sound of loving or dying, equally muted. He looks at O. "Oya?"

She nods.

He says, "A good name. I'm sorry I forgot it."

She smiles, and he thinks that if nothing is good after this moment, he could be content. And then he thinks that's the stupidest thought he has ever had, because he wants everything to be even better. He calls, "Mr. Bossman Sevenday, sir? I've got your rock." He holds out the cloth bag.

As Bossman Sevenday reaches for it, Street thinks about jerking the stone out. But it belongs to Bossman Sevenday, who must know how to show it to the dead without forgetting who he is. Maybe his dark glasses let him look on the stone. Street could knock off the glasses. The idea is tempting, but it doesn't seem like a good idea to risk making Death like him even less. Letting Bossman take the bag, Street says, "I'm glad to have this straightened out. Taking something from Bossman Sevenday! You know only a fool would do that."

"Yes, I do," says Bossman Sevenday, laughing as he takes Street's arm. "Walk with me."

O says, "The gem's back. Everything is back the way it should be now."

Bossman Sevenday says, "Not quite. Someone stole from me."

Street almost smiles in pride, then stops himself. "Not really, Mr. Bossman Sevenday, sir. You've got the rock back. And if you've got it, it's like it was never gone, so no one could say anything was taken. Not really. If you see what I mean."

Bossman Sevenday laughs. "They'll talk, Trickster. Which is why you must come with me now."

Street says, "Oya, want to wait outside for me? I shouldn't be long."

Bossman Sevenday shakes his head and laughs louder. "Ah, Trickster, don't ask her to be that patient."

Street says, "You're taking me now?"

Bossman Sevenday nods.

"And I'm not coming back?"

Bossman Sevenday nods again.

"I didn't expect this."

Bossman Sevenday says, "Expecting things is not one of your gifts, Trickster."

O says, "Bossman, I'm asking—"

Bossman Sevenday shakes his head. "Some things I must do with no thought of others."

Street says, "I can't believe it. No one'll believe it at first."

Bossman Sevenday says, "Believe what?"

Street drops to his knees. "Oya! See me here before the Bossman!"

As O squints at him, Bossman Sevenday says, "Begging won't save you."

"I'm not begging." Street clasps his hands together.

Bossman Sevenday says, "Sure looks like—"

Street cries, "Thank you, Mr. Bossman Sevenday, sir! Thank you!"

Bossman Sevenday frowns.

Street glances at O, "You see how happy I am? You tell everyone of Bossman Sevenday's kindness! You tell 'em to stop fearing him, because he's the most forgiving gentleman there could be!"

O nods hesitantly.

Street looks back up at Bossman Sevenday. "I was terrified you'd kick me out in the world without my memories, and folks would laugh at me for the rest of my life as the poor fool who tried to steal from you. I thought I'd suffer and suffer as the proof that no one should mess with you."

Bossman Sevenday says, "You will—"

Street cries louder, "Now Oya's seen how you'll even forgive a trickster who was fool enough to steal from you. People will come up to you and say you're the gentlest gentleman of all!" Street leans forward and kisses Bossman's cold shoes. "See, Oya! Tell 'em how grateful I was when you left me!" He kisses Bossman's shoes again. The leather is even colder against his lips. "Bless you, Bossman Sevenday! Bless you!"

Bossman Sevenday looks at O, then at Street. Smoke comes from behind his round sunglasses, and they begin to glow red, and he says, "Get. Up."

Street says, "Are we going now, Bossman?" He scrambles to his feet and grins. "I can't wait!"

Bossman Sevenday's face is a flaming skull as he screams, "Get out! You get out of here this instant!"

Street says, "But Bossman, haven't you forgiven—"

O grabs his wrist and jerks him toward the door.

Street says, "No, O! I beg you! Don't make me go back!"

They stumble down the long hall. The tiles rock beneath them as the earth quakes. Doors blow open. Harsh winds like arctic storms and scorching desert gales buffet them from each door that they pass, and they hear screams and wails of despair. And as they run, Street shouts, "Let me go back, O! Please!"

Ms. Brigitte stands at the front door. She glares at them, then throws the doors wide and shouts, "You deserve no less!"

"No! Please, no!" cries Street. He and O plunge down the steps and leap into the Zephyr and race away from Bossman Sevenday's home.

And, as they go, Street is not sure whether the sound that he hears is Bossman's rage or his laughter.

9

Street stretches in the car as they cruise into the city. O looks at him and says, "I don't think you know the meaning of subtlety."

Street nods. "I'm not the only one."

O says, "You don't have your memories."

Street says, "I know life's good, and you're the best there is. What else do I need to know?"

O laughs. "Not one thing at all."

Street says, "So everyone in our crowd has a purpose?"

O nods. "More or less. And duties with the purpose."

Street says, "What about me?"

O shakes her head.

Street laughs. "So my only purpose—" He smiles smugly at O. "—is to be."

O smiles back. "A pain."

He shrugs. "Well, yes. Everyone's good at something."

Dream Catcher

Will Shetterly

Dear John Marshall,

My name is Crosses Water Safely. At school, I was called my white name, Janine Skunk. I didn't know my real name then. You always held your nose and waved your hand in front of your face when you saw me, and everyone laughed. Grandmother says skunks are beautiful and smart. She says anyone who can trick Rabbit is smart, and Rabbit knows to leave Skunk alone.

Grandmother dreamed my real name. She saw me in a storm in the front of a canoe. Many people were in the canoe, and they were all scared. But I was not scared. The people stopped being scared when they saw I was not scared. And then the storm went away.

Grandmother lives on a reservation up north. Father said she is a bush Indian. And he laughed like you always did at school, John Marshall. My mother looked down and did not say anything. I want to be a bush Indian when I grow up.

Grandmother came to stay with us last fall. She came because Father told her I was having bad dreams. He laughed when she showed up at our door. He said she was a bad dream herself, and where would she sleep? She said she would sleep on the floor of my room if she had to. She came because she had made something for me. A dream catcher.

Grandmother said all dream catchers look like spider webs. It doesn't matter what they're made of. She made the frame of mine with basswood twine and birch branches. The colored string came from a Hudson Bay store. You hang the dream catcher in your window. Bad dreams get caught in it, but good dreams pass right through.

When we hung the dream catcher in my room, Grandmother asked if I remembered the bad dreams. She looked at me very hard and said it was important. I said not really. She asked if I remembered anything about them. I said maybe. She asked what I remembered. I said red eyes. She asked what else. I just shook my head and laughed like the dreams were silly.

I didn't have any bad dreams that night. In the morning, Grandmother looked at the dream catcher and looked at me and smiled. I smiled at her, too. I wanted her to stay with us forever.

That was the day I took the dream catcher to Show and Tell and told how Grandmother made it for me. Our teacher said it was a good report. But in the hall, you grabbed the dream catcher and said a skunk should be able to scare away bad dreams with its stink. When you threw it down the hall, I was glad it didn't break.

That night, Father asked Grandmother if she wasn't tired of sleeping on my floor. She said she didn't mind. I didn't have any bad dreams that night, either. In the morning, I looked hard at the dream catcher, but I couldn't see any dreams. Grandmother said I didn't know how to look. But someday I would see everything better.

That day, you asked if my grandmother had made me a brain catcher, 'cause I could sure use one. Also, Father asked me to go to the park and play softball with him. I said I was tired. Mother said I was always tired and always in my room and I should go.

When we came back, Father said he needed a shower. Mother said he sure did. Father said I should shower too. I said I was okay. He laughed like I was very funny and said to come on, don't waste water. Then he saw Grandmother looking, and he said oh, forget it.

After dinner, he brought home a brand new living room couch that folded out into a bed. He said Grandmother should sleep comfortably, since she wanted to stay with us forever. Grandmother said he did not have to do that. He said it was done, and he wanted her to be comfortable. He took a big drink of beer and he didn't say anything else. Grandmother looked at me and didn't say anything, either.

At bedtime, she said if I needed her, I should just call. I could not answer. I laughed like it was okay and went into my room and put on the nightlight and got into bed.

I lay there for a long time, trying to go to sleep. I told myself it was okay with Grandmother in the next room. But it wasn't okay with Mother in the next room.

Then I heard him standing outside the door. I smelled him there. I prayed for him to go away, and I told God I was sorry for whatever I had done. Then he opened the door and whispered my white name. I tried not to hear. When he got into the bed, I tried not to look. He turned my face so I had to look. He said he loved me. His eyes were all bloodshot.

When the door opened, he jumped up and pointed at me and said, "She wanted—" and "You don't think I was going to—" and "I was drunk, I didn't know—"

Grandmother came straight to me and hugged me. She wrapped my blanket around me real tight. She said, "We're going."

Father said, "It's not what you're thinking! You can't believe—"

Grandmother led me to the dream catcher and took it down from the window.

"She's my daughter!" Father yelled. "You're not taking her—"

Grandmother held up the dream catcher and said, "Look."

He looked at it, and then at her, and then at me. I looked at the dream catcher. Grandmother handed it to me. I hugged it. Father screamed and ran out.

Mother was in the hallway. She did not say anything as we went out. Father was in the living room, curled up in a ball and gasping. Grandmother did not slow down.

I am living on the reservation now. I have two best friends, Adam Mishenene and Martha Kwandibens. I have a dog, Socks. He walks funny because he was hit by a car, but he will fetch anything. I have to talk to a counselor every week who thinks if I say everything that happened, it will be better. Mother and Father have to see a counselor too. Maybe we will be a family again this summer. I said I would give it a try, anyway, and everyone cried.

I wrote to my old teacher, asking how everyone was. She said you had been taken away, John Marshall. When I saw that, I was happy. Then she said your parents had been doing something bad to you for a long time. That is why I am sending you what's with this letter. You hang it in the window, and only the good dreams come through.

Your friend,

Crosses Water Safely (Janine Skunk)

Stories by Emma Bull

The Princess and the Lord of Night

Emma Bull

This story is for Carolyn Brust, with best wishes.

Once upon a time there was a princess who had everything she wanted. She had a horse as white as the high clouds of a summer sky who could run from one end of the kingdom to the other in a day. She had a walnut-brown dog who understood anything she said. She had an ash-gray cat as swift as a blink and as clever as six professors. She had a crow as black as the inside of an inkwell who could recite every poem ever written. She had a velvet cloak as blue as twilight that could turn its wearer invisible.

Whenever the princess said she wanted anything—or even when she looked as if she might want something—the king and the queen, her father and mother, hurried to give it to her. For the Lord of Night had put a curse on the princess when she was born, that if ever she wanted something she couldn't have, the kingdom would fall into ruin and the king and queen would die.

Some people, if they got everything they wanted, would become spoiled and silly before they could turn around once. But the princess had seen her mother and father hurrying to get her whatever she wanted, afraid that the Lord of Night might appear in a burst of green smoke and destroy the kingdom if they failed.

The princess felt terrible about it, so she tried to delight in all she had instead of longing for more. Still, there were her horse, and her dog, and her cat, and her crow, and her cloak, which she had wanted and gotten, and she was glad to have them.

On the morning of her thirteenth birthday, the princess woke very early and sat straight up in bed. She had dreamed of something she wanted, and now that she was awake, she found she wanted it more

85

than ever. But she resolved not to tell the king and queen about it. She would go out and get it for herself.

So she mounted her white horse, who could run from one end of the kingdom to the other in a day. She called her brown dog, who understood everything she said. She put her gray cat, swift as a blink and clever as six professors, on the saddle before her. She set the crow that could recite all the world's poems on her shoulder, and tucked the velvet cloak that could make her invisible into the saddle case. Then she rode out into the kingdom to look for what she wanted.

She hadn't been riding for an hour before she met a young man sitting on a stone by the side of the road. He'd covered his face with both hands, and she thought he might be crying.

"What is your trouble?" the princess called to him, from high atop her white horse.

"Oh," he said, looking up at her, "my mother is wasting away with sickness. I have a charm to cure her, but I have to use it before the sun goes down, and she lives far away, on the edge of the sea. I can never reach her in time."

"Well," said the princess, "I want your mother to be well and you to be happy. Take my horse, and you'll be there in time for dinner."

At that, the young man leaped up, full of hope. The princess unstrapped the saddle case and set it on the ground. Then she helped him mount the white horse, and watched as they disappeared, fast as the wind, bound for the edge of the sea.

"That's a start to my journey," said the princess, and went on down the road with her dog, her cat, her crow, and the case that held her cloak.

A little farther along the way she entered a forest, and in the forest under a tree she met a ragged, weeping little girl.

"Whatever is the matter?" asked the princess.

"I've lost our sheep," the little girl sobbed, "the ones I was driving to market to sell. They took fright and scattered into the trees. Now I'll have to go home with nothing, and all my brothers and sisters will go cold and hungry."

"That would be a sorry thing," said the princess. "I want you to stop crying, and your family to be well. Here, I shall give you my dog, who understands speech. Tell her to round up all your sheep and help you drive them to market, and she'll do just as you say."

86

The little girl called to the dog, which bounded up to her. As the princess set off again, she heard the sheep maaa-ing and baaa-ing as the dog drove them out of the woods.

"I've miles to go yet," the princess said to herself, and went on down the road with her cat, her crow, and her cloak.

She was growing hungry, so when she came to a cottage she decided to stop and ask if anyone there could spare her a bit of bread. When she knocked on the door there was no answer. But she thought she heard a noise inside, so she opened the door and stepped in.

An old woman sat on a stool there, weeping into her apron.

"Why do you weep so, Grandmother?" asked the princess.

"It's the rats!" wailed the old woman. "They've eaten my corn and my oats and my wheat, and tonight they'll finish my barley. And that's all I have to keep me from starving."

"Then dry your tears," the princess bid her. "I want you to be merry, and your larder to be full. So you may have my cat. There's no rat in all the world can outrun or outsmart him. And when I return home, I'll send you corn and oats and wheat to replace what you've lost, and a cow to milk besides."

The old woman leaped up with a shout and threw her arms around the princess. Before she could say "Farewell," the cat had killed three rats and was hunting a fourth.

"One foot in front of the other," the princess said, and went on down the road with her crow and her cloak.

In a little while, she came to a house that stood all alone. There she saw a man sitting on the front step. Tears streamed down his face, but he never made a sound.

"Heavens, what's amiss?" asked the princess.

He shook his head and beckoned her closer. When she put her face down next to his, he whispered, "My poor daughter has fallen under an enchantment. She can neither move nor speak, and the only way to break the spell is to talk to her for three days and three nights. I've talked for a day and a night and half a day, and now I'm so hoarse I cannot talk at all. What can I do to help my girl?"

"I've just the thing," said the princess. "I want your daughter to go free and you to get your voice back, so I'll give you my crow who can recite every verse in the world. Just let him perch by your daughter's right hand, and she'll have poems and songs until she can sing them herself."

At that the man flung his hat into the air and took the crow with great delight.

"The path to home's not easy yet," the princess said, and went on down the road, carrying the case that held her cloak that could turn its wearer invisible.

At last she came to a place where the land was hilly, and great boulders stood all around. It was a strange place, and smelled of magic. As she rounded a bend in the road, she came upon a little boy sitting on the ground with his face hidden in his arms.

"Are you not well?" asked the princess, but cautiously, because she knew one should be cautious in such a place.

The boy looked up, and she saw it wasn't a boy at all, but a very small brown man with long pointed ears, and a long, long moustache that reached to his waist, and sharp black eyes in a face as wrinkled as a raisin. "Why do you ask?" he said.

"Because I will help if I can," the princess said.

"No one can help," said the little brown man. "The Lord of Night has stolen away my magic in a box of elder wood, and set a beast to guard it. The beast has six eyes on each side of its head. It never eats and it never sleeps. What can you do about that?"

"I've a score of my own to settle with the Lord of Night," the princess told him, "but if I didn't, I would still give you my cloak, because I want you to have justice. Wrap it around you, and you'll be as invisible as air. Then you may walk past the beast as you please, and take your magic back."

The little man gathered up the velvet cloak and looked long at her with his fierce black eyes. "This is a good favor you've done me," he said, "and I would do one for you. But without my magic, I haven't much."

He pulled a fine gold ring with a blue stone off his thumb. "Still, you may have this from me," said the little brown man. "If you keep the stone turned in, what people tell you will come true. But if you turn the stone out, then promise what they will, everything they say will end up false."

"Thank you very much," the princess replied, "and I'll take care with it."

She blinked, and the little man was gone, because he'd wrapped himself in her cloak.

"Journey's end," the princess said. She put the little man's ring in her pocket and set out home again by the shortest way.

When she reached the palace, her mother and father ran out to meet her.

"Daughter, tell me quickly. Is there anything you want?" the queen asked, full of fear.

"Why do you want to know?" said the princess.

"Because the Lord of Night is here," answered her father the king, "and he says we must give up our kingdom and our lives because the curse has come to pass."

"Oh," said the princess. "Well, tell him if he'd like to know what I want, he'll have to ask me himself. Bring him to me."

The king and queen hurried back to the palace. In a moment, the Lord of Night himself, dressed all in black and with eyes like little flames, came out to meet her. The king and queen followed behind him, their faces pale as milk.

"I think there is something you want," he said, in a voice like wind hissing through dead leaves.

"And what would that be?" said the princess, as bravely as she could, though she was terrified. She had never before been face to face with the Lord of Night.

"Your horse and your dog are gone, and your cat and your crow."

"That they are," the princess answered. "A young man has the horse, a little girl has the dog, an old woman has the cat, and a man and his daughter have the crow." But the princess said nothing about her cloak, because the Lord of Night hadn't.

"I gave the wasting sickness to the young man's mother," the Lord of Night said, cracking his fingers one by one. "I frightened the little girl's sheep, so that they would all be lost in the forest. I sent the rats to eat the old woman's grain, and I laid the enchantment on the man's daughter so that she could neither move nor speak. I did all that to trap you. I made you give up the things you want."

"That's not true," the princess replied. "I gave away my horse to the young man because I wanted him to save his mother. I gave my dog to the little girl because I wanted her to get her sheep to market. I gave my cat to the old woman because I wanted her to have enough to eat. I gave my crow to the man because I wanted his daughter to move and speak again. And I wanted all of them to be happy. I got just what I wanted."

"It's not so!" cried the Lord of Night. "You want something. You've wanted something since this morning, and haven't got it. I know, I can smell it all around you!"

"Now that," said the princess, "is a fact, and I'll tell you what it is. I want to be free of your curse." And she slipped her hand in her pocket, where she'd put the ring the little brown man had given her.

"Never!" the Lord of Night shrieked. "You'll bear that curse until the end of your life."

But as he spoke, the princess popped the fine gold ring on her finger and turned the blue stone to face out. Then she took her hand out of her pocket and showed the ring to the Lord of Night.

He stared in dread at the ring with its blue stone sparkling at him like laughter. "Where did you get that ring? Where?" he screamed.

"I think you know where," said the princess, "and I think you know this ring. A little brown man gave it to me, and told me that if I turned it so that the stone faced out, anything said to me would be made false. And that's what I did when you spoke. Now my curse is gone, for you did the uncursing yourself."

"Then the little brown man shall pay for it," vowed the Lord of Night in a fury.

"Will he? But he gave me the ring in return for my cloak that makes its wearer invisible, and if he hasn't used it by now, I'd be surprised."

"No! No!" the Lord of Night howled, and disappeared in a burst of green smoke.

The king and queen were overjoyed. They announced a great celebration to be held the very next night in the palace. The princess invited the young man, the little girl, the old woman, and the man and his daughter.

The young man brought his mother, who was as hale and rosy as if she'd never been sick in her life. The little girl brought her parents and her brothers and sisters, all dressed in handsome new clothes they'd bought with money from selling their sheep. The old woman brought a sweet, spicy cake she'd made from her flour. The man and his daughter danced the night away, and the daughter sang like a flute as she danced.

The princess invited the little brown man, too, but if he was there, no one saw him. Everyone who came said there had never been a better party or a better reason to have one, and all of them lived happily ever after.

Man of Action

Emma Bull

My therapist had quite a lot to say
When I explained I was unmoved by chocolates and bouquets.
"What are you looking for in love," she asked, "that you can't find?"
I said, "The smell of cordite would brighten up my day."
Does he wear his jacket loose to hide the holster?
Does he keep his schedule free to cut and run?
I'm the girl dressed in black in the Lotus Elan
And I'm looking for a man of action.
She says I long to nurture secretly,
But sensitive and sweet gives me a case of ennui.
See, I want a hero from a Hong Kong action flick
With a brand new Smith & Wesson and a taste for irony
Does his hair smell like the smoke from burning buildings?
Does he have a dragon tattoo on his arm?
I'm the girl on the train with the timer for the bomb
And I'm looking for a man of action.
I could be happy with a man who's built for speed
A heat trace like an F-16, a ruthless sense of style
Strange clicking on his phone line, scars he can't explain
Who never takes the first cab and who doesn't often smile.
Afraid I'm gonna have to miss our session
Hope you've got another patient due to make confession
I'll be at the airport in my trenchcoat and my shades
Looking for a long-legged dark-haired indiscretion.
Does he drive like hell-hounds know his license number?
Does he always sit where he can see the door?
I'm the girl on the bridge with the bag full of money
I'm the girl at the stick of the black helicopter
And I'm looking for a man of action.

The Last of John Ringo

Emma Bull

You were dead, all but the bullet.
Was there a shining, sober moment,
A choice, a rightness,
Like the one between the trigger pulled
And the target struck,
When the end seemed the only, perfect one?
Last waltz, last chord, and home in the moonlight?
Or was it disarray on discord—
One thing forgotten, another misplaced,
A third mishandled, a fourth dropped unheeded—
Until your life, continued,
Would have been bootless, horseless,
A cartridge belt upside down:
Fool's motley for a dying boomtown?
There was water in the mines.
There was no next town,
No next good game.
The sunset only day's end,
Not a curtain before the next grand act,
Not a promise to ride on toward.
So you chose, or the gods chose for you.
Untidy life, snagged to knots with other lives,
Gives way at last to one smooth course of myth.
From your black-oak wayside seat
It was a snarl beyond your picking-out.
But those who lived dug channels for your past,
Made art of you,
And art makes sense.
So crude despair or drunk mischance gave place

To murder: thundering vengeance come at last.
That's an end that makes a tale;
That's a villain makes a hero.
The point of all your restless, angry life
Was that it ended. Choice, chance, or retribution:
How would you have lived, knowing your dead man's fame?
A final joke: the boomtown survived.
It breathes now as a place you'd not have lived in,
But dead, you are a model citizen,
Necessary, as all coins have two sides.
To those who want forever for their names
You say, "Choose big enemies, and hope for bigger lies.
Then sit down by the road."
You were dead. But not for long.

De la Tierra

Emma Bull

The piano player drums away with her left hand, dropping all five fingers onto the keys as if they weigh too much for her to hold up. The rhythms bounce off the rhythms of what her right hand does, what she sings. It's like there's three different people in that little skinny body, one running each hand, the third one singing. But they all know what they're doing.

He sucks a narrow stream of Patrón over his tongue and lets it heat up his mouth before he swallows. He wishes he knew how to play an instrument. He wouldn't mind going up at the break, asking if he could sit in, holding up a saxophone case, maybe, or a clarinet. He'd still be here at 3 a.m., jamming, while the waiters mopped the floors.

That would be a good place to be at 3 a.m. Much better than rolling up the rug, burning the gloves, dropping the knife over the bridge rail. Figuratively speaking.

They aren't that unalike, she and he. He has a few people in his body, too, and they also know what they're doing.

The difference is, his have names.

"*¿Algo mas?*" The wide-faced waitress sounds Salvadoran. She looks too young to be let into a bar, let alone make half a bill a night in tips. She probably sends it all home to *mami*. The idea annoys him. Being annoyed annoys him, too. No skin off his nose if she's not blowing it at the mall.

He actually *is* too young to legally swallow this liquor in a public place, but of course he's never carded. A month and a half and he'll be twenty-one. Somebody ought to throw a party. "*Nada. Grácias.*"

She smiles at him. "Where you from? Chihuahua?"

"Burbank." Why does she care where he's from? He shouldn't have answered in Spanish.

97

"No, your people—where they from? My best friend's from Chihuahua. You look kinda like her brother."

"Then he looks like an American."

She actually seems hurt. "But everybody's from someplace."

Does she mean "everybody," or "everybody who's brown like us?" "Yep. Welcome to Los Angeles."

He and the tequila bid each other goodbye, like a hug with a friend at the airport. Then he pushes the glass at the waitress. She smacks it down on her tray and heads for the bar. There, even the luggage disappears from sight. He rubs the bridge of his nose.

Positive contact, Chisme answers from above his right ear. Chisme is female and throaty, for him, anyway. *All numbers optimal to high optimal. Operation initialized.*

He lays a ten on the table and pins the corner down with the candle jar. He wishes it were a twenty, for the sake of the Salvadoran economy. But big tippers are memorable. He stands up and heads for the door.

Behind him he hears the piano player sweep the keys, low to high, and it hits his nerves like a scream. He almost turns—

Adrenal limiter enabled. Suppression under external control.

Just like everything else about him. All's right with the world. He breathes deep and steps out into the streetlights and the smell of burnt oil.

The bar's in Koreatown. The target is in downtown L.A. proper, in the jewelry district. Always start at least five miles from the target, in case someone remembers the unmemorable. Show respect for the locals, even if they're not likely to believe you exist.

He steps into the shadow that separates two neon window signs and slips between, fastlanes. He's down at Hill and Broadway in five minutes. He rubs the bridge of his nose again. *Three percent discharge*, says Chisme. After three years he can tell by the way it feels, but it's reflex to check.

The downtown air is oven-hot, dry and still, even at this hour, and the storm drains smell. They'll keep that up until the rains come and wash them clean months from now. He turns the corner and stops before the building he wants.

There's a jewelry store on the first floor. Security grills lattice the windows, and the light shines down on satin-upholstered stands with nothing on them. Painted on the inside of the glass is, "Gold Mart/Best prices on/Gold/Platinum/Chains & Rings." Straight up, below the fifth floor windows, there's a faded sign in block letters: "Eisenberg & Sons".

Time to call another of the names. He massages his right palm with his left thumb.

Magellan responds. Not with words, because words aren't what Magellan does. Against the darkness at the back of the store white lines form, like a scratchboard drawing. He knows they're not really inside the store, but his eye doesn't give a damn. The pictures show up wherever he's looking. This one is a cutaway of the building: the stairwell up the left side, the landings, the hallways on each floor. And the target, like a big lens flare...at the front of the fourth floor.

They're always on the *top* floor. Always. He focuses on the fifth floor of the diagram and massages his hand again. The zoom-in is so fast he staggers. *Vertical axis restored*, Chisme murmurs.

The fifth floor seems to be all storage; the white lines draw wire-frame cartons and a few pieces of broken furniture in the rooms.

Not right, not right. Top floor makes for a faster getaway, better protection from the likes of him. Ignoring strategy can only mean that the strategy has changed. He probes his upper left molar with his tongue, and Biblio's sexless whisper, like sand across rock, says, *Refreshing agent logs. Information updated at oh-two-oh-three.*

Fifteen minutes ago is good enough. He thinks through the logs, looking for surprises, new behaviors, deviations in the pattern. *Nada.* His fourth-floor sighting will be in the next update as an alert, an anomaly. He's contributed to the pool of knowledge. Whoopee for him.

He stands inside the doorway, trying to look like scenery, but every second he waits makes it worse. If the target gets the wind up, a nice routine job will have gone down the crapper. And if the neighborhood watch spooks and the LAPD sends a squad, the target will for sure get the wind up.

But it's not routine. He knows it, he's made and trained to know it. The target is not where it ought to be. The names are no help: they follow orders. Just as he does. *No te preocupes, hijo.* Do the job until it does for you; then there'll be another just like you to clean up the mess, and you'll be a note in the logs.

Blood pressure adjusted, Chisme notes. Not an admonishment, just a fact. The names give him facts. It's up to him what to do with them. To hell with the neighborhood watch. He touches thumb to middle finger on each hand, stands still, breathes from the belly. Chisme isn't the only one who can do his tune-up.

He takes the chameleon key from his pocket, casual as any guy who's left something on his desk at work—oops, yeah, officer, the wife'll kill me if I don't bring those tickets home tonight. The key looks like a brass Schlage; he could hand it to the cop and smile. But when it goes in the lock—

He feels it under his fingers, like a little animal shrugging. It's changing shape in there, finding the right notches and grooves and filling them. When it feels like a brass key again, he turns it, and the lock opens easy as a peck on the cheek.

Thirty seconds on the alarm, according to the documents in the archives of the security service that installed it. Biblio tells him what to punch on the keypad, and the display stops flashing, "ENTER CODE NOW" and offers him a placid, "SYSTEM DISARMED". This part is never hard. If a target showed up in one of the wannabe mansionettes on Chandler at four in the morning, he could walk right in and the homeowner would never know.

If nothing went wrong after the walking-in part, of course.

The stairs in front of him are ill-lit, sheathed in cracked linoleum and worn rubber nail-down treads. He smells dust, ammonia, and old cigarette smoke. But not the target, not yet.

He starts up toward the next floor.

•

The evening before, he got an official commendation for his outstanding record. He had to go to Chateau Marmont, up the hill from Sunset, to get it, and on a Friday, too, so he had to pay ten dollars for valet parking to get his head patted. Good dog. If he could fastlane on his own time, it would solve so many problems. But hey, at least there was still such a thing as "his own time."

She was out on the patio by the pool, stretched in a lounge chair. From there a person could see a corner of the Marmont bungalow where Belushi had overdosed. He was pretty sure she knew that; they liked things like celebrity death spots.

Some of them almost anyone could recognize—if almost anyone knew to look for them. They're always perfect, of their kind. That's why so many of them like L.A., where everybody gets extra credit for looking perfect. Try going unnoticed in Ames, Iowa, looking like that.

She had wavy golden hair to her shoulders, and each strand sparkled when the breeze shifted it. She wore a blue silk halter top, and little white shorts that showed how long and tan her legs were. She could've been one of those teen-star actresses pretending to be a Forties pin-up, except that she was too convincing. She sipped at a *mojito* without getting any lipstick on the glass.

For fun, he jabbed his molar with his tongue to see if Biblio could tell him anything about her—name, age, rank. *Nada, y nada mas.* None of them were ever in the database. Didn't hurt to try, though.

"Your disposal record is remarkable," she said, with no preface.

"I do my job." He wondered what other agents' records were. He was pretty sure there were others, though he'd never met them. She didn't ask him to sit down, so he didn't.

"A vital one, I assure you." She gazed out at the view: the L. A. basin all the way to Santa Monica, just beginning to light up for the night, and a very handsome sunset. No smog or haze. Could her kind make that happen, somehow? They'd more or less made him, but he was nothing compared to a clear summer evening in Los Angeles.

She turned to look at him fully, suddenly intent. "You understand that, don't you? That your work is essential to us?"

He shrugged. A direct gaze from one of them had tied better tongues than his.

"You're saving our way of life—even our lives themselves. These others come from places where they're surrounded by ignorant, superstitious peasants. They have no conception of how to blend in here, what the rules and customs are. And their sheer numbers..." She shook her head. "A stupid mistake by one of them, and we could all be revealed."

"So it's a quality-of-life thing?" he asked. "I thought the problem was limited resources."

She pressed her lips together and withdrew her gaze. The evening seemed immediately colder and less sweetly scented. "Our first concern, of course. We're very close to the upper limit of the carrying capacity of this area. Already there are..." (she closed her tilted blue eyes for a moment, as if she had a pain somewhere) "...empty spots. We are the guardians of this place. If we let these invaders overrun it, they'll strip it like locusts, as they strip their native lands."

A swift movement in the shrubbery—a hummingbird, shooting from one blossom to another. She smiled at it, and he thought, *Lucky damned bird*, even though he didn't want to.

"I still don't get it," he said, his voice sounding like a truck horn after hers. "Why not help them out? Say, '*Bienvenidos*, brothers and sisters, let's all go to Disneyland?' Then show them how it's done, and send them someplace where they can have their forty acres and a mule? They're just like you, aren't they?"

She turned from the bird and met his eyes. If he thought he'd felt the force of her before, now he knew he'd felt nothing, nothing. "Have you seen many of them," she asked, "who are just like me?"

He's seen one or two who might have become like her, in time, with work. But none so perfect, so powerful, so unconsciously arrogant, so serenely *sure*, as she and the others who hold his leash.

•

He's on the first landing before he remembers to check the weapon. Chisme monitors that, too, and would have said something if it wasn't registering. But it's not Chisme's ass on the line (if, in fact, Chisme *has* one). Trust your homies, but check your own rifle.

He holds his left palm up in front of him in the gloom and makes a fist, then flexes his wrist backward. At the base of his palm the tiny iron needles glow softly, row on row, making a rosy light under his skin.

He used to wonder how they got the needles in there without a scar, and why they glow when he checks them, and how they work when he wants them to. Now he only thinks about it when he's on the clock. Part of making sure that he can still call some of the day his own.

When he finishes here, he'll be debriefed. That's how he thinks of it. He'll go to whatever place Magellan shows him, do whatever seems to be expected of him, and end by falling asleep. When he wakes up the needles will be there again.

He goes up the stairs quiet and fast, under his own power. If he fastlanes this close, the target will know he's here. He's in good shape: he can hurry up three flights of stairs and still breathe easy. That's why he's in this line of work now. Okay, that and being in the wrong place at the right time.

102

Introspection is multitasking, and multitasking can have unpleasant consequences. That's what the names are for, *hijo*. Keep your head in the job.

Half the offices here are vacant. The ones that aren't have temporary signs, the company name in a reasonably businesslike typeface, coughed out of the printer and taped to the door. Bits of tape from the last company's sign still show around the edges. The hallway's overhead fluorescent is like twilight, as if there's a layer of soot on the inside of its plastic panel.

At least it's all offices; one less problem to deal with, *grácias a San Miguel.* Plenty of the buildings on Broadway are apartments above the first two floors, with Mom and Dad and four kids in a one-bedroom with not enough windows and no air conditioning. People sleep restless in a place like that.

Which makes him wonder: why *didn't* the target pick a place like that? Why make this easier?

On the fourth floor, the hall light buzzes on and off, on and off. He feels a pre-headache tightness behind his eyebrows as his eyes try to correct, and his heart rate climbs. Is the light the reason for this floor? Does the target know about him, how he works, and picked this floor because of it?

Chisme gives his endocrine system a twitch, and he stops vibrating. He's a well-kept secret. And if he isn't, all the more reason to get this done right.

He walks the length of the hallway, hugging the wall, pausing to listen before crossing the line of fire of each closed door. He doesn't expect trouble until the farthest door, but it's the trouble you don't expect that gets you. Even to his hearing, he doesn't make a sound.

Beside the last door, the one at the front of the building, he presses up against the wall and listens. A car goes through the intersection below; a rattle on the sidewalk may be a shopping cart. Nothing from inside the room. He breathes in deep and slow, and smells, besides the dry building odors, the scent of fresh water.

He probes his right palm with his thumb, and when Magellan sends him the diagram of the fourth floor, he turns his head to line it up with the real surfaces of the building. Here's the hall, and the door, and the room beyond it. There's the target: shifting concentric circles of light, painfully bright. Unless everything is shot to hell, it's up against

103

the front wall, near the window. And if everything *is* shot to hell, there's nothing he can do except go in there and find out.

At that, he feels an absurd relief. *We who are about to die.* From here on, it's all action, as quick as he can make it, and no more decisions. Quick, because as soon as he fastlanes the target will know he's here. He reaches down inside himself and makes it happen.

He turns and kicks the door in, and feels the familiar heat in nerve and muscle tissue, tequila-fueled. He brings his left arm up, aims at the spot by the window.

Fire, his brain orders. But the part of him that really commands the weapon, whatever that part is, is frozen.

•

The *coyotes* mostly traffic in the ones who can pass. After all, it's bad for business if customers you smuggle into the Promised Land are never heard from again by folks back in the old 'hood.

But sometimes, if cash flow demands, they make exceptions. *Coyotes* sell hope, after all. Unreasonable, ungratifiable hope just costs more. The *coyotes* tell them about the Land of Opportunity and neglect to mention that there's no way they'll get a piece of it.

Then the *coyotes* take their payment, dump them in the wilderness, and put a couple of steel-jackets in them before leaving.

He's done cleanup in the desert and found the dried-out bodies, parchment skin and deformed bone, under some creosote bush at the edge of a wash. The skin was often split around the bullet holes, it was so dry. Of course, if they'd been dead, there wouldn't have been anything to find. Some that he came across could still open their eyes, or speak.

•

Maybe in the dark this one can pass. Maybe she looks like an undernourished street kid with a thyroid problem. In the pitch-dark below an underpass from a speeding car, maybe.

She should never have left home. She should be dying in the desert. She should be already dead, turned to dust and scattered by the oven-hot wind.

Her body looks like it's made of giant pipe cleaners. Her long, skinny legs are bent under her, doubled up like a folding carpenter's ruler, and the joints are the wrong distance from each other. Her ropy arms are wrapped around her, and unlike her legs, they don't seem jointed at all—or it's just the angle that makes them seem to curve like tentacles.

And she's white. Not Anglo-white or even albino-white, but white like skim milk, right down to the blueish shadows that make her skin look almost transparent. Fish-belly white.

Her only clothing is a plaid flannel shirt with the sleeves torn off, in what looks like size XXL Tall. It's worn colorless in places, and those spots catch the street light coming through the uncovered window. The body under the shirt is small and thin and childlike. Her head, from above, is a big soiled milkweed puff, thin gray-white hair that seems to have worn itself out pushing through her scalp.

The office is vacant. An old steel desk stands on end in the middle of the room. Empty filing cabinet drawers make a lopsided tower in a corner. Half a dozen battered boxes of envelopes are tumbled across the floor, their contents spilled and stained. But the room's alive with small bright movements.

It's water—trickling down the walls, running in little rivulets across the vinyl flooring, plopping intermittently in fat drops from the ceiling. Water from nowhere. From her.

He hears the words coming out of his mouth even as he thinks, *This isn't going to work.* "I'm here to send you back." Once one of the poor bastards becomes his job, there's no "sending back". His left arm is up, his palm turned out. He should fire.

The milkweed fluff rocks slowly backward. Her face is under it. Tiny features on an outthrusting skull, under a flat, receding brow, so that her whole face forms around a ridge down its middle. Only the eyes aren't tiny. They're stone-gray without whites or visible pupils, deep-set round disks half the size of his palm.

She opens her little lipless mouth, but he doesn't hear anything. She licks around the opening with a pale-gray pointed tongue and tries again.

"Eres un mortal."

You're a mortal. A short speech in a high, breathy little-girl voice, but long enough to hear that her accent is familiar.

105

He's light-headed, and his ears are ringing. He needs adjusting. Damn it, where's Chisme?

Wait—he knows what this is. He's afraid.

She's helpless, not moving, not even paying attention. All he has to do is trigger the weapon, and she'll have a hundred tiny iron needles in her. Death by blood poisoning in thirty seconds or less—quicker and cleaner than the *coyote's* steel-jacketed rounds would have been. Why can't he fire?

He tries again, in Spanish this time—as if that will make it true. "I'm sending you back."

Something around her brows and the corners of her eyes suggests hope. She rattles into speech, but he can't make out a word of it. He recognizes it, though. It's the *Indio* language his grandmother used. He doesn't know its name; to his *abuela*, it was just speaking, and Spanish was the city language she struggled with.

He can't trust his voice, so he shakes his head at her. Does she understand that? His left arm feels heavy, stretched out in front of him.

Suddenly anger cuts through his dumb-animal fear. She's jerking him around. She found out somehow where his mother's family is from, and she's playing him with it. He doesn't have to make her understand. All he has to do is shoot her.

"You are not of the People, but you are of the land." She's switched back to Spanish, and he hears the disappointment in her voice. "You cannot send me back to something that is not there."

"Whose fault is that?" *Don't talk to her!* But he's angry.

"I do not know who it was." She shakes her head, less like a "no" than like a horse shaking off flies. "But the spring is gone. The water sank to five tall trees below the stone. The willows died when they could not reach it."

Willows and cottonwoods mark subsurface water like green surveyor's flags all through the dry country. He remembers willows around the springs in the hills behind his grandmother's village. "So you're going to move north and use up everything here, too?"

"¿*Que*?" Her white, flattened brow presses down in anger or confusion, or both. "How can I use up what is here? Is it so different here, the water and the land and the stone?"

There has to be a correct answer to that. Those who sent him after her probably have one. But he's not even sure what she's asking, let

106

alone what he ought to answer. *Nothing, you moron.* And what did he expect her to say? "Sí, sí, I'm here to steal your stuff"? They both know why she's here. If she'd just make a move, he could trigger the weapon.

"We keep, not use. How to say..." She blinks three times, rapidly, and it occurs to him that that might be the equivalent, for her, of gazing into space while trying to remember something. "Protect and guard. Is it not so here? Mortals use. We protect and guard. They ask for help—water for growing food, health and strength for their children. They bring tobacco, cornmeal, honey to thank us. We smell the presents and come. Do the People not do this here?"

He tries to imagine that piece of blonde perfection by the Chateau Marmont pool being summoned by the smell of cornmeal and doing favors for *campesinos*.

The word triggers his memory, like Chisme toggling his endocrine system. He recalls his last visit to his *abuela's* house, when he was eight. She was too weak to get out of bed for more than a few minutes at a time. She was crying, yelling at his mom, saying that somebody had to take the tamales to the spring. His mom said to him, as she heated water for his bath, "You see what it's like here? When your cousins call you *pocho*, you remember it's better to be American than a superstitious *campesino* like them."

He'd grown up believing that, until *they* found him, remade him, and sent him out to do their work. In that hot, moist room he feels cold all over. To hide it, he laughs. "Welcome to the Land of the Free, *chica*. No handouts, no favors, no fraternizing with the lower orders."

Her eyes darken, as if a drop of ink fell into each one. Fear surges in him again. *You should have shot her!* But tears like water mixed with charcoal well up, spill over, draw dark gray tracks on her white, sloping cheeks. "Please—it is not true, tell me so. I have nowhere to go. The machines that are loud and smell bad come and tear the trees from the soil, break mountains and take them away. They draw the water away from the sweet dark places under the earth. Poison comes into the water everywhere, how I do not know, but creatures are made sick who drink it. I tried to stay by the spring, but the water was gone, and the machines came. There was no room for me."

"There's no room for you here," he snaps. But he thinks, You're so skinny, Jesucristo, you could live in a broom closet. There must be some place to fit you in.

She shakes her head fiercely, smears the gray tears across her cheeks with her fingers. "Here there are places where the machines do not go. I know this. The People here are *inmigrantes* from the cold lands—they must know how it is. They will understand, and let us help them guard the land."

Already there are…empty spots, the blonde by the pool had said. But just this one little one? Would she be so bad?

No. All of his targets were each just one. Together they were hundreds. "They're guarding it from all of you, so you don't use everything up. Like locusts."

She goes still as a freeze-frame. "Mortals use. The People guard and protect. Surely they know this!"

What is she saying? "The power. Whatever it is, in the land. It's drying up."

"The People let the magic run through us like water through our fingers. We do not hoard it or hide it or wall it in. If we did, it would dry up, yes. Who told you this lie?"

"They did. The ones like you." *Have you seen many who are just like me?* he hears the blonde saying, in that voice that made everything wise and true.

She hasn't moved, but she suddenly seems closer, her eyes wider, her hair shifting like dry grass in the wind. There's no wind. He wants to back away, run.

And he remembers that night in his grandmother's house, after the fight about the tamales. He remembers being tucked up in blankets on the floor, and not being able to sleep because it stayed in his head—the angry voices, his *abuela* crying, his *mamá* cleaning up after dinner with hard, sharp movements. Nobody's mad at you, he'd told himself. But he'd still felt sick and scared. So he was awake when the *tap, tap, tap* sounded on the window across the room. On the glass bought with money his mother had sent home. And he'd raised his head and looked.

The next morning he'd told his mother he'd had a bad dream. That was how he'd recalled it ever since: a bad dream, and a dislike for the little house he never saw again. But now he remembered. That night he saw the Devil, come to take his mother and grandmother for the sin of anger. He'd frozen the scream in his throat. If he screamed, they would wake and run in, and the Devil would see them. If it took him instead, they would be safe.

What he'd seen, before he'd closed his eyes to wait for death, was a white face with a high, flattened forehead, gray-disk eyes, and a lipless mouth, and thin white fingers pressed against the glass. It was her, or one of her kind, come down from the spring looking for the offering.

"It is not true," she hisses, thrusting her face forward. "None of my kind would say that we devour and destroy. This is mortals' lies, to make us feared, to drive us away!"

He *is* afraid of her. He could snap those little pipe cleaner arms, but that wouldn't save him from her anger. It rages in the room like the dust storms that can sand paint off a car.

She has to be wrong. If she isn't, then for three years he has—He had no choice. Did he? Three years of things, hundreds of them, that should have lived forever.

"Your kind want you kept out," he spits back at her. "You don't get it, do you? They sent me to kill you."

He'd thought she was still before. Now she's an outcrop of white stone. He can't look away from her wide, wide eyes. Then her mouth opens and a sound comes out, soft at first, so he doesn't recognize it as laughter.

"You will drive us back or kill us? You are too late. Jaguars have come north across the Rio Grande. The wild magic is here. We will restore the balance in spite of the ignorant *inmigrantes*. And when we are all strong again, they will see how weak they are alone."

She moves. He thinks she's standing up, all in one smooth motion. But her head rises, her arms shrink and disappear, her bent legs curve, coil. He's looking into her transformed face: longer, flatter, tapered, serpentine. The flyaway hair is a bush of hair-thin spines. Rising out of it are a pair of white, many-pronged antlers.

Their points scrape the ceiling above his head. The cloud of tiny iron needles fills the air between him and her and he thinks, *Did I fire?*

But by then she's behind him. There's a band of pressure around his chest. He looks down to see her skin, silver-white scales shining in the street light, as the pressure compresses his ribs, his lungs. She's wrapped around him, crushing him.

Chisme will know when he stops breathing. When it's too late. The room is full of tiny stars. She's so strong he can't even struggle, can't cry because he can't breathe. He wants so much to cry.

The room is black, and far, far away. He feels a lipless mouth brush his forehead, and a voice whisper, "*Duermes, hijo, y despiertas a un mundo mas mejór.*" The next world is supposed to be better. He hopes that's true. He hopes that's where he's going.

•

He lies with his eyes closed, taking stock. His ribs hurt, but he's lying on something soft. Hurt means he's not dead. Soft means he's not on the floor of that office in the jewelry district, waiting for help.

He listens for the names. Nothing. He's alone in his head.

He opens his eyes. The light is low, greenish and underwatery, and comes from everywhere at once. He's back in their hands, then.

At the foot of whatever he's lying on, a young guy looks up from a sheet of paper. Brown hair, hip-nerd round tortoishell glasses, oxford-cloth button-down under a cashmere sweater under a reassuring white coat. For a second he thinks he was wrong and this is a hospital, that's a doctor.

"Hey," says the guy. "How do you feel?"

Come on, lungs, take in air. Mouth, open. "Crummy." He sounds as if his throat's full of mud.

The guy draws breath across his teeth—a sympathy noise. "Yeah, you must have caught yourself a whopper."

This one's remarkably human, meaning damned near unremarkable. But the lenses in the glasses don't distort the eyes behind them, because of course, they don't have to correct for anything. He's never seen one of them so determined to pass for normal. Is there a reason why this one's here now? Are they trying to put him at ease, off his guard?

"Actually," he answers, "it was a little kid who turned into a big-ass constrictor snake."

"Wow. Have you ever gotten a shape-changer before?"

Bogus question. The guy knows his whole history, knows every job he's done. But there's no point in calling him on it. "Yeah."

A moment of silence. Is he supposed to go on, talk it out? Is this some kind of post-traumatic stress therapy they've decided he needs? Or worse—is he supposed to apologize now for screwing up, for letting her get by him?

110

The guy shrugs, checks his piece of paper again. "Well, you're going to be fine now. And you did good work out there."

Careful. "Any job you can walk away from."

"Quite honestly, we weren't sure you had. Your 'little kid' put out enough distortion to swamp your connection with us. As far as we can tell it took almost thirty minutes for it to dissipate, after you...resolved the situation. Until then, we thought you'd been destroyed. Your handlers were beside themselves."

Handlers—the names. He wonders what "beside themselves" looks like for Chisme and Biblio and Magellan, or whatever those names are when they aren't in his head. He's never heard emotion out of any of them.

He stares at the young guy, handsome as a soap opera doctor. He starts to laugh, which hurts his ribs. Has he dealt with shape-changers before? Hell, which of them *isn't* a shape-changer? However they do it, they all look like what you want or need to see. Except the ones, bent and strange, who can't pass. "I wasn't sure I killed her."

The young guy winces. "Killed" is not a nice word to immortals, apparently. "The site was completely cleansed. Very impressive. And I assure you, I'm not the only one saying so."

"That's nice." He's never failed to take out his target before this. He doesn't know what punishment it is that he seems to have escaped. For this one moment, he feels bulletproof. "I talked to her, before I did it."

Surprise—and alarm?—on the young guy's face. "By the green earth! Are you nuts? You must have been warned against that."

"She said her kind—your kind—aren't a drain on the local resources. Or aren't supposed to be. She implied you'd forgotten how it's done."

The soap-opera features register disgust. "Just the sort of thing one of them would say. They're ignorant tree-dwellers. They have no idea how complex the modern world is. You know what they're like."

He doesn't, actually. He's supposed to kill them, not get acquainted with them. "Her folks were here first," he says, as mildly as he can.

The young guy frowns, confused. "What does that have to do with it?" He shakes his head. "Don't worry, we understand these things. We know what we're doing. You can't imagine what it would be like if we let down our guard."

Pictures come into his head—from where? A picture of jaguars, glimmering gold and black like living jewelry, slipping through emerald leaves; of blue-and-red feathered birds singing with the sweet, high voices of children; of human men and women sitting with antlered serpents and coyote-headed creatures, sharing food and stories in a landscape of plenty; of the young white-coated guy, on a saxophone, jamming with the piano player in the Koreatown bar while a deer picked its way between the tables.

"You'll be fine now," the young guy repeats. "Get some sleep. When you wake up you'll be back home. I think you can expect a week or two off—go to Vegas or something, make a holiday of it."

Of course, "get some sleep" is not just a suggestion. The guy makes a pressing-down motion, and the greeny light dims. He can feel the magic tugging at his eyelids, his brain. The young guy smiles, turns away, and is gone.

It's a good plan—but not Vegas, oh, no. He'll wake up in his apartment. He'll get up and pack...what? Not much. Then he'll head south. Past the border towns and the *maquiladoras*, past the giant commercial fields of cotton and tomatoes scented with chemicals and watered from concrete channels.

He wonders if they'll be able to track him, if they'll even care that he's gone. For them, the world must be full of promising, desperate mortals. He'll lose the names, the senses, the fastlane, but he'll be traveling light; he won't need them.

Eventually he'll get to the wild places, rocky or green, desert or forest or shore. Home of the ignorant, superstitious peasants. That's where he'll stop. He'll bake tortillas on a hot, flat stone, lay out sugar cane and tobacco.

Maybe nothing will come for them. Maybe he won't even be able to tell if anything's there. But just in case, he'll tell stories. They'll be about how to get past people like him, into the land where the magic is dying because it can't flow like water.

Then he'll move on, and do it again. Nothing makes up for the ones he's stopped, but he can try, at least, to replace them.

Sleep, child, she'd said, *and wake to a better world.* He'd thought then she'd meant the sleep of death, but if she'd wanted to kill him, wouldn't he be dead? He relaxes into the green darkness, the comforting

112

magic. When he wakes this time, it'll be the same old world. But some morning, for someone, someday, it will be different.

What Used to Be Good Still Is

Emma Bull

Porphyry is a volcanic rock. Maybe that's why it happened. Maybe it was because the hill that became a pit was named Guadalupe, for the Virgin of Guadalupe, who appeared in a vision to a Mexican peasant a long time ago. Maybe it's because walls change whatever they enclose, and whatever they leave out.

And maybe it could have happened anywhere, any time. But I don't believe that for a second.

I expect I wouldn't have taken too much notice of Sara Gutierrez if my pop hadn't. I was a senior at Hollier High School, varsity football first string, debating team, science club. Sara was the eighth-grade sister of Alfred Gutierrez, who I knew from football. But the Gutierrezes lived in South Hollier, down the slope from the Dimas shaft, on the other side of Guadalupe Hill, and we lived on Collar Hill above downtown with the lawyers and store owners and bankers. Alfred and I didn't see much of each other outside of football practice. The only time my father saw Alfred's father was when Enrique Gutierrez had his annual physical at the company hospital, or if he got hurt on the job and Pop had to stitch him up.

But one night I was up studying and heard Pop in the kitchen say, "I don't know if that youngest Gutierrez girl is simple or plain brilliant."

Pop didn't talk about patients at home as a rule, so that was interesting enough to make me prick up my ears.

"Probably somewhere in between, like most," Mom said. Mom didn't impress easily.

"She came into the infirmary today with her chest sounding like a teakettle on the boil. If I can keep that child from dying of pneumonia or TB, I'll change my name to Albert Schweitzer." He paused, and I knew Mom was waiting for him to come back from wherever that thought had led him. She and I were used to Pop's parentheses. "Anyway, while I'm writing up her prescription, she says, 'Doctor Ryan, what makes a finch?'"

"I don't suppose you told her, 'God,'" Mom said with a sigh.

"I didn't know what to say. But when she saw I didn't get her drift, she asked why are house finches and those little African finches that Binnie Schwartz keeps in her parlor both finches? So I started to tell her about zoological taxonomy—"

"I just bet you did," Mom said. I could hear her smiling.

"Now, Jule—"

"Go on, go on. I won't get any peace 'til you do."

"Well, then she said, 'But the finches don't think so. We're human beings because we say we are. But the finches don't think they're all finches. Shouldn't that make a difference?'"

A pause, and the sound of dishes clattering in the wash water. "Sara Gutierrez spends too much time on her own," Mom said. "Invalids always think too much."

I don't remember what Pop replied to that. Probably he argued; Pop argued with any sentence that contained the word "always."

By the time I came home for the summer after my first year of college, the matter was settled: Sara Gutierrez was bright. She'd missed nearly half her freshman year in high school what with being out sick, but was still top of her class. Pop bragged about her as if he'd made her himself.

She was thin and small and kind of yellowish, and you'd hardly notice if she was in the same room with you. The other girls in town got permanent waves to look like Bette Davis. Sara still looked like Louise Brooks, her hair short, no curl at all. But that summer I saw her at the ballpark during one of the baseball games. She looked straight at me in the stands. There was something in her eyes so big, so heavy, so hard to hang onto that it seemed like her body would break from trying to carry it.

Nobody ever suggested that Sara was bright at anything likely to be of use to her. A long while later I looked her up in the *Hollier Hoist*, the high school yearbook, to see what her classmates must have made of her. She'd been a library monitor. That was all. No drama society, no debating team, no booster club, no decorating committee for the Homecoming dance.

I guess she saved her debating for me. And she danced, all right, but you won't find that in the yearbooks.

Hollier was a mining town—founded in the 1880s by miners and speculators. The whole point of life here was to dig copper out of the ground as cheap as possible, and hope that when you got it to the surface you could sell it for a price that made the work worthwhile. The town balanced on a knife edge, with the price of copper on one side, and the cost of mining it on the other.

And that didn't apply only to the miners and foremen and company management. If copper did poorly, so did the grocers, mechanics, lawyers, and schoolteachers. What came up out of those shafts fed and clothed us all. Pop was a company doctor. Without copper, there was no company, no one to doctor, no dinner on the table, no money for movies on Saturday, no college tuition. He used to say that Hollier was a lifeboat, with all of us rowing for a shore we couldn't see. The company was the captain, and we trusted that the captain had a working compass and knew how to read it.

Underground mining's expensive. The shafts went deeper and deeper under the mountains following the veins of high-grade ore, the pumps ran night and day to pump out the water that tried to fill those shafts, and the men who dug and drilled and blasted had to be paid. But near the surface, under what farmers call dirt and miners call *overburden*, around where the rich veins used to run, there was plenty of low-grade ore. Though it didn't have as much copper in it, it could be scraped right off the surface. No tunnels, no pumps, and a hell of a lot fewer men to pay.

Guadalupe Hill was a fine cone-shaped repository of low-grade ore.

The summer after my sophomore year at college, I came home to find the steam shovels scooping the top off Guadalupe Hill. You could see the work from the parlor windows on Collar Hill, hear the roar and crash of it funneled up the canyon from the other side of downtown. Almost the first thing I heard when I got off the train at the depot was the warning siren for a blast, and the dynamite going off like a giant bass drum. From the platform I could see the dust go up in a thundercloud; then the machinery moved in like retrievers after a shot bird.

As Pop helped me stow my suitcase in the trunk of the Hudson, I said, "I'd sure like to watch that," and jerked my head at Guadalupe Hill.

"I'd take you over now, but your mother would fry me for supper."

"Oh, I didn't mean before I went home." I would have meant it, but I knew he'd be disappointed in me if I couldn't put Mom before mining.

Once I'd dropped my suitcase in my room and given Mom a kiss and let her say I looked too thin and didn't they feed me in that frat house dining room, Pop took me down to watch the dig.

It was the biggest work I'd ever seen human beings do. Oh, there'd been millions of dollars of copper ore taken out of the shafts in Hollier. Everyone in town knew there were a thousand miles of shafts, and could recite how many men the company employed; but you couldn't *see* it. Now here was Guadalupe Hill crawling with steam shovels and dump trucks, men shouting, steam screeching, whistles, bells. It went as smooth and precise as a ballet troupe, even when it looked and sounded like the mouth of Hell.

And the crazy ambition of the thing! Some set of madmen had wanted to turn what most folks would have called a mountain inside out, turn it into a hole as deep and as wide as the mountain was tall. And another set of madmen had said, "Sure, we can do that."

Later I wasn't surprised when people said, "Let's go to the moon," because I'd seen the digging of Guadalupe Pit. It was like watching the building of the pyramids.

Pop stopped to talk to the shift boss. Next to that big man, brown with sun and streaked with dust, confident and booming and pointing with his square, hard hands, Pop looked small and white and helpless. He was a good doctor, maybe even a great one. His example had me pointed toward pre-med, and medical school at Harvard or Stanford if I could get in. But looking from him to the shift boss to the roaring steam shovels, I felt something in me slip. I wanted to do something big, something that people would see and marvel at. I wanted people to look on my work and see progress and prosperity and stand in awe of the power of Man.

Over dinner, I said, "It makes you feel as if you can do anything, watching that."

"You can, if you have enough dynamite and a steam shovel," Pop agreed as he reached for a pork chop.

"No, really! We're not just living on the planet like fleas on a dog anymore. We're changing it to suit us. Like sculptors. Like—"

"God?" Mom said, even though I'd stopped myself.

"Of course not, Mom." But I'd thought it, and she knew it. She also knew I was a college boy and consequently thought myself wiser than Solomon.

Conversation touched on the basketball team and the repainting of the Women's Club before I said carefully, "I've been wondering if I'm cut out for med school."

Guess I wasn't careful enough; Pop gave me a look over his plate that suggested he was onto me. "Not everyone is."

"I don't want to let you down."

"You know we'll be proud of you no matter what," Mom replied, sounding offended that she had to tell me such a thing.

"I'm thinking of transfering to the Colorado School of Mines."

"Might need some scholarship money—being out of state," said Pop. "But your grades are good. The company might help out, too." He passed me the mashed potatoes. "You don't have to be a doctor just because I am."

"Of course not." I needed to hear him say so, though.

We sat in the parlor after dinner. Pop got his pipe going before he said, "The Gutierrez family isn't doing so well. Tool nippers got laid off at the Dimas shaft, and Enrique with 'em. I think it hit Sara hard."

At first I thought he was talking about Mrs. Gutierrez; I don't know that I'd ever heard her first name. Then I remembered Sara.

"You might take the time for a chat if you see her." He took his pipe out of his mouth and peered at it as if it were a mystery. "She asks about you."

If there's a young fellow who can remain unmoved by the knowledge that a girl asks about him, I haven't met him.

Sara was working in the Hollier Library for the summer. I found an excuse to drop in first thing next day. I came up to the desk and called to the girl on the other side who was shelving reserved books, "Is Sara Gutierrez working today?"

Of course it was her. When I look back on it, it seems like the most natural thing in the world that the girl would straighten up and turn

119

'round, and there she'd be. Her hair still wasn't waved, and she wasn't pink and white like a girl in a soap ad. But she wasn't thin anymore, either. Her eyes were big and dark under straight black brows, and she looked at me as if she were taking me apart to see what I was made of. Then she said, without a hint of a smile, "She'd better be, or this whole place'll go to the dickens."

I'd planned to say hello, pass the time of day for a few minutes. But a little fizz went up my backbone, and I heard myself say, "Must be awful hard for her to get time off for lunch."

"She'd probably sneak out if someone made her a decent offer."

"Will the lunch counter at the drug store do?"

Sara looked at me through her eyelashes. "Golly, Mr. Ryan, you sweet-talked me into it."

"I'll come by for you at the noon whistle."

She had grilled cheese and a chocolate phosphate. Funny the things you remember. And she said the damnedest things without once cracking a smile, until I told her about my fraternity initiation and made her laugh so hard she skidded off her stool. By the time I asked for the check I'd gotten a good notion of how to tell when she was joking. And I'd asked her to go to the movies the next night, and she'd said yes.

I picked her up for the movie outside the library, and when it was over, I proceeded to drive her home. But at the turnoff for the road to South Hollier, she said, "I can walk from here."

I turned onto the road. "Not in the dark. What if you tripped in a hole, or met up with a javelina—"

"I'd rather walk," she said, her voice tight and small.

I didn't think I'd said or done anything to make her mad. "Now, don't be silly." I remembered Pop saying that Sara seemed to take her father's layoff hard. Was that what this was about?

"Really—" she began.

In the headlights and the moonlight I could see two tall ridges of dirt and rock crossways to the road on either side, as if threatening to pinch it between them. Two corrugated iron culvert pipes, each as big around as a truck, loomed in the scrub at the roadside.

"Where'd that come from?"

She didn't answer. The Hudson passed between the ridges of dirt, and I could see the lights of the houses of South Hollier in front of me. I pulled over.

"Are they building something here?" I asked.

Sara sat in the passenger seat with her hands clenched in her lap and her face set, looking out the windshield. "It's Guadalupe Hill," she said at last.

"What?"

"They have to put it someplace. The tailings will make a new line of hills around South Hollier on the east and south."

I tried to imagine it. North and west, the neighborhood ran right up to the mountain slopes. This would turn South Hollier into the bottom of a bowl with an old mountain range on two sides and a new one on the others.

"What about the road?"

"That's what the pipes are for."

"You mean you'll drive through the pipe, like a tunnel?"

"One for each direction," she answered.

"Well, I'll be darned." The more I thought about it, the cleverer it was. Wasn't it just like mining engineers to figure out a way to put a tailings dump where it had to go without interfering with the neighborhood traffic?

Sara shook her head and pleated her skirt between her fingers. I put the Hudson into gear and drove down the road into South Hollier.

At her door, I asked, "Can I see you again?"

She looked up into my face, with that taking-me-apart expression. At last she said, "'May I.' College man."

"May I?"

"Oh, all right." Her eyes narrowed when she was teasing. Before I knew what had happened, she was on the other side of her screen door. Based on her technique, I was not the first young man to bring her home. "Good night, Jimmy."

I drove back to Collar Hill with vague but pleasant plans for the summer.

She met me for lunch a couple times a week, and sometimes she'd let me go with her and carry her packages when she had errands to the Mercantile or the Fair Store. Once she wanted sheet music from the

Music Box, and she let me talk her into a piano arrangement of a boogie woogie song I'd heard at a college party.

"Should I hide it from my mama?" she asked, with her eyes narrowed.

"I'll bet she snuck out to the ragtime dances."

"Oh, not a good Catholic girl like my mama."

"Mine's a good Catholic girl, too, and she did it."

Sara smiled, just the tiniest little smile, looking down at the music. For some reason, that smile made my face hot as a griddle.

Sara wouldn't go to a movie again, though, or the town chorus concert or the Knights of Columbus dance. I asked her to the Fourth of July fireworks, but she said she was going with her family.

"I'll look for you," I said, and she shrugged and hurried away.

The fireworks were set off at the far end of Panorama Park, down in the newer neighborhood of Wilson where the company managers lived. Folks tended to spread their picnic blankets in the same spot every year. The park divided into nations, too, like much of Hollier. A lot of the Czech and Serbian families picnicked together, and the Italians, and the Cornishmen; the Mexicans set up down by the rose garden, at the edge of the sycamores. The Gutierrez family would be there.

I got to the park at twilight, and after saying hello to a few old friends from high school, and friends of Mom and Pop's, I pressed through the crowd and the smells from all those picnic dinners. When I got to the rose garden it was almost dark, but I found Alfred Gutierrez without too much trouble.

"You looking for Sara?" he said, with a little grin.

"I told her I'd come 'round and say hi." I was above responding to that grin.

"She's around here someplace. *Hola, Mamá*," he called over his shoulder, "where'd Sara go?"

Mrs. Gutierrez was putting the remains of their picnic away. She looked up and smiled when she saw me. "Hello, Jimmy. How's your mama and papa?"

"They're fine. I just wanted to say hello..."

Mrs. Gutierrez nodded over her picnic basket. "Sara said she had to talk to someone."

Was it me? Was she looking for me, out there in the night, while I looked for her? There was a bang—the first of the fireworks. "Will you tell her I was here?"

Alfred grinned again, and Mrs. Gutierrez looked patient in the blue light of the starburst.

I watched the fireworks, but I didn't get much out of them. Was Sara avoiding me? Why wouldn't she see me except when she was downtown; in the daytime, but never the evenings? Could it be she was ashamed of her family, so she wouldn't let me pick her up at home? The Gutierrez family wasn't rich, but neither were we. No, it had to be something about me.

It wasn't as if we were sweethearts; we were just friends. I'd go back to college in September, she'd stay here, and we'd probably forget all about each other. We were just having fun, passing the time. She was too young for me to be serious about, anyway. So why was she giving me the runaround?

By the time the finale erupted in fountains and pinwheels, I'd decided two could play that game. I'd find myself some other way to pass the time for the next couple months, and it wouldn't be hard to do, either.

That was when I saw her, carried along with the slow movement of people out of the park, her white summer dress reflecting the moon and the street lights. She was holding someone's little girl by the hand and trying to get her to walk, but the kid had reached that stage of tired in which nothing sounded good to her.

"Hi, Sara."

"Jimmy! I didn't see you there."

I wanted to say something sophisticated and bitter like, "I'm sure you didn't," but I remembered that I'd resolved to be cool and distant. That's when the little girl burst into noisy, angry tears.

"Margie, *Margarita*, I *can't* carry you. You're a big girl. Won't you please—"

I scooped the kid up so quickly that it shocked the tears out of her. "A big girl needs a bigger horse than Sara," I told her, and settled her on my shoulders, piggyback-fashion.

We squeezed through the crowd without speaking until we got to Margie's family's pickup truck. The Gutierrez family was riding with them, and I had to see Alfred smirk at me again. Folks started to settle into the back of the truck on their picnic blankets. Something about Sara's straight back and closed-up face, and the fact that she still wasn't talking, made me say, "Looks kind of crowded. I've got my pop's car here..."

Mrs. Gutierrez looked distracted and waved her hands over picnic basket, blankets, sleeping kids, and folded-up adults. "Would you—? Sara, you go with Jimmy. I don't know how..." With that, she went back to, I think, trying to figure out how they'd all come in the truck in the first place.

Sara turned to me, her eyes big and sort of wounded. "If you don't mind," she mumbled.

We were in the front seat of the Hudson before I remembered my grudge. "Now, look, Sara, you've been dodging me—"

She was startled. "Oh, no—"

"I just want to say you don't have to. We've had some fun, but if you think I'm going to go too far or make a pest of myself or hang on you like a stray dog—"

The force of her head-shaking stopped me. "No, really, I don't."

"What's up with you, then? We're just friends, aren't we?"

Sara looked at her knees for a long time, and I wondered if I'd said something wrong. "That's so," she said finally. "We are."

She sounded as if she were deciding on something, planting her feet and refusing to be swayed. I'd only started on my list of grievances, but her tone made me lose my place in the list. "I guess I'll take you home, then."

We talked about fireworks as I drove: which we liked best, how we'd loved the lights and colors but hated the bang when we were kids, things we remembered from past July Fourths in the park. But as I turned down her road and headed toward South Hollier, Sara's voice trailed off. At the tailings ridge, I stopped the car.

"Darn it, Sara, why should I care where you live? Is that what this is about, why you go all stiff and funny?"

She stared at me, baffled-looking. "No. No, it's that..." She reached for the door handle. "Come with me, will you, Jimmy?"

In the glare of the headlights, she picked her way up to the foot of the tailings. I was ready to grab her elbow if she stepped wrong; the ground was covered with debris rolled down from the ridge top, rocks of all sizes that seemed to want to shift away under my feet or turn just enough to twist my ankle. But she went slow but steady over the mess as if she'd found a path to follow.

She stopped and tipped her head back. The stars showed over the black edge of the tailings, and I thought that was what she was looking at. "Can you tell?" she asked.

"Tell what?"

Sara looked down at her feet for the first time since she got out of the car, then at the ridge, and finally at me. "It doesn't want to be here."

"What doesn't?"

"The mountain. Look, it's lying all broken and upside down—overburden on the bottom instead of the top, then the stone that's never been in sunlight before. It's unhappy, and now it'll be a whole unhappy ring around South Hollier." She turned, and I saw two tears spill out her eyes. "We've always been happy here before."

For an instant I thought she was crazy; I was a little afraid of her. Then I realized she was being poetic. Pop had said her dad's layoff had hit her hard. She was just using the tailings as a symbol for what had changed.

"You'll be happy again," I told her. "This won't last, you'll see."

She looked blank. Then she reached out toward the slope as if she wanted to pat it. "This will last. I want to fix it, and there's nothing..." She swallowed loudly and turned her face away.

I couldn't think of a way to fix things for her, and I didn't want to say anything about her crying. So I turned back to the tailings ridge, textured like some wild fabric in the headlights. "That gray rock is porphyry, did you know?"

"Of course I do." The ghost of her old pepper was in that. I suppose it was a silly question to ask a miner's daughter.

"Well, do you know it's the insides of a volcano?"

She looked over her shoulder and frowned.

"The insides of a want-to-be volcano, anyway," I went on. "The granite liquifies in the heat and pushes up, but it never makes it out the top. So nobody knows it's a volcano, because it never erupted."

Sara had stopped frowning as I spoke. Now she turned back to the tailings with an expression I couldn't figure out. "It wanted to be a volcano," she murmured.

I didn't know what else to say, and she didn't seem to need to say anything more. "I ought to get you home," I said finally. "Your mom will be wondering."

When we stopped in front of her house, Sara turned to me. "I only told you that, about the...about the mountain, because we're friends. You said so yourself. I wouldn't talk about it to just anybody."

"Guess I won't talk about it at all."

She smiled. "Thank you, Jimmy. For the ride, and everything." She slid out of the passenger side door and ran up to her porch. She ran like a little kid, as if she ran because she could and not because she had to. When she got to the porch she waved.

I waved back even though I knew she couldn't see me.

Mom asked me the next day if I'd drive her up to see her aunt in Tucson. We were halfway there before she said, "Are you still seeing Sara Gutierrez?"

I was about to tell her that I'd seen her the night before, when I realized that wasn't how she meant "seeing." "We're just friends, Mom. She's too young for me to think of that way."

"Does she think so, too?"

I thought about last night's conversation. "Sure, she does."

"I know you wouldn't lead her on on purpose, but it would be a terrible thing to do to her, to make her think you were serious when you aren't."

"Well, she doesn't think so." Mom was just being Mom; no reason to get angry. But I was.

"And it would break your father's heart if you got her in trouble."

"I'm not up to any hanky-panky with Sara Gutierrez, and I'm not going to be. Are you satisfied?"

"Watch your tone, young man. You may be grown up, but I'm still your mother."

I apologized, and did my best to be the perfect son for the rest of the trip. But the suggestion that anyone might think Sara and I would be doing things we'd be ashamed to let other people know about—it hung around like a bad smell, and made me queasy whenever I remembered it.

Did people see me with Sara and think I was sneaking off with her to—My God, even the words, ones I'd used about friends and classmates and strangers, were revolting. Somewhere in Hollier, someone could be saying, "Jimmy Ryan with the youngest Gutierrez girl! Why, he probably dazzled her into letting him do whatever he wanted. And you know he won't think about her for five minutes after he goes back to college."

When Mom and I got back from Tucson, I rang up Sam Koslowsky, who I knew from high school, and proposed a little camping and fishing in the Chiricahuas. He had a week's vacation coming at the garage, so he liked the notion.

For a week, I didn't see Sara, or mention her name, or even think about her, particularly. I hoped she'd gotten used to not seeing me, so when I came back, she wouldn't mind that I stopped asking her out or meeting her for lunch.

It would have been a fine plan, if Mom hadn't wanted me to go down to the library and pick up the Edna Ferber novel she had on reserve. When I saw that the girl at the desk wasn't Sara, I let my breath out in a whoosh, I was so relieved. Maybe relief made me cocky. Whatever it was, I thought it was safe to go upstairs and find a book for myself.

Sara was sitting cross-legged on the floor in front of the geography section, her skirt pulled tight down over her knees to make a hammock for the big book in her lap. She looked up just as I spotted her. "Jimmy, come look at this."

It was as if she hadn't noticed I'd been gone—as if she hadn't noticed I wasn't there five minutes earlier. She had a wired-up look to her, as if she had things on her mind that didn't leave room for much else, including me. Wasn't that what I'd wanted? Then why was I feeling peeved?

I looked over her shoulder at the book. At the top of the page was a smudgy photograph of Mount Fuji, in Japan. Sara jabbed at the paragraphs below the photo as if she wanted to poke them into some other shape. "Mount Fuji," I said, as if I saw it every day.

"But that's not just the name of the mountain. The mountain's a goddess, or *has* a goddess, I'm not sure which. And her name is Fuji. And look—" Sara flipped pages wildly until she got to one with a turned-down corner (I was shocked—a library assistant folding corners) and another photo. The mountain in this one was sending up blurry dark smoke. "Here, Itza—Itzaccihuatl in Mexico. Itza is sort of a goddess, too. Or anyway, she's a woman who killed herself when she

127

heard her lover died in battle, and became a volcano. And there's a volcano goddess in Hawaii, Pele."

"Sure. All right," I said, since she seemed to want me to say something.

"And there's more than that. Volcanoes seem extra-likely to have goddesses, all over the world."

I laughed. "I guess men all over the world have seen women blow their tops."

Instead of laughing, or pretending to be offended, she frowned and shook her head. "There's so much I need to know. Did you want to go to lunch? Because I'm awfully sorry, I just don't have time."

That reminded me that I was annoyed. "I just came to get a book. People do that in libraries." I pulled one down from the shelf above her head and walked off with it. The girl at the desk giggled when she checked it out, and it wasn't until I was outside that I found I was about to read *A Lady's Travels in Burma*. Between that and Mom's Edna Ferber, I figured I was punished enough for being short with Sara.

I waited a week before I stopped by the library again. Again she was too busy for lunch, but as I moved to turn from the desk, she said, "I really am sorry, Jimmy." She didn't look like a girl giving a fellow the brush-off. In fact, something about her eyebrows, the tightness of her lips, made her look a little desperate.

I could be busy, too, I decided, and with better reason. I wrote to the Colorado School of Mines to ask what a transfer required in the way of credits, courses, and tuition. I wrote to some of the company's managers, in town and at the central office, inquiring about scholarship programs for children of employees who wanted to study mining and engineering. I gathered letters of recommendation from teachers, professors, any Pillar of the Community who knew me. Pop helped, and bragged, and monitored my progress as if he'd never had visions of a son following him into medicine.

In mid-August, I got a letter from the School of Mines, conditionally accepting me for the engineering program. All I had to do was complete a couple of courses in the fall term, and I could transfer in January. I took it down to Pop's office as soon as it came, because he was almost as eager as I was.

He was with a patient. I sat in the waiting room for a few minutes, but I felt silly; waiting rooms are for patients. I ducked into the little room that held Pop's desk and books and smelled like pipe tobacco. The transom over the door between it and the examining room was open, and the first words I heard were from Sara. I should have left, but I didn't think of it.

"See, Margarita? Just a sprain. But don't you go near the tailings again."

"*You* do," said a little voice with a hint of a whine.

"I'm grown up."

"When I'm grown up, can I?"

"Maybe," said Sara, something distant in her voice. "Maybe by then."

"Tailings dumps shift and settle for a while," Pop agreed on the other side of the door. "They're not safe at first for anybody. *Including* grown-ups."

"Have...have many people been hurt, in South Hollier?" Sara sounded as if she wanted Pop to think it was a casual question. But I knew her better.

"Some sprains and bruises. Probably some scrapes that I never see, but only minor things. Folks just can't seem to stay off a hill or a high building, whatever you tell 'em. Especially the little ones," Pop added in a new, dopey voice. Margie squealed, as if maybe Pop had tweaked her ear.

I was mostly packed and ready to head back to college when Lucas Petterboro, three years old, wandered away from his yard in South Hollier and out to the new tailings dump. From what could be told after the fact, it seemed he'd caused a little slide clambering up the slope, which had dislodged a much larger rock, which had produced a still larger slide. Searchers found his shoe at the bottom of the raw place in the dump, which gave them an idea where to start digging.

Pop and Mom and I went to the funeral. Pop had delivered Luke. Everyone in South Hollier was there, and so were a lot of other people, mining families, since the Petterboros had been hard-rock miners down the Princess Shaft for thirty years. Mom sat beside Mrs. Petterboro at the cemetery and held her hand; Pop talked to Joe Petterboro, and now and then touched him lightly on the shoulder. The pallbearers were South Hollier men: Mr. Dubnik, who'd won the hard-rock drilling contest three years running; Mr. Slater, who ran a little grocery out of the front of his house; Fred Koch, who'd been in my class and who was

129

clerking in a lawyer's office downtown: and Luis Sandoval, the cage operator for the Dimas Shaft. It was a small coffin; there was only room for the four of them. The children of South Hollier stood close to their parents, in their Sunday clothes, confused and frightened. Their mothers and fathers held their hands and wore the expression folks get when something that only happens to other people happens to one of their own.

And me? There wasn't a damned thing for me to do.

So when Sara came up to me, her eyes red in a white face, and slipped her hand into mine, I wanted to turn and bawl like a baby on her shoulder. If she'd spoken right away, I would have.

"So," I said at last, harsher than I'd meant to. "Guess that mountain's still unhappy, huh?"

She let go of my hand. "Yes. It is." She pulled her sweater close around her, though the sun was warm. "It keeps me awake at night. The engineers say the ridge ought to be stable, but there was a slide last week that came within three feet of the Schuellers' back door."

"Too much rain this summer." That made her shrug, which made me look closer at her. "What do you mean, it keeps you awake? Worrying won't help."

Her eyes were big and haunted and shadowed underneath. "I can hear the mountain, Jimmy."

Her mom called Sara's name. Sara shot me a last frightened look and went to her.

I went back to college the day after the funeral. I sat on the train still seeing that look, still hearing Sara say, "I can hear the mountain." I told myself it was poetry again, and banished her voice. But it always came back.

I shut it out with work. By the time the term ended and I packed all my worldly goods on the train for home, I'd gotten top grades in my classes, a scholarship from the company, and an invitation to visit my fraternity's house on the School of Mines campus at my earliest convenience.

I walked in the back door of the house on Collar Hill and smelled pipe tobacco, ginger snaps, and baking potatoes. I saw the kitchen linoleum with the pattern wearing away in the trafficked spots, saw Mom's faded flowered apron and felt her kiss on my cheek. Suddenly I felt safe. That was the first I knew that I hadn't felt safe for a long time, and that the feeling building in me as the train approached Hollier wasn't anticipation, but dread.

"You'll have to go find us a Christmas tree," Mom said to me over dinner. "Your father's been so busy lately that it's full dark before he gets home."

"And your mom won't let me buy a Christmas tree in the dark anymore," Pop added.

"Oh, the poor spavined thing you brought home that year! You remember, Jimmy?"

It was as if I'd been away for years. I shivered. "Why so busy, Pop?" If it was the tailings, if it was South Hollier...

"Mostly a bumper crop of babies—"

"Stephen!" Mom scolded.

"—along with winter colds and pneumonia and the usual accidents. Price of copper is up, the company's taken more men on for all the shifts, and that just naturally increases the number of damned fools who let ore cars run over their feet."

"Right before I left, the Petterboro baby—"

"Lord, yes. Nothing that bad since, thank God."

"Then the tailings are safe?"

Pop cocked his head and frowned. "Unless you run up to the top and jump off. It's true, though, that the South Hollier dump made more trouble in the beginning and less now than any others. I guess they know what they're doing, after all."

The tightness went out of my back. It was all right. Of course Sara hadn't meant it literally, what she'd suggested at the funeral. And now everything was fine.

When I saw Sara on Main Street the next afternoon, on her way to catch the trolley home, I knew that something wasn't fine at all. Her cheeks were hollow, her clothes hung loose on her, and the shadows around her eyes were darker than when I left.

"You've been sick again," I said, before I realized how rude it would sound.

"No. Ask your dad." She thumped her knuckles against her chest. "Lungs all clear."

"But—" I couldn't tell her she looked awful; what kind of thing was that to say? "Pop's car's down the block. Can I drive you someplace?"

"I'm just headed home."

"Why, I know right where that is!" I sounded too hearty, but she smiled.

"There's still room, with all that chemistry and geometry in there?"

"The brain swells as it fills up. My hat size gets bigger every year."

"Oh, so it's learning that does that."

When we got to the tailings, I saw that the culvert pipes were in place on the roadway, and the fill crested over them about six feet high. I steered the car into the right-hand pipe. I felt like a bug washed down a drain as the corrugated metal swallowed the car and the light. The engine noise rang back at us from the walls, higher and shrill. I wanted to crouch down, to put the Hudson in reverse, to floor it.

"Looks like they've moved a lot of stone since summer." I watched her out of the corner of my eye as I said it.

She nodded. It wasn't the old nervous silence she used to fall into near the tailings. She wasn't stiff or tense; but there was a settled quality to her silence, a firmness.

"Pop says the dump's quit shifting."

Sara looked at me as we came out of the pipe and into South Hollier. "That's right." She made it sound like a question.

I didn't know what to answer, so instead I asked, "Is your dad back at work?"

"They brought him on as a mechanic at the pit. He likes it. And it means he'll get his full pension after all."

South Hollier was now enclosed in its bowl, a Medieval walled town in the Arizona mountains. It looked constrained, like a fat woman in a girdle. But kids played in front yards, women took wash off their clotheslines, smoke rose from chimneys. Everything was all right.

Except it wasn't. Something was out of whack.

When I pulled up to Sara's front door, I said, "We're still friends?"

She thought about it. I realized I liked that better than if she'd been quick to answer. "We are."

"Then I'll say this, one friend to another. Something's eating you, and it's not good. Tell me. I'll help."

Sara smiled, a slow one that opened up like flower petals. We heard her screen door bang, and looked to see her mom on the front porch.

"Jimmy!" Mrs. Gutierrez called. "Jimmy Ryan, when did you get home? Come in for coffee!"

Sara gave a little laugh. "Don't argue with my mama."

I went in, and got coffee Mexican style, with a little cinnamon, and powdered-sugar-dusted cookies. Mrs. Gutierrez skimmed around her scoured red-and-yellow kitchen like a hummingbird. But here, too, something wasn't right.

Mrs. Gutierrez gave Sara a pile of magazines to take to a neighbor's house. When we heard the screen bang behind her, Mrs. Gutierrez turned to me. "You see how she is?"

"Has she been sick?"

Mrs. Gutierrez twisted the dishrag between her hands, and I was reminded of Sara twisting at her skirt, the first night I'd driven her home. "When... At night, late, she goes to bed. She says she's going to bed. But I lie awake in the dark and hear her go out again. It's hours before she comes back."

I felt so light-headed I almost couldn't see. "Is it some boy?" I was scared at how angry I sounded. "Is she—" Everything else stuck in my throat. I had no business being angry. I was furious.

But Mrs. Gutierrez shook her head. "Do you think I would let that go on? Almost I wish it were. Then we'd have shame or a wedding, but not this—this fading away."

It was true. Sara was fading away.

"What can I do?"

"Find out what's happening. Make her stop."

So I began to meet her for lunch. She wasn't too busy anymore, but she was always tired. Still, she smiled at me, the kind of weary, gentle smile that women who work too hard wear, and let me take her to the drug store lunch counter. I made her eat, which she didn't mind doing, but didn't seem to care much about, either.

"Are you going to tell me what's wrong?" I asked every time. And every time, she'd say "Nothing," and make a joke or turn the subject.

One day—I know the date exactly, December 12—I badgered her again.

"There's nothing wrong, Jimmy. Everything's fine now."

"That sounds like things used to be wrong. What's changed?"

Sara gave a little frustrated shrug that made her collarbone show through her blouse. "You remember I told you we used to be happy? Well, we're happy again. That's all."

"Your mom's not happy."

"Yes, she is—she's just looking for something to be unhappy about. Is that why you're always nagging me? Because she told you to?"

"Well, why shouldn't she? You're skin and bones, she says you don't sleep, you sneak out of the house—"

Sara's face stopped me. It was like stone, except for her eyes, which seemed to scorch my face as she looked at me. "You know what you are, Jimmy Ryan? You're a busybody old woman. Keep your nose out of my business from now on!"

She spun around on her counter stool and plunged out of the drugstore.

By the time I got out to the sidewalk she was gone. She wasn't at the library, or the high school.

That night I picked at my dinner, until Mom said, "Jimmy, are you sick?"

"I had a big lunch, I guess. Pop, can I borrow the car tonight?"

"Sure. What you got planned?"

I felt terrible as I said, "Supposed to be a meteor shower tonight. I thought I'd drive out past Don Emilio and watch."

This time he didn't give me a look across the table. I almost wished he had.

I drove out the road toward South Hollier at about 9 p.m. I didn't know when the Gutierrez family went to bed, but I didn't want to arrive much past that time, whatever it was. I parked the car off the road just before the culvert-pipe tunnels and walked the rest of the way.

The night was so clear that the starlight was enough to see by. I circled South Hollier, only waking up one dog in the process, until I found a perch where I could see the front and back doors of the Gutierrez house. That put me partway up the lower slopes of the tailings dump. I'd thought there was another house or two between theirs and the dump; had they been torn down to make room?

It got cold, and colder, as I waited. I wished I had a watch with a radium dial. Finally I saw movement; I had to blink and look away to make sure it wasn't just from staring for so long at one spot.

Sara was a pale smudge, standing in her back yard in a light-colored dress, her head tipped back to see the stars, or the ridge top. She set out to climb the slope.

She wasn't looking for me, and I was wearing a dark wool coat. So I could follow her as she climbed, up and up until she reached the top of the ridge. I had the sense to stay down where I wouldn't show up against the sky.

Sara stood still for a moment, her head down. Then she lifted her face and her arms. She began a shuffling step, rhythmic, sure, as if the loose stones she danced over were a polished wood floor. About every five steps she gave a spring. Sometimes she'd turn in place, or sweep her arms over her head in a wide arc. I followed her as she moved along the ridge, until in one of her turns the starlight fell on her face. It was blank, entranced. Her eyes were open, but not seeing.

I couldn't stand it. "Sara!"

She came back to her own face; I don't know any other way to say it. She came back, stumbled, and stopped. I scrambled up the slope to her, and grabbed her shoulders as she swayed. They were thin as bird bones under my hands.

"Sara, what *is* this? What the hell are you doing out here?" My voice sounded hollow and thin, carried away by the air over the ridge.

"Jimmy? What are you doing here?"

I felt my face burn. The only true answer was "Spying." I felt guilty enough to be angry again. "Trying to find out what you wouldn't tell me. Friends don't lie to each other."

"I haven't...I haven't lied to you."

"You said everything was fine!"

She nodded slowly. "It is, now."

"You're sleepwalking on the tailings!"

Her face took on a new sharpness. "You think I'm sleepwalking?"

"What else?"

"Oh, God." She scrubbed at her face with both hands. "Don't you remember, when I told you about Fuji and the others?"

I let go of her shoulders. For the first time I felt, in my palms, the heat of her skin, that radiated through the material of her dress. "This isn't some bunk about the mountain?"

"I had to fix it. There wasn't anybody else who could."

"You're not fixing anything! This is just a pile of rocks that used to be a hill!"

"Jimmy. I *am* the mountain."

She stood so still before me, so straight and solid. And I was cold all the way through, watching the light of the stars waver through the halo of heat around her.

135

"Sara. Please, this is—Come down from here. Pop will help you—"

Her eyes narrowed, and her head cocked. "Can he dance?"

She was still there, still present in her crazy head. The rush of relief almost knocked me over. What would I have done if she'd been lost—if I'd lost her?

If I'd lost her. Before my eyes I saw two futures stretching out before me. One of them had Sara in it, every day, for every minute. The other... The other looked like bare, broken rock that nothing would grow on.

The shock pushed the words out of my mouth. "I love you, Sara."

She shook her head, wide-eyed. "Oh..."

"Marry me. I'm going to Colorado next month, you can go with me. You can finish school there—"

Sara was still shaking her head, and now her eyes were full of tears and reflected stars. She reached out a hand, stretching it out as if we were far, far apart. "Oh, Jimmy. I want—Oh, don't you see?"

"Don't you care for me, Sara?"

She gave a terrible wordless cry, as if she were being twisted in invisible hands. "I can't leave!"

"But for you and me—"

"There are more people than just us. They need me."

"Your folks? They've got your brothers. They don't need you the way I do."

"Jimmy, you're not listening. I *can't* leave. I'm the mountain."

Her face wasn't crazy. It was streaked with tears and a deep, adult sorrow, like the saints' statues in St. Patrick's Church. Sara reached out to me the way Mary's statue reached down from her niche over the altar, pity and yearning in the very finger-joints. I saw the waving heat around her, and the stars in her eyes and her hair.

I stepped back a pace. I couldn't help it.

I saw her heart break. That's the only way I can describe what I watched in her face. But when it was done, what was left in her eyes and her mouth and the way she held her head was strong and certain and brave.

"Goodbye, Jimmy," she said. She turned, sure-footed, and ran like a deer along the tailings ridge into the night.

I think I shouted her name. I know that something set the dogs barking all over South Hollier, and eventually Enrique Gutierrez was shaking me by the shoulders.

When Sara hadn't come home by morning, we called the police. Mr. and Mrs. Gutierrez were afraid she'd broken her leg, or fallen and been knocked out. I couldn't talk about what I was afraid of, so I agreed with them, that that could have happened.

Every able-bodied person in South Hollier joined the search. Everyone thought it would be over in an hour or so. By afternoon the police had brought dogs in, and were looking for fresh slides. They didn't say they were looking for places where the rocks might have engulfed a body.

If she was out there, the dogs would have found her. Still, I had to go down to the station, because I was the last one to see her, because the girl at the lunch counter had heard our fight. And God knows, I must have seemed a little crazy. I told them what I'd seen and what we'd said. I just didn't tell them what I thought had happened.

I didn't transfer to the Colorado School of Mines. Leveling mountains didn't appeal to me anymore. I went back to pre-med, and started on medical school at the University of Arizona. When Pearl Harbor was bombed, I enlisted, and went to the Pacific as a medic.

After the war, I finished medical school and hired on as a company doctor at the hospital in Hollier. Pop had passed, and Mom was glad to have me nearby. I couldn't live in the house on Collar Hill, though, that looked down the canyon to where Guadalupe Hill had been. I found a little house in South Hollier, small enough for a bachelor to handle.

The Gutierrez house was gone. As the dump grew, it needed a bigger base, and the company bought the house and knocked it down to make room for more rock. Mr. and Mrs. Gutierrez bought a place down at the south end of Wilson, and while they were alive, I used to visit and tell them how their old neighbors were getting on.

I'd lived in South Hollier for a couple of months before I climbed the slope of the tailings one December night and sat in the starlight. I sat for maybe an hour before I felt her beside me. I didn't turn to look.

"The mountain's happy now," I said. My voice cracked a little.

"I'm happy," she said. "Be happy for me, Jimmy."

"Who's going to be happy for me?"

137

"I'll do that. Maybe someday you will, too."

I shook my head, but it seemed silly to argue with her.

"What used to be good still is," she said. "Remember that." And after a minute, "I take care of everybody, but you most of all."

"I'll die after a while and save you the trouble."

"Not for a long time." There was motion at the corner of my eye, and I felt warm lips against my cheek. "I love you, Jimmy."

Then there was nothing beside me but a gust of cold wind.

I'd watched the mining of Guadalupe Hill, and thought men could do anything, be anything, conquer anything. I'd thought we'd cure cancer any day.

Now Guadalupe Pit is as deep as Guadalupe Hill once was high, and next to it there's a second pit that would hold three Guadalupes. Both pits are shut down, played out. There's no cure for cancer, the AIDS quilt is so big that there's no place large enough to roll the whole thing out at once, and diabetes has gone from a rarity to an epidemic.

But in South Hollier there's a ridge that could have been nothing more than a heap of barren, cast-off rock; and a cluster of buildings that could have slowly emptied and died inside their wall. Instead there's a mountain with a goddess, and a neighborhood that rests safe and happy, as if in her warm cupped hands.

For Elise Matthesen, and the necklace of the same title.

Joshua Tree

Emma Bull

My name is Tabetha Sikorsky. Yes, that's usually spelled "Tabitha," but spelling has never been my mom's hot subject. I'm not sure what my dad's hot subject is, but I hope it's wood shop, since he's now living in Phoenix nailing roofing on tract houses.

That beats the hell out of being a manicurist in the middle of the desert in the most horrible town in the world. Which is what my mom is. Which makes me the daughter of a manicurist in the middle of, etc., etc. No comment on where that falls on the beats-the-hell scale.

I'm sixteen. The school district thinks I'm seventeen (when they think of me), because my mother faked my birth certificate to get me into kindergarten when I was four. Kindergarten is free daycare. It wasn't till third grade that I realized my real age wasn't a secret of Defense Department proportions, and Mom and I wouldn't go to jail if it came out that she'd forged my birth certificate. But it was still a while before I stopped getting dizzy and sick to my stomach every time someone asked, "And how old are you, sweetie?"

I don't want anyone to think my mom doesn't love me. I've seen her with people she's said "I love you" to, and I figure she does a better job of loving me than she does with most of them. She just has a short attention span. I bet I was 24/7 interesting when I was the new Cabbage Patch baby, but now I'm only intermittently riveting. I try not to use it up.

We live in a town that wouldn't exist if it weren't for the Marine base. They put military bases in the middle of nowhere because real towns wouldn't take that crap. In our case, they put the base in the center of hundreds of miles of desert and let a town happen around it, like a parasite. That's us: Tapewormville.

If you're just driving through, it probably looks like a thriving little burg. Look! They've got a Seven-Eleven *and* a Circle K! If you stay, you

139

have time to notice that the successful businesses deal in the following: barbering (there are more "MARINE HAIRCUTS" signs in town than stop signs) liquor (drink here, or take-out); fast food (pizza delivery is big); strippers; and auto body shops. The body shops are because, after coming into town to drink and watch girls take off their tops, the Maggots try to drive back to the base. It's not just an economy, it's a whole ecosystem.

Not that the only people on base are the Maggots. The officers are mostly older, married with kids, even. Even Marines grow up eventually. Still, it's like living in an occupied country. I read someplace that people in Guam want the U.S. military base out of there, but they're afraid the economy would tank. Well, here we are: Guam with no ocean.

Normal towns have plenty of laundromats and supermarkets and clothing stores and stuff. Not base towns. The base has its own washing machines. It has a mess hall and a commissary. Uniforms come with the gig. And for everything else, like videos and cigarettes and magazines that aren't Soap Opera Digest, there's the PX. So that leaves the townies' needs, which can be met by one scabby Wal-Mart twenty miles away.

It's probably pretty clear that I'm not a base kid. I was born a townie, and I'm scared shitless that I'll die one. I'm more scared of that than car wrecks, earthquakes, or AIDS. This is the kind of town you can't possibly stay in all your life. So why are there so many people here who've done exactly that?

That's the real reason the town hates the base. On base, people get reassigned, moved around, resign their commissions.

They can leave.

Which raises an interesting question: To get out of this town, do I have to join the Marines?

I'm writing this because Ms. Grammercy gave us an over-the-weekend assignment for Junior English: write our autobiographies. She had to explain to the back of the room what "autobiography" means. Okay, that's not fair. I already knew, and Maryanne Krassner probably knew, because she reads them if they're by actors. But I could see the rest of the townies in the back two rows hearing "autobiography" and thinking, "Cars?"

I thought it was a bullshit assignment. We're in high school. How much autobiography are we supposed to have? But I've sort of gotten into it.

To encourage our creativity (she actually said that) Ms. G. gave us a list of questions we could start with. Here they are:

1. What is your name?
2. How old are you?
3. Who are your parents? What do they do?
4. Do you have brothers or sisters?
5. Where were you born? What is your hometown like?
6. What career do you want to pursue?
7. What is your favorite kind of music?
8. What person has had the most influence on your life?
9. What problem in the world is most important to you?

Here's what I wrote to turn in:

My name is Tabetha Sikorsky. I'm seventeen years old. My mother's name is Cheryl and she's a manicurist. My father's name is Arthur and he does construction in Phoenix. My mother and father are divorced. I don't have any brothers or sisters. I was born here. It's small but okay. I would like a career at a store maybe a record store. My favorite music is Eminem. The person who had the most influence on my life was Ms. Keating my 3rd grade teacher because she was smart and still pretty. I think the problem in the world that's most important to me is pollution.

I think it's a masterpiece. Especially considering what I had to work with.

I picked Eminem from an unbiased study of the T-shirts in Mr. Kuyper's Geography class. Two Jennifer Lopez, one U-2, two Bone Thugs 'n' Harmony, three Led Zeppelin (and isn't that sad?), four Eminem. The Ms. Keating thing I just thought was funny. As for the world problem—oh, excuse me, "the problem in the world"—how am I supposed to pick one? Global warming, poverty, war, torture, nuclear waste disposal, the whole damn government, everybody else's government. I was sitting next to the trash can, and I had an inch left before the margin, so I settled on "pollution." If you cross the margin lines on your notebook paper, Ms. G. takes points off. It's as if we're figure skaters and she's the Russian judge.

I take it back about not being able to write your autobiography at sixteen/seventeen. I just realized I know everything that will happen in Ms. G.'s class on Monday. I'll pass my homework over Luis Perez's shoulder, and he'll make a big deal of reading it and laughing before he passes it up. (I was going to write that I wanted a career as an exotic dancer, but then I remembered Luis. He stifled my creativity.) Piper Amendola will toss back her Pantene Pro-V hair and hand in twenty typed pages with the comment that she found the assignment "really useful and interesting." Ms. G. will tell the front of the room that they're all clever and going to heaven or college, whichever comes first, and the back of the room that we don't seem to be trying.

And if I know what will happen Monday, why shouldn't I know what will happen next month, in ten years, everything right up to when I die? I can write my whole life story now. But some things are too big a waste of time even for me.

•

Monday went as predicted, except I forgot to mention the hangover from Janelle's birthday party. I knew I'd have one; I just forgot to mention it.

The party Janelle told her stepmom about was on Saturday. But Sunday we went over to Little Mike's rec room for the real thing.

When I was a kid, and I thought about what I'd have when I got my own place, it looked a lot like Little Mike's. It's embarrassing to write that. Black-light posters, for godsake. A couple crisscross strings of Christmas lights "for atmosphere" (of what? Trailer-park holiday cheer?). A black vinyl couch that makes fart sounds when you move around on it, no matter what you're wearing. A red shag carpet that smells like dog pee when you're close enough—like when you sit on the floor (I only did it once). And the incense, of course. "African Love." I think he bought it at a truck stop.

But Mike's okay. He's always up for hosting a party, as long as you give him money for the beer. If you want pot, though, you have to bring your own. He doesn't want to violate his parole. I don't have the heart to tell him that supplying alcohol to minors has got that covered already.

I really thought I'd get through Sunday night without a crappy moment. TLC was playing loud on Mike's stereo, my third beer was in my hand, Janelle was sitting beside me singing along, Barb and Nina were dancing and pretending they didn't notice the guys watching them.

Then suddenly, boom. Everything sucked. I have no idea what set it off. Nina was shaking her big butt and her big boobs, and I could tell that in her head she looked like Lisa "Left Eye". But she really just looked sloppy and sad. Barb's water bra bounced up and down, and the guys watched like the young males in the herd watch the female who's going into heat, planning to be first with the most when she's ready (in this case, after one more beer).

Suddenly everyone in the room seemed to be on the fast track to pregnancy, jail, or a seasonal job on the line at a fruit packing plant. Including me.

I looked at Janelle, and she wasn't singing along anymore. For a second I thought maybe she felt it, too. The crappy mood almost lifted. Then I realized what was actually up with her face, and helped her outside to puke.

Little Mike's place is at the edge of town. His backyard is basically miles of sand, rocks, and mesquite. There's even a joshua tree right behind the garage, a pretty sickly-looking one (though how can you tell with joshua trees?) with its two branches twisted like rejects from a grade school pipe cleaner project.

I held Janelle's hair out of her face while she did the deed. Janelle never just throws up and gets on with her life. It's a big production number that goes on forever. The motion sensor light over the back door had turned off by the time she got serious about it.

Janelle sounds like she's dying when she pukes, so I tried to distract myself, but the desert in the dark doesn't provide much material. I pretended the tree was a psycho killer with two heads sneaking up on a houseful of naughty, naughty teenagers. A psycho killer with shaggy, spiky hair. Stupid hair. Stupid psycho killer, making your big move on a bad hair day. Don't you want your picture in the paper?

Janelle and I became best friends in fifth grade. Actually, we became twins. I stole Mom's paring knife, and we cut our thumbs and pressed them together in a sacred ritual in Janelle's garage. We wore the same

143

clothes, loved the same bands, crushed on the same TV stars, had the same opinions—I bet it drove everyone nuts.

We recruited Barb and Nina to the posse the next year. It was girl heaven. Sleepovers at my house, when my mom would give us manicures at the kitchen table. Parties at Nina's, whose dad works in the bakery at Costco. Afternoons riding Barb's uncle's horses. Saturdays when we'd dress up in clothes Janelle's stepmom was giving away and pretend we were making a music video.

It was at Nina's quinceañera that I first made a joke that Janelle, Barb, and Nina didn't get. It didn't happen again for a while, but that was the first one.

I handed Janelle a couple of tissues and let her swish her mouth out with my beer (then let her keep the bottle). "Thanks, Beth," she said, "you are the best friend ever. I just really love you."

I don't know why, but the puker/hair-holder relationship generates these feelings of intimacy. It wears off in about an hour, or sooner if you screw it up.

"Do you ever think that growing up isn't as good as it was supposed to be?" I said.

Our moving around had turned the light back on, so we could even see each other. Her face was still blotchy and pale, and the dark liner around her lips was smeared. "What?" she said.

"When we were little kids, it just felt like we were on this big adventure. Now it's like we're on a guided tour of a landfill. Do you know what I mean?"

She frowned. "If you don't want to be at my party, you don't have to stay."

"It's not the party! But don't you ever feel like there's something really important out there, that we aren't getting?" You'd think I'd have learned to cut my losses by now.

"Oh, God, Beth, I get enough Jesus crap from my stepmom." She took a big swallow of beer and said, "I'm going back in."

Of course, I did, too. Everything was swell. I had another beer, and we were all laughing and happy. Wahoo.

Here's what I think I'm having trouble with: this *is* what happiness is. When I was a kid, I thought I'd just get happier and happier as I got older, and have more things to be happy about. I based this theory on observation of select adults. The problem with my results is that I couldn't tell the difference then between happy and fake-happy. Now I know you pretend to be just frigging ecstatic over everything, maybe because you're so glad it's not worse. Pleased to meet you! means, Thank God you're not a cop! or, I love this car! means, At least it's not a '78 Datsun with bald tires and bad hoses!

But sometimes I can still have these moments of total happiness. And I feel as if every time I pretend to be happy, I'm scaring that real happiness off.

I rode my bike home from the party. Randy Nesterhoff offered me a ride, but the car smelled like Southern Comfort from six feet away. I'm stupid, but at least I'm selective about it.

•

I don't know why I'm still writing this shit down. If I wanted to keep a diary, this wouldn't be the way I'd do it. And for sure no one is ever going to see this. Unlike the masterpiece version, which I turned in Monday morning. (Got it back today. C-, with my carefully omitted commas written in, in red. Got to give Ms. G. something to do.)

Maybe what I'm doing, writing this, is what Piper's crew do when they're crammed in front of the girls' room mirror before first period (and just incidentally, hogging the sinks). "Eeuw, is that a zit?" "Is my hair too straight?" "I just got this lip gloss, is it, like, okay?" I'm holding up these words to my face so I can check myself out. Looking for normal in there somewhere, or even a good sort of abnormal.

Piper and Co. take that whole "the few, the proud" thing pretty seriously—their folks are officers, so they're sweetly condescending to the base kids whose fathers are mere grunts, and treat the townies the way the Spanish missionaries treated the Indians. Make yourselves useful and don't talk back, or we'll shoot you. I'm pleased to say that Piper hasn't once figured out a way I can be useful to her.

Bigots are people who say, "I don't hate all [fill in the blank] people. Why, some of my best friends are [ditto]." I'm proud to say I'm not a bigot. None of my friends are kids from the base.

As far as I know, the only good thing that ever came off that base was Steve. Mom dated him ("dated" meaning "slept with") for nine months, when I was twelve/thirteen. He didn't treat me like an adult, exactly. It was more that I was a real person to him, not someone he

145

had to impress on the way to impressing Mom. He figured out that I really wanted a mountain bike, and gave it to me for my birthday.

Then he got transferred. I didn't find out for almost a year that he asked Mom to marry him when it happened. He wanted to take us with him.

Obviously, we didn't go. Mom had a huge fight with him instead. Don't ask me to explain that.

He's in Saudi Arabia now. Another desert.

I think sometimes I should do with Piper what the Indians did with the missionaries. Be polite but stupid to her face, and sabotage the hell out of her when she's not looking. But I can't keep my mouth shut. Today she and Kristin Gold and Amber Janeke were hanging around Piper's locker, which is annoyingly close to mine. I passed them on my way to get my geography book, and Piper said, "Do you smell something?" Smothered laughter from Kristen and Amber.

So I stopped. "Probably," I said. "Your locker door's open."

It took her a second to get it. By that time I had my locker open and my book out. (Being fast on your locker combination is a survival skill.) I smiled at her, slammed the door, and hauled it for class. I was so proud of that one that I raised my hand when Mr. Kuyper asked where Mongolia is. Adrenaline is a dangerous drug.

And of course, I came back after class and found the entire contents of my locker on the hall floor. Note to self: check door after slamming to ensure latching has occurred.

There are at least two sets of Rules for Life, as far as I can tell. There are the ones that get you picked up by the cops or taken to the assistant principal's office if you break them: Don't leave school grounds, don't spray paint stop signs, don't drink, don't drop firecrackers in the toilets.

But there's a different set that you really can't break if you don't want your life to suck relentlessly. At the head of the list, Rule Number One: Don't get noticed. As long as you stay exactly the person everyone thinks you're supposed to be, you're fine. Piper can answer questions and get A's on homework because that's who she's supposed to be. I'm supposed to be someone else. Usually I have that person nailed. But sometimes I lose perspective and do something inconsistent.

Then I have to put my crap back in my locker, get my gym shoes out of the toilet, prove to Janelle that I'm not dissing her party, and give the wrong answer to a question I shouldn't have stuck my hand in the air over anyway. But that's fair. High school exists to teach you the rules, and I figure I'm getting a solid B average.

•

Ring ring! Life changes. How can you not love telephones? For better or worse, *ring ring!* and presto, there's something different in your ear from what you were doing or thinking a second ago. Even if it's about replacement windows or something.

But it might not be. What if it's NASA, and they want you to know the shuttle is making an emergency landing, and it looks as if touchdown is going to be somewhere around your bathtub, and you might want to evacuate your neighborhood?

Raves are not on the list of approved uses for National Monuments, I bet. But it's tough to police a national monument that's hundreds of thousands of acres wide, full of blind canyons and dry washes. What makes Joshua Tree a monument, anyway, like the Lincoln Memorial? And why is it a national monument *and* a national park? Who decides this stuff?

Anyway, now Saturday night is spoken for.

Mom answered the phone, so after I hung up, she had to know who it was. It's hard to explain a phone call from a stranger who asks for you by name, then only has fifteen seconds of things to say. I told her it was the library, and a book I'd reserved was in. Thank god she has no idea when the library closes.

Mom shares the school district's expectations for her daughter. I think that's because the school district is her most dependable source of information on me. We aren't home together much. It makes the library excuse risky, though, since she has no idea how much I read, and based on my grades, I shouldn't know when the library's open, either.

"What book?" she asked.

I was in the middle of dialing Bob Esquivel. I turned the phone off and tried to look dazed while I figured out an answer.

I guess Mom and I really haven't seen much of each other lately, because I was surprised at how tired she looks. There are two deep lines between her eyebrows and this heaviness around the corners of her mouth, as if she's been having a bad day for the last 365. When I was really little and Dad still lived with us, she had cheerleader hair, blonde and thick and long. When people talk about hair like ripe wheat, I figure that's what they mean. Now her hair looks more like dry grass before the fall wildfires, the life sucked out.

"Just a book for school," I said, then, thinking of Mr. Kuyper, "about China."

"Don't they have the right books in the school library? You'd think they'd have what the teachers are teaching, for godsake."

"It's not like you're paying extra, Mom. The library's free."

"Nothing's free. Those books cost tax money."

What do you say to that? Better books than a bomber? Maybe I looked a little too stupid, because she stomped out to the kitchen.

She cheered up after she found out there was lasagna in the fridge. It's weird—cooking is the only thing I'm supposed to do well that I'm actually good at.

And I cheered up because Bob was home and up for Saturday night.

I don't know how they do these things in cities, but out here, if you want to find the party, it helps to have a global positioning system. Seriously. Bob Esquivel's the only other person in town I know who likes to rave. He has a GPS and a dirt bike, and a profile like Keanu Reeves. He graduated last year, and the high school halls are dark and drab since then. Okay, they were dark and drab before that, but for some of us, birds sang and the ceiling rained flowers if he met our eyes as we passed on the way to class. The "us" did not include Janelle, Nina, and Barb, who thought his hair was too long.

Raving is one of the things I don't have in common with those guys. The first rave I ever went to, Janelle went, too. After fifteen minutes, I was bouncy and breathless and felt like a little kid who'd just discovered a fully-equipped secret fort. Janelle hated the music, thought all the people were freaks, and was afraid to touch anything for fear of getting AIDS or TB. Janelle believes everything she reads on the Internet.

Given that I'm not exactly the life of the party at parties, I suppose it's weird that I'd drag my ass into the desert in the dark to hear some DJ spin for a bunch of X-heads wearing glow-necklaces.

Well, surprise.

The way to get through normal life is to pretend it isn't getting to you. If you let on that you're hurt, the other animals will turn on you and tear you to pieces. Don't attract the attention of predators.

But in the dark in the desert, with a pile of speakers the size of our house kicking out the groove, and everyone around me faceless and trancing, it's different. Then I can scream loud as I want, and sometimes everyone around me does, too, as if for once I'm not the only one who wants to scream. I can stamp as if everything I hate is down there in the dirt and I can smash it to bits. I can jump up and down and flap my arms like a nut, just because maybe the DJ will see the top of my head and then I can imagine the groove is just for me.

Most of all, when I'm out there banging up against dozens of strangers and sharing their sweat, I'm alone. Yes, alone. So I'm safe. I'm free.

I should have mentioned the park earlier. I usually think of this place as being divided into two cultures, the base and the townies. But it's really three parts, and the third one is the park. That's a whole different culture.

There's the rangers, who live here but not quite *here*—I don't know how to explain it. Then there are day visitors, campers, backpackers, rock climbers, driving through town on Highway 62 in shiny SUVs and rental cars. Lots of Eddie Bauer and Northface logos on clothes, lots of bright-colored nylon gear. They stop for breakfast at the Lucky Lizard or La Boule (the only places in town with real coffee, and I'm counting our house) and fill 'er up with premium, but that's it for their contact with the other two cultures.

If this were the Middle Ages, we'd be the peasants, and the Marine base would be the landowners. The park would be the Church, with its own walls and special rules, and the monks being contemplative in their monastery. With pilgrims in really nice wagons.

The Marines ship people out, the tourists come and leave. But the peasants are forever. The only escape the park offers is the occasional rave, and that's like getting drunk—it's temporary.

It's a really good temporary, though.

•

How can you do something so crappy to your kid as to move her to a new school in spring of junior year? I guess the Marines don't exactly ask first, but wasn't there an aunt she could have stayed with?

Naturally, Ms. G. stood her up in front of the class and introduced her, as if this were third grade. I don't remember her name—I was too busy feeling sorry for her, and being mad at myself for wasting time feeling sorry for her.

She looked like David Bowie dressed up like Audrey Hepburn. Little black sheath dress, bangle bracelets, big sunglasses pushed up into her hair, which is white-blonde and short and sticks up. Fishnet stockings (tramp!) and Converse hi-tops (weirdo!). She looked out over the rest of us with these huge round brown eyes, like a deer who has no idea that that thing in your hands is a shotgun.

Sure enough, when the bell rang, Randy Nesterhoff sauntered up to where New Girl was stuffing her books into the biggest purse in the world. "Man, you don't have any tits at all, do you?" he said. His buddies snickered behind him.

She looked up and kind of blinked her eyes wider—it's not easy to describe. "Neither do you," she said.

"Yeah, well, I'm a *guy*."

Her eyebrows went up. "You are?" She shouldered the monster purse and walked out. Randy's crew laughed and Randy turned purple.

Me, I was revising my opinions about deer.

The second incident, at lunch, was even more interesting. Amber and Piper had set up the ballot box for Junior Formal king and queen at the end of the cafeteria line, so there was no dodging it.

"Did you vote yet, Beth?" Amber cooed as I went by with my tray. The way she asked made it a joke. Only not funny.

"You should vote for yourself," Piper added. "Then at least you'd get a vote."

Somebody behind me said, "What was your name again? Piper?"

I had to turn and look. It was New Girl.

Piper opened her mouth, but New Girl finished, "No, I must have misheard. I mean, you're a girl, not a light plane."

For a second, I adored New Girl. Then she turned to me and said, "And you don't look like a Beth."

It's one thing to step into the searchlight yourself. Dragging someone else in with you is rude. "My parents couldn't spell 'Goddess,'" I said, and bolted for the table where Janelle and Barb were sitting.

They asked me about New Girl. God knows, they couldn't help but notice her. I just said she was in my English class.

But I thought about it for a long time. New Girl is an equal-opportunity insulter: Randy the townie and Piper the officer's brat both got a faceful. She doesn't care if she sticks out like the proverbial thumb, and she has no clue about the class structure.

Obviously, Dead Chick Walking.

•

I don't know how to tell this. I don't even know if it happened. But if it didn't happen, what did?

I'm really careful about what I drink at a rave. Beer out of a bottle, watch it being opened, then don't let the bottle out of my sight. Keg beer, watch the cup all the way from the tap to my hand, and then don't let the cup out of my sight. Never hard liquor, because the bottle stays open too long. What did I say earlier about only being selectively stupid? You never know when somebody'll decide to spring enlightenment on you unannounced.

I have to cover that because that's the first thing you think—it's still what I think, except I know it can't be true. Unless I drank so much that I don't remember being stupid—eating a brownie or drinking out of someone's canteen. But I wouldn't do that. I'm always careful.

Okay, this is making me cry. And the tears really sting, which makes me feel sorry for myself, so I want to cry even more. Stupid, stupid, stupid. But I feel like I was abducted by aliens or something, as if there was a piece of my life when I lay bare-assed under a big light and everyone stared at me *only I can't remember it*. Instead there's this thing I do remember that can't have happened.

Must not be crying next time Mom comes in.

Mom stayed home from work to take care of me. She hasn't done that since I was in third grade. She's taking the emergency room nurse's instructions pretty seriously. She pops in to check the Gatorade level in my glass, and no matter how much I've drunk, she makes me drink more, and then she refills it. You'd think I'd be peeing like a horse. Shows how dried-out I am.

151

She came in when I was writing. I told her this was homework. That was the first time she sounded pissed off since it happened. She said, "The school won't expect you to do your damn homework with your brains cooked out." I remember it exactly because I liked the image. My skull like a busted pressure cooker, and all my nutritious brains coming out like steam.

I wouldn't hurt as much if I'd lie still, but if I don't write this, I think it instead, and it goes round and round until it's a little brain tornado. At least if I write it down, it seems like it goes in a straight line. And on one of these Gatorade runs, Mom will tell me to quit or else, so I want to do as much as I can before then.

She was so scared in the emergency room.

It was a great party Until. Riding there with my arms around Bob's waist—I feel stupid about it now, but I thought, Tonight he'll see me dancing, and he'll be really into me. We'll dance together like Belle and the Beast, alone in the desert and as the sun comes up he'll kiss me. It makes me feel crappy just to write it, but I have to.

We got to the last set of coordinates, which turned out to be an alley between two long rockpiles, and followed the line of tiki torches stuck in the rock cracks over our heads. At the end of the alley I could feel the space open up, as if there wasn't anything for my body's sonar to ping off of. The sky was like a black sequined dress—no moon, but all the stars in the universe, gathered to watch.

The party was marked off by a huge circle of torches ten feet high. Outside the circle, I couldn't see a thing. I knew there was a lot of *there* out in the dark, but I couldn't tell if the desert went up or down on either side, or just lay flat forever. The DJ stand was at one end of the circle, with its red work lights and secret movements—not whole people, just parts moving in and out of the light. There must have been a hundred people in the circle, being restless and noisy.

We stepped out of the alley—and an organ chord swelled up from everywhere. The whole circle went dead quiet. It was like the party had been waiting for us.

Bob went to find the beer. I wanted to follow him, but that chord began to throb, right in time to my heart. I ran toward the torches. The chord turned into the intro to an old Prince song, with the DJ scratching it so it had a new rhythm. Then he let the song go.

I let me go. I was sweating like a hog in about a minute, when he started cross-fading between Prince and the Ramones. Someone near me started to laugh, as if they'd got a joke.

He spun up some Moby after that, and I danced till my legs felt wobbly. Then I found the kegs and got a big red plastic cup of beer. It was thin and acidy, but it was like cold lemonade after dancing. I chugged it.

I like remembering the beginning of the night. I just want to write about dancing and getting my buzz on, and the cool things I saw in the circle. I did see cool things, like the woman who'd glued rhinestones to her arms and chest and face in patterns until she was one shining diagram, and the guy who'd smeared the stuff inside the Cyalume lightsticks on his hands and was drawing patterns in the dark as he danced. There were a bunch of people in masks made of leaves and feathers, dancing together, and when the torchlight shone in their eyes, it was like seeing a coyote watching you through the bushes. They were cool enough that I figured they'd come in from L.A.

I danced and drank until I didn't feel either cool or uncool. The point wasn't see-and-be-seen. The point was to be there, part of this mob in the dark. I felt as if I had to be there, or there'd be a break in the circuit, that the juice wouldn't flow. If I stopped dancing, there'd be a rolling blackout. If I stopped dancing, even the DJ wouldn't be able to mix. I was invisible, unnoticed—but connected and necessary.

But I did stop dancing, didn't I?

I went for beer—and there was Bob. He was shiny in the torch light, and his shirt was unbuttoned. He looked like a big, sweaty romance novel cover. "Beth," he said. "You look way hot."

I pretty much stopped breathing. "So do you."

"Yeah." He grinned and flapped his shirt. He meant temperature-hot. I replayed the conversation—okay, then so did I.

"You know, I really like you," he added.

I was drinking beer. It slopped over my upper lip, down my chin, and onto my tank top. "I like you, too," I got out past the back of my hand as I wiped my face.

"I like that shirt. You should wear more clothes like that."

It was just a tank top. I wanted him to like me, not my clothes.

"You should wear it without a bra, though. If you wore tight clothes, guys would notice you more."

153

Okay, he'd found the Ecstasy. Sure he liked me—right then, he liked *everyone*. But maybe he liked me a little bit more...?

"Hello, Goddess," said a voice off to my right. It was New Girl.

"Huh-uh," Bob said. "This is Beth."

New Girl shook her head. She looked even more deer-like in the dark, with her eyes black and shining. She'd stuck a line of sparkly bindi down her cheek below one eye, like tears. Her hair in the torches made her head look like a little moon. She had on a black sleeveless T-shirt with a glitter snake on it.

"You can't be a Beth. What's your real name?" she asked. She didn't look at Bob.

"Tabetha," I said.

"Excellent! The Goddess Tab, who dances in the desert to bring secrets to the surface!"

"Ooo-kay. Way too much X." I turned to get away and drink my beer. Inside my head I was yelling "Follow me!" at Bob. Instead, New Girl followed, and Bob trailed after.

"No X. I don't do that stuff. It's too embarrassing afterward," said New Girl. "It makes me tell people I can't stand that they're wonderful human beings."

My sentiments exactly, but I wasn't going to tell her so. "What the hell is your name?" I asked.

"Alice. The female incarnation of the Hanged Man from the tarot. A woman on a perilous quest of self-discovery down the rabbit hole of life."

I actually opened my mouth to blow her off when I realized that I was hearing the kind of thing that I think but never say. "Is it really Alice?"

"Uh-huh. Is it really Tabetha?"

"Yeah."

"Well, then we know each other's true names. And you know what that means."

And I actually did. Jesus, nobody else in town would, but I did. All those years of reading weird shit, and it finally seemed as if it had a point.

That's when Bob said, "You talk really strange. Either of you give blow jobs?"

I don't know what I was about to say or do before Bob's little conversation starter, but suddenly I was scared of whatever it was. Real terror, like I'd almost walked in front of a speeding car and barely jumped back in time. I don't remember what I said, but I chugged my beer and headed straight for the center of the circle where it was darkest.

Even that was no good. If something got slipped into my beer, it must have been before that, because suddenly I didn't feel safe. The whole mob was watching me, waiting for me to do something I wasn't supposed to. But what was I supposed to? No matter how loud the music was, every noise I made was louder. When I moved, I was in someone's face. I wasn't connected anymore. And "darkest" wasn't dark enough to hide in. I had to get away.

I shoved out of the dancers, past the torches, and stumbled over rocks and tufts of grass. Then I just kept going. After a minute my eyes adjusted to the starlight, as much as they ever would.

Everything was horrible. Bob wasn't going to kiss me under the sunrise. I was the slut with beer on her shirt who'd maybe do him because it wasn't as if guys liked me. And Alice New Girl had seen the whole thing.

That's when I put my foot in a hole, twisted my ankle, and fell down. Another wake-up call. I just sat there and cried like a jerk.

I had to go back to the circle. To being who I'm supposed to be— too stupid to bruise, too dumb to imagine, hard and happy and in hiding. I'm the tortoise, pulling my body parts back under cover, saying, Who, me? Oh, I'm just a rock.

Of course, I couldn't find the circle.

They'd made it hard to find, because if you could see it from anywhere, then so could the rangers. But I couldn't hear it, either. I'd gone a lot further than I thought.

I got scared. That's what screws you when you're lost in the desert. I should have stayed where I was till morning. I could have been right next to a park road. Instead I went stumbling through the dark.

I remember the sun coming up. I was in the middle of a plain, and the plain had joshua trees all over it, spaced out like an orchard without rows. Real trees, maybe thirty or forty feet high, not like the crummy little tree behind Mike's garage. Every one had a big crown of twisty branches, but there was no shade. When the wind blew, it hissed through the leathery knife-blade leaves, but nothing moved.

Rockpiles stuck up around the plain. I couldn't tell how far away they were. No road, no trails. Not even footprints.

I just kept walking. I didn't know what else to do. Little lizards slid off rocks when my shadow fell on them. Ravens flew over, making ugly laughing sounds. A rabbit with black ear tips crossed in front of me and didn't even look at me. A coyote sat and scratched his ear with a hind leg, then trotted off between the rocks. It got hotter and hotter. I remember noticing I wasn't sweating anymore.

Now comes the part I remember that didn't happen. I don't know when, except that there was still enough light to see by.

I thought it was a tree. I saw its feet first, and they were twisted and dry and dark like juniper roots. Its legs were like the trunks of the big joshua trees, corky-looking bark where the old leaves have fallen away. Above that, dry leaves hung on it like brown daggers overlapping. Only its head and hands were green. Knobs of green sword leaves like the ends of the joshua tree branches. Mistletoe was scattered around its head, the dark red strands like tiny bones. It had a face, but it was made of leaves, so I almost had to imagine it, like seeing pictures in clouds. That bent leaf in the middle is the nose, that line of leaf-ends there, that's the mouth. And those deep pits between the leaves are where its eyes would be.

Inside my head I was flailing and screaming, but my body wasn't doing anything. I think I was either passed out or close to it. It was like having a bad dream—you want it to go away, but it doesn't occur to you that you can do anything about it.

It bent over as if it was trying to look into my face. I guess I must have been sitting or lying down. Maybe. It had to bend practically in half. Then it picked up a rock and cut its hand open.

That sounds nasty, but it was just interesting at the time. It cut a long gash in the bark of its palm. Water, or maybe sap, oozed up out of the cut and filled its cupped hand. It stuck its hand out under my nose.

Now I understand about animals being able to sniff out water. The water smelled like being alive. Everything else in the world was dying, in different ways and at different speeds, but that water was alive forever.

So I drank it. I was so thirsty I'd stopped feeling it, but all of a sudden I couldn't get enough to drink. (So much for Miss I'm-careful-what-I-swallow. But since it couldn't have happened, does that time count?)

And that's it. I don't remember anything else, even in little confetti bits like I remember the rest. There's just nothing between that and when I woke up in the morning at the edge of the park where the all-terrain vehicle freaks go to play. Some vroom-vroomer saw me sit up on my sand dune and nine-one-oned.

I have a hideous sunburn (blisters in places) and I'm massively dehydrated. But I overheard the doctor tell the nurse he thought I was lying about being out there for two nights and a day. I wasn't messed up enough. And for sure I was lying either about where I started or about being on foot, because it was twenty miles from there to the place I was found.

Sure, whatever. I'm lying. That works for me.

•

Our dog died when I was eleven/twelve. Oh, boo hoo, right? Well, yeah—he was a great dog, and I'd grown up with him. But what was important, because I hadn't expected it, was the way it changed things between Mom and me. We did a lot of talking in between the crying, about important stuff. I don't know why grief made us feel as if it was safe to take the lids off. But it turned a crappy experience into a pretty good one, and for a while, we were closer than we'd been since I was tiny.

My point is, sometimes truly crappy experiences have a crowbar effect on the rest of your life. Everything shakes loose. Then you can let it go back to the way it was, or you can step in and make something happen, something that might be permanent.

Janelle, Nina, and Barb came over yesterday after school. You'd think I had cancer. Lots of hushed voices and sentences trailing off. Of course, me being lost in the desert is about the most interesting thing that's happened to any of us for years, so I understand that they'd want to get some mileage out of it. It made me feel like a museum exhibit.

Then Barb and Nina had to go babysit Nina's brothers. So I told Janelle about Bob at the rave.

"So did you do it?" Janelle asked.

157

"Do what?"

"Blow him. You *didn't?*" She squeaked that last bit. "Beth, I thought you were into him!"

I couldn't think of a thing to say. No joke, no verbal shrug, no cover story, nothing.

"Oh, god." Janelle looked disgusted. "He was supposed to say, 'I love you. I've always loved you.' Right?"

"Of course not!" Well, yes. Was that wrong? If it wasn't wrong, why had I denied it?

"Hel-lo! Guys have to know there's something in it for them. It's just, you know, biology. You love them before the blow job, and they love you after."

"Don't you ever both love each other at the same time?"

Blank stare from Janelle.

It was worse than not speaking the same language. At least with languages there's a chance you'll have a word for the concept.

I told her I was tired. Actually I was kind of sick to my stomach. She suddenly remembered to talk as if I was dying. And brain damaged. "You take care of yourself, hon. Okay?" Then she left.

That was when I had my big revelation. I didn't want to be just like Janelle anymore. I *couldn't* be. I wasn't built with the right parts or something. I guess I'd hoped that, if I stuck with her, she'd want to be more like me. But what was there about me that screamed "role model"?

Being like Janelle wouldn't save me from my life. And being like me wouldn't save Janelle. The people from the Titanic might have found some floating debris to hang onto, but they were still in the middle of the North Atlantic.

I said it was a revelation. I didn't say it made me insanely happy.

After dinner (frozen pizza—I'm the cook, after all), Mom came to my bedroom door and said, "There's a girl who says she's in your English class and has your homework assignment." She was half-frowning—not angry, just trying to figure out how she felt about this. "Alice somebody?"

Oh, god. Alice New Girl, witness to my shame, calling to find out if I had committed seppuku like a smart person. Well, I had to face the world eventually. Make like a rock, I told myself. "Sure. Where's the phone?"

158

"She's not on the phone," said Mom. "She's here."

I had only seconds to get my ducks in a row. All I could do was tug the sheet up straight and make my face blank. In that last moment I saw my bedroom as others see it: the matching furniture bought during my ten-minute girlie phase in fifth grade, now with the white laminate chipped off the corners. The dark blue mini-blinds with the puffy valance (Wal-Mart!) that grotesquely needed dusting. Clothes tossed everywhere. Invalid crap on the nightstand.

Alice came in. She wore black capri pants and a red bowling shirt with "Stan" embroidered over the pocket, and had the giant purse over her shoulder. Her face was world-class blank. "Hi," she said.

My mom took that as some kind of signal, because she left. Alice instantly closed the door and plopped down on the floor beside the bed. "Oh, jeez, Tab, you look *awful!* I'm so sorry. I tried to follow you at the rave, but I lost you in the dancers. Then I went back and tried to get that idiot guy to help me find you, but he was so full of Happy-Shiny he couldn't find his own head. How do you feel?"

Like I'm in the path of Hurricane Alice, I wanted to say. "Okay, considering."

"Considering that you could still be out there, bleaching like a cow skull?"

"With the ravens picking out my eyes," I said, just to see if she'd be grossed out.

"And the kangaroo rats stealing away your hair to make their nests," she said gleefully.

I tried not to grin. "The search party would never find me, but I'd be all around them."

"Part of the desert forever!" Alice finished. "It sounds like a song."

"Or an *Outer Limits* episode. You brought my English homework?"

She made a spitting noise. "That was just an excuse. I'm grounded. Nothing else would have got me past the parental units, short of climbing out a window." She looked at the wall over my head. "Where's that?"

When I did my frantic life-flashes-before-my-eyes view of the bedroom, I'd forgotten the tree picture over the bed. It's a blown-up color photo I got at a church rummage sale, nothing fine art about it. In the picture, a path climbs a hill in the foreground, around these big oak trees and a couple of good-sized rocks, then curves out of sight.

159

When I first saw it, I had this *hunger* to get into the picture, to follow that path. I can still stare into it and imagine walking around those rocks, into the shade of the trees, and seeing what's on the other side of the hill.

"I don't know where it is." Then I amazed myself, because my mouth opened again, and out came, "It's a picture about possibilities. About wanting. The path always goes out of sight." I didn't just figure that out, but I hadn't planned to tell anyone. Now to see what Alice would do to my exposed throat...

Alice looked very serious and intense. "What do you want when you look at it?" she asked.

I didn't feel like I could lie. I'd started this, after all. And the tree picture is one of the few things I'd grab if the house caught fire. I shrugged (which reminded me about the sunburn). "I don't know. I just want."

A big grin spread across her face. "Yes! Just like 'Malibu'!"

"What?"

"Hole! Courtney Love! On *Celebrity Skin*... You haven't heard it?"

She grabbed up the giant purse and pulled out a portable CD player. At first I thought there were morning glories glued all over it. Then I saw some of them were scuffed, and I realized they were painted on. Amazing.

Alice handed me the headphones. "'Malibu' makes me feel the same way. Like there's a road in front of me, and I have to find a way to get on it and see where it goes, or I'll go nuts." She looked up to make sure I had the phones on and pushed "play."

Wistful, jangly, beautiful guitars in my ears, and a girl singing, talking right to me. I mean, *spooky* to me—the voice wanted to know how I'd gotten so screwed up, and how I'd held it together in spite of it. And then it said, Hey, meet me halfway, *chica*, and the two of us can maybe save your stupid life, okay?

Even with the sunburn, I got goosebumps.

When the chorus started, Alice sang along, as if she knew without listening exactly how long the first verse was. Then she grabbed the phones off my ears.

"Hey!" I said.

"I can't not listen to it. We need a boombox."

I pointed to my desk. She jumped up, found mine (under a pair of jeans), and put the disk in. The song started over, and Alice bumped the volume up.

"Play it again," I said when it stopped.

After a couple more plays, we were singing along with Courtney as loud as we could. About a place where the ocean would wash away all the bullshit. A place to live, not just survive.

"Have you ever been?" Alice asked.

"What, to Malibu?" I laughed. "No chance."

"But it's only three hours away! Well, L. A. is. When my dad told me we were coming to California, I went nuts. But it seems like nobody here has ever been to L. A...." Alice grabbed her spiky hair and pulled it. "Three hours away there are great bands and dance clubs and juice bars and history and art and *the ocean*, and we're missing it! There are surfers and pelicans and movie stars!"

"All in the same place?" I asked, trying not to laugh.

"Yes! And you and I have got to go."

It wasn't like with Janelle, when I knew I was trying to fit my sticking-out pieces into the empty spot in the puzzle. It was as if I'd had a dream every night that I couldn't remember, and Alice had remembered it for me.

I know where that path in the picture comes out. On the other side of that hill is Malibu.

Mom must have heard us singing and shrieking, because she came in and said I had to rest.

"I'll bring your homework tomorrow." Alice winked.

"Don't forget your CD." I really didn't want to remind her.

"You can borrow it," she said.

Mom came back after she shooed Alice out. I asked, "Have you ever been to the ocean?"

She stared at me for a second. "No."

"Alice and I are going."

"Oh? When's that happening?"

"I don't know yet. But we will."

She gave me such a funny look—as if I'd surprised her, as if she felt sorry for me. Or for her. But she just said, "Drink your Gatorade."

I've listened to the whole album about a dozen times already.

Today I told Alice what happened when I was in the desert. She's the only person I've told. It was like having to be honest about how I felt about the tree picture: either I wasn't going to say anything about what happened after I ran off, or I had to tell her the whole thing.

I was afraid she would be different when I came back to school. I had visions of her being tight with Piper, pretending I'd become See-Through Girl. I know all about survival tactics, after all.

And, okay, I was afraid of the way I'd be—that I'd go back to sticking with Janelle and our posse. Because I *do* know about survival. I didn't know if I could resist that yummy, cozy, Supposed to Be hiding place.

But it was as if Alice and I were wired up like Secret Service guys. We could watch the crowd for snipers while we had each other's backs. I've started raising my hand in class. I just laughed and walked away when Amber called me "Gross Peeling Thing". I'm not alone, like the tree behind Little Mike's garage. I'm a forest, like the trees in the park.

The park is why I had to tell Alice. "Let's go out there this Saturday," she said today after sixth period.

"Why?" The bottom fell out of my stomach.

"Joshua Tree is a big deal. I read about it. It's this amazing ecosystem that doesn't exist anywhere else. And so far I've only seen it in the dark."

"It's the desert. There, I saved you so much time."

"Tab!" Then she looked at me with her eyes squinched up. "Is this anything I should know about?"

Even when I was behaving like a psych case, she didn't insist I tell her my deepest, darkest secrets. So of course I had to.

I told her about the creature in the desert, about waking up on the other side of the park, and the doctor saying I was lying.

Alice didn't say anything right away. I got scared. "It was probably heatstroke," I added, and heard the flatness in my voice.

She shook her head. "I don't think so."

That scared me even more. "Why not? It was heatstroke, LSD, or I'm insane! What do you mean, 'I don't think so'?"

"Remember your lips?"

I was about to yell at her, but she looked so serious.

"Lips dry out worse than any other part of your face, because they don't have any oil glands," she went on. "When I came to see you right after it happened, you looked like you'd just come off a barbecue grill. But your lips didn't. They weren't even dry."

I think every hair on my body stood straight up. "When I drank out of its palm—"

"You put your mouth in the water."

This Saturday we're spending the day in the park. We're going to bike in, and pack a lunch and huge amounts of water. Alice has a guide to the birds and animals and plants, and the plan is to see how many we can check off.

It's funny, but I'm not worried about seeing the joshua tree thing again. I think if something like that happens to you, you get one shot. You can do what you want with it, but that taste of live magic is one per customer.

Now that I'm not trying to be who I'm supposed to, I've started to wonder about the rest of the world. Is everybody wearing a disguise with the zipper stuck? Are all the supposed-to-bes big fat lies? If so, how about the desert? I know what it's supposed to be: no water, no life, everything poisonous, pointy, or otherwise out to get you.

I was supposed to be a loser. Maybe the desert and I have something in common.

Can't wait to talk this over with Alice.

Silver or Gold

Emma Bull

Moon Very Thin sat on the raised hearth—the only place in the center room out of the way—with her chin on her knuckles. She would have liked to be doing something more, but the things she thought of were futile, and most were undignified. She watched Alder Owl crisscross the slate floor and pop in and out of the stillroom and the pantry and the laundry. Alder Owl's hands were full of things on every crossing: clean clothes, a cheese, dried yellow dock and feverfew, a tinderbox, a wool mantle. She was frowning faintly all over her round pink face, and Moon knew that she was reviewing lists in her head.

"You can't pack all that," said Moon.

"You couldn't," said Alder Owl. "But I've had fifty years more practice. Now remember to cure the squash before you bring them in, or there'll be nothing to eat all winter but onions. And if the squirrels nest in the thatch again, there's a charm—"

"You told me," Moon sighed. She shifted a little to let the fire roast a slightly different part of her back. "If I forget it, I can look it up. It's awfully silly for you to set out now. We could have snow next week."

"If we did, then I'd walk through it. But we won't. Not for another month." Alder Owl wrapped three little stoneware jars in flannel and tucked them in her wicker pack.

Moon opened her mouth, and the thing she'd been busy not saying for three days hopped out. "He's been missing since before Midsummer. Why do you have to go now? Why do you have to go at all?"

At that, Alder Owl straightened up and regarded her sternly. "I have responsibilities. You ought to know that."

"But why should they have anything to do with him?"

"He is the prince of the Kingdom of Hark End."

165

Moon stood up. She was taller than Alder Owl, but under that fierce gaze she felt rather stubby. She scowled to hide it. "And we live in Hark End. Hundreds—thousands of people do. A lot of them are even witches. They haven't all gone tramping off like a pack of questing youngest sons."

Alder Owl had a great many wrinkles, which deepened all over her face when she was about to smile. They deepened now. "First, youngest sons have never been known to quest in packs. Second, all the witches worth their salt and stone have tried to find him, in whatever way suits them best. All of them but me. I held back because I wanted to be sure you could manage without me."

Moon Very Thin stood still for a moment, taking that in. Then she sat back down with a thump and laced her fingers around her knees. "Oh," she said, halfway between a gasp and a laugh. "Unfair, unfair. To get at me through my pride!"

"Yes, my weed, and there's such a lot of it. I have to go, you know. Don't make it harder for me."

"I wish I could do something to help," said Moon after a moment.

"I expect you to do all your work around here, and all of mine besides. Isn't that enough?" Alder Owl smoothed the flap down over the pack and snugged the drawstring tight.

"You know it's not. Couldn't I go with you?"

Alder Owl pulled a stool from under the table with her foot and sat on it, her hands over her knees. "When I travel in my spirit," she said, "to ask a favor of Grandmother, you can't go with me."

"Of course not. Then who'd play the drum, to guide you back?"

Alder Owl beamed. "Clever weed. Open that cupboard over the mantel-shelf and bring me what you find there."

What Moon found was a drum. It was nothing like the broad, flat, cowhide journey-drum, whose speech echoed in her bones and was like a breathing heartbeat under her fingers, whose voice could be heard in the land where there was no voice. This drum was an upright cylinder no bigger than a quart jar. Its body was made of some white wood, and the skins of its two heads were fine-grained and tufted with soft white hair around the lashings. There was a loop of hide to hold it with, and a drumstick with a leather beater tucked through that.

Moon shook her head. "This wouldn't be loud enough to bring you home from the pump, let alone from—where are you going?"

166

"Wherever I have to. Bring it to me."

Moon brought her the drum, and Alder Owl held it up by the loop of hide and struck it, once. The sound it made was a sharp, ringing tok, like a woodpecker's blow.

Alder Owl said, "The wood is from an ash tree planted at the hour of my birth. The skins are from a ewe born on the same day. I raised the ewe and watered the tree, and on my sixteenth birthday, I asked them for their lives, and they gave them gladly. No matter how far I go, the drum will reach me. When I cannot hear it, it will cease to sound.

"Tomorrow at dawn, I'll leave," Alder Owl continued. "Tomorrow at sunset, as the last rind of the sun burns out behind the line of the Wantnot Hills, and at every sunset after, beat the drum once, as I just did. "

Moon was a little shaken by the solemnity of it all. But she gathered her wits at last and repeated, "At sunset each day. Once. I'll remember."

"Hmph. Well." Alder Owl lifted her shoulders, as if solemnity was a shawl she could shrug away. "Tomorrow always comes early. Time to put the fire to bed."

"I'll get the garden things," Moon said. She tossed her cloak on and went out the stillroom door into the night.

Her namesake was up, and waxing. Alder Owl would have good light, if she needed to travel by night. But it would be cold traveling; frost dusted the leaves and vines and flagstone paths like talcum. Moon shivered and sighed. "What's the point of having an able-bodied young apprentice, if you're not going to put all that ableness to use?" she muttered to the shifting air. The cold carried all her S's off into the dark.

She pinched a bloom from the yellow chrysanthemum, and a stalk of merry-man's wort from its sheltered bed. When she came back into the house she found that Alder Owl had already fed the fire and settled the logs with the poker, and fetched a bowl of water. Moon dropped the flowers into it.

"Comforter, guard against the winter dark," Alder Owl said to the fire, as always, as if she were addressing an old friend. She stirred the water with her fingers as she spoke. "Helpmeet, nourisher of flesh and heart, bide and watch, and let no errant spark leap up until the sun should take thy part."

Firelight brushed across the seamed landscape of Alder Owl's face, flashed yellow in her sharp, dark eyes, turned the white in her hair to ivory. Tomorrow night, Moon thought, she won't be here. Just me. She could believe it only with the front of her mind, where all untested things were kept. The rest of her, mind and lungs and soles of feet, denied it.

Alder Owl flicked the water from her hand onto the hearth, and the line of drops steamed. Then she handed the bowl to Moon, and Moon fed the flowers to the fire.

After a respectful silence, Moon said, "It's water." It was the continuation of an old argument. "And the logs were trees that grew out of the earth and fed on water, and the fire itself feeds on those and air. That's all four elements. You can't separate them."

"It's the hour for fire, and it's fire that we honor. At the appropriate hours we honor the other three, and if you say things like that in public, no educated person in the village will speak to you." Alder Owl took the bowl out of Moon's hands and gathered her fingers in a strong, wet clasp. "My weed, my stalk of yarrow. You're not a child anymore. When I leave, you'll be a grown woman, in others' eyes if not your own. What people hear from a child's mouth as foolishness becomes something else on the lips of a woman grown: sacrilege, or spite, or madness. Work the work as you see fit, but keep your mouth closed around your notions, and keep fire out of water and earth out of air."

"But—"

"Empty the bowl now, and get on to bed."

Moon went into the garden again and flung the water out of the bowl—southward, because it was consecrated to fire. Then she stood a little while in the cold, with a terrible hard feeling in her chest that was beyond sadness, beyond tears. She drew in great breaths to freeze it, and exhaled hard to force the fragments out. But it was immune to cold or wind.

"I'd like to be a woman," she whispered. "But I'd rather be a child with you here, than a woman with you gone." The sound of the words, the knowledge that they were true, did what the cold couldn't. The terrible feeling cracked, melted, and poured out of her in painful tears. Slowly the comforting order around her, the beds and borders Alder Owl had made, stopped the flow of them, and the kind cold air wiped them off her face.

At dawn, when the light of sunrise lay tangled in the treetops, Alder Owl settled her pack on her back and went out by the front door. Moon went with her as far as the gate at the bottom of the yard. In the uncertain misty land of dawn, Alder Owl was a solid, certain figure, cloaked in shabby purple wool, her silver and black hair tucked under a drunken-brimmed green hat.

"I don't think you should wear the hat," Moon said, past the tightness in her throat. "You look like an eggplant."

"I like it. I'm an old woman. I can wear what I please."

She was going. What did one say, except "Goodbye," which wasn't at all what Moon wanted? "When will you come back?"

"When I've found him. Or when I know he can't be found."

"You always tell me not to try to prove negatives."

"There are ways," Alder Owl replied, with a sideways look, "to prove this one."

Moon Very Thin shivered in the weak sun. Alder Owl squinted up at her, pinched her chin lightly. Then she closed the gate behind her and walked down the hill. Moon watched her—green and purple, silly and strong—until the trees hid her from sight.

She cured the squash before she put them in the cellar. She honored the elements, each at its own hour. She made cheese and wine, and put up the last of the herbs, and beat the rugs, and waxed all the floors against the coming winter muck. She mended the thatch and the fence, pruned the apple trees and turned the garden beds, taking comfort from maintaining the order that Alder Owl had established.

Moon took over other established things, too. By the time the first snow fell, her neighbors had begun to bring their aches and pains to her, to fetch her when a child was feverish, to call her in to set a dog's broken leg or stitch up a horse's gashed flank. They asked about the best day to sign a contract, and whether there was a charm to keep nightshade out of the hay field. In return, they brought her mistletoe and willow bark, a sack of rye flour, a tub of butter.

She didn't mind the work. She'd been brought up for it; it seemed as natural as getting out of bed in the morning. But she found she minded the payment. When the nearest neighbor's boy, Fell, trotted up to the gate on his donkey with the flour sack riding pillion, and thanked her, and gave it to her, she almost thrust it back at him. Alder Owl had given her the skill, and had left her there to serve them. The payment should be Alder Owl's. But there was no saying which would appear first, Alder Owl or the bottom of the sack.

"You look funny," Fell said.

"You look worse," Moon replied, because she'd taught him to climb trees and to fish, and had thus earned the privilege. "Do you know those things made out of wood or bone, with a row of little spines set close together? They call them 'combs'."

"Hah, hah." He pointed to the flour. "I hope you make it all into cakes and get fat." He grinned and loped back down the path to the donkey. They kicked up snow as they climbed the hill, and he waved at the crest.

She felt better. Alder Owl would never have had that conversation.

Every evening at sunset, Moon took the little drum out of the cupboard over the mantel. She looked at it, and touched it, and thought of her teacher. She tried to imagine her well and warm and safe, with a hot meal before her and pleasant company near. At last, when the rim of the sun blinked out behind the far line of hills, she swung the beater against the fine skin head, and the drum sounded its woodpecker knock.

Each time Moon wondered: Could Alder Owl really hear it? And if she could, what if Moon were to beat it again? If she beat it three times, would Alder Owl think something was wrong, and return home?

Nothing was wrong. Moon put the drum away until the next sunset.

The Long Night came, and she visited all her neighbors, as they visited her. She brought them fir boughs tied with bittersweet, and honey candy, and said the blessing-charm on their doorsteps. She watched the landscape thaw and freeze, thaw and freeze. Candle-day came, and she went to the village, which was sopping and giddy with a spell of warmer weather, to watch the lighting of the new year's lamps from the flame of the old. It could be, said the villagers, that no one would ever find the prince. It could be that the King of Stones had taken him beneath the earth, and that he would lie there without breath, in silence, forever. And had she had any word of Alder Owl, and hadn't it been a long time that she'd been gone?

Yes, said Moon, it had been a long time.

The garden began to stir, almost invisibly, like a cat thinking of breakfast in its sleep. The sound of water running was everywhere, though the snow seemed undisturbed and the ice as thick as ever. Suddenly, as if nature had thrown wide a gate, it was spring, and Moon was run off her legs with work. Lambing set her to wearing muddy paths in the hills between the cottage and the farmsteads all around. The mares began to foal, too. She thanked wisdom that women and men, at least, had no season.

She had been with Tansy Broadwater's bay thoroughbred since late morning. The foal had been turned in the womb and tied in his cord, and Moon was nearly paralyzed thinking of the worth of the two of them, and their lives in her hands. She was bloody to the elbows and hoarse with chanting, but at last she and Tansy regarded each other triumphantly across the withers of a nursing colt.

"Come up to the house for a pot of hot tea," Tansy said as Moon rinsed soap off her hands and arms. "You won't want to start out through the woods now until moonrise, anyway."

Moon lifted her eyes, shocked, to the open barn door. The sun wore the Wantnot Hills like a girdle.

"I have to go," she said. "I'm sorry. I'll be all right." She headed for the trail at a run.

Stones rolled under her boots, and half-thawed ice lay slick as butter in the shadows. It was nearly night already, under the trees. She plunged down the hill and up the next one, and down again, slithering, on all fours sometimes. She could feel her bones inside her brittle as fire-blasted wood, her ankles fragile and waiting for a wrench. She was afraid to look at the sun again.

The gate—the gate at the bottom of the path was under her hands. She sobbed in relief. So close... She raced up through the garden, the cold air like fire in her lungs. She struggled frantically with the front door, until she remembered it was barred inside, that she'd left through the stillroom. She banged through the stillroom door and made the contents of the shelves ring and rattle. To the hearth, and wrench the cupboard door open . . .

The drum was in her hands, and through the window the sun's rind showed, thin as thread, on the hills. She was in time. As the horizon closed like a snake's eyelid over the disk of the sun, Moon struck the drum.

There was no sound at all.

Moon stared at the drum, the beater, her two hands. She had missed, she must have. She brought the beater to the head again. She might as well have hit wool against wool. There was no woodpecker knock, no sharp clear call. She had felt skin and beater meet, she had seen them. What had she done wrong?

Slowly Alder Owl's words came back to her. *When I cannot hear it, it will cease to sound.* Moon had always thought the drum would be hard to hear. But never silent. *Tell me if you can't hear this,* she thought wildly. Something else they'd said as she left, about proving negatives—that there were ways to prove the prince couldn't be found.

If he were dead, for example. If he were only bones under the earth.

And Alder Owl, beyond the drum's reach, might have followed him even to that, under the dominion of the King of Stones.

She thought about pounding the drum; she could see herself doing it in her mind, hammering at it until it sounded or broke. She imagined weeping, too; she could cry and scream and break things, and collapse at last exhausted and miserable.

What she did was to sit where she was at the table, the drum on her knees, watching the dark seep in and fill the room around her. Sorrow and despair rose and fell inside her in a slow rhythm, like the shortening and lengthening of days. When her misery peaked, she would almost weep, almost shriek, almost throw the drum from her. Then it would begin to wane, and she would think, *No, I can bear it,* until it turned to waxing once again.

She would do nothing, she resolved, until she could think of something useful to do. She would wait until the spiders spun her white with cobwebs, if she had to. But she would do something better than crying, better than breaking things.

The hide lashing of Alder Owl's drum bit into her clenched fingers. In the weak light of the sinking fire, the wood and leather were only a pale mass in her lap. How could Alder Owl's magic have dwindled away to this—a drum with no voice? What voice could reach her now?

And Moon answered herself, wonderingly: *Grandmother.*

She couldn't. She had never gone to speak with Grandmother herself. And how could she travel there, with no one to beat the drum for her when she was gone? She might be lost forever, wandering through the tangled roots of Grandmother's trees.

Yet she stood and walked, stiff-jointed, to the stillroom. She gathered up charcoal and dried myrtle and cedar. She poured apple wine into a wooden cup, and dropped in a seed from a sky's-trumpet vine. It was a familiar set of motions. She had done them for Alder Owl. She took down the black-fleeced sheepskin from the wall by the front door, laid it out on the floor, and set the wine and incense by it, wine to the east, charcoal to the south. Another trip, to fetch salt and the little bone-handled knife—earth to the north, the little conical pile of salt, and the knife west, for air. (Salt came from the sea, too, said her rebellious mind, and the knife's metal was mined from earth and tempered with fire and water. But she was afraid of heresy now, afraid to doubt the knowledge she must trust with the weight of lives. She did as she'd been taught.)

At last she took the big drum, the journey-drum, out of its wicker case and set it on the sheepskin. The drum would help her partway on her travels. But when she crossed the border, she would have to leave body, fingers, drum all at the crossing, and the drum would fall silent. She needed so little: just a tap, tap, tap. Well, her heart would have to do.

Moon dropped cross-legged on the sheepskin. Right-handed she took up the knife and drew lightly on the floor around herself as if she were a compass. She passed the knife to her left hand behind her back, smoothly, and the knife point never left the slate. That had been hard once, learning to take the knife as Alder Owl passed it to her. She drew the circle again with a pinch of salt dropped from each hand, and with cedar and myrtle smoking and snapping on their charcoal bed. Finally she drew the circle with wine shaken from her fingers, and drank off the rest. Then she took up the drum.

She tried to hear the rhythm of her breathing, of her heart, the rhythm that was always inside her. Only when she felt sure of it did she begin to let her fingers move with it, to tap the drum. It shuddered under her fingers, lowing out notes. When her hands were certain on the drum head, she closed her eyes.

A tree. That was the beginning of the journey, Moon knew; she was to begin at the end of a branch of the great tree. But what kind of tree? Was it night, or day? Should she imagine herself as a bird or a bug, or as herself? And how could she think of all that and play the drum, too?

Her neck was stiff, and one of her feet was going to sleep. You think too much, she scolded herself. Alder Owl had never had such trouble. Alder Owl had also never suggested that there was such a thing as too much thinking. More of it, she'd said, would fix most of the world's problems.

Well, she'd feel free to think, then. She settled into the drumbeat, imagined it wrapped around her like a featherbed.

—A tree too big to ever see all at once, one of a forest of trees like it. A tree with a crown of leaves as wide as a clear night sky on a hilltop. Night time, then. It was an oak, she decided, but green out of season. She envisioned the silver-green leathery leaves around her, and the rough black bark starry with dew in the moonlight. The light came from the end of the branch. Cradled in leaves there was a pared white-silver crescent, a new moon cut free from the shadow of the old. It gave her light to travel by.

The rough highroad of bark grew broader as she neared the trunk. She imagined birds stirring in their sleep and the quick, querulous chirk of a squirrel woken in its nest. The wind breathed in and out across the vault of leaves and made them twinkle. Moon heard her steps on the wood, even and measured: the voice of the drum.

Down the trunk, down toward the tangle of roots, the knotted mirror-image of the branches above. The trunks of other trees were all around her, and the twining branches shuttered the moonlight. It was harder going, shouldering against the life of the tree that always moved upward. Her heartbeat was a thin, regular bumping in her ears.

It was too dark to tell which way was down, too dark to tell anything. Moon didn't know if she'd reached the roots or not. She wanted to cry out, to call for Grandmother, but she'd left her body behind, and her tongue in it.

A little light appeared before her, and grew slowly. There were patterns in it, colors, shapes—she could make out the gate at the bottom of the garden, and the path that led into the woods. On the path—was it the familiar one? It was bordered now with sage—she saw a figure made of the flutter of old black cloth and untidy streamers of white hair, walking away from her. A stranger, Moon thought; she tried to catch up, but didn't seem to move at all. At the first fringes of the trees the figure turned, lifted one hand, and beckoned. Then it disappeared under the roof of the woods.

Moon's spirit, like a startled bird, burst into motion, upward. Her eyes opened on the center room of the cottage. She was standing unsteadily on the sheepskin, the journey drum at her feet. Her heart clattered under her ribs like a stick dragged across the pickets of a fence, and she felt sore and prickly and feverish. She took a step backward, overbalanced, and sat down.

"Well," she said, and the sound of her voice made her jump. She licked her dry lips and added, "That's not at all how it's supposed to be done."

Trembling, she picked up the tools and put them away, washed out the wooden bowl. She'd gathered up the sheepskin and had turned to hang it on the wall when her voice surprised her again. "But it worked," she said. She stood very still, hugging the fleece against her. "It worked, didn't it?" She'd traveled and asked, and been answered, and if neither had been in form as she understood them, still they were question and answer, and all that she needed. Moon hurried to put the sheepskin away. There were suddenly a lot of things to do.

The next morning she filled her pack with food and clothing, tinderbox and medicines, and put the little ash drum, Alder Owl's drum, on top of it all. She put on her stoutest boots and her felted wool cloak. She smothered the fire on the hearth, fastened all the shutters, and left a note for Tansy Broadwater, asking her to look after the house.

At last she shouldered her pack and tramped down the path, through the gate, down the hill, and into the woods.

Moon had traveled before, with Alder Owl. She knew how to find her way, and how to build a good fire and cook over it; she'd slept in the open and stayed at inns and farmhouses. Those things were the same alone. She had no reason to feel strange, but she did. She felt like an imposter, and expected every chance-met traveler to ask if she was old enough to be on the road by herself.

She thought she'd been lonely at the cottage; she thought she'd learned the size and shape of loneliness. Now she knew she'd only explored a corner of it. Walking gave her room to think, and sights to see: fern shoots rolling up out of the mushy soil, yellow cups of wild crocuses caught by the sun, the courting of ravens. But it was no use pointing and crying, "Look!", because the only eyes there had already seen. Her isolation made everything seem not quite real. It was harder each night to light a fire, and she had steadily less interest in food. But

175

each night at sunset, she beat Alder Owl's drum. Each night it was silent, and she sat in the aftermath of that silence, bereft all over again.

She walked for six days through villages and forest and farmland. The weather had stayed dry and clear and unspringlike for five of them, but on the sixth she tramped through a rising chill wind under a lowering sky. The road was wider now, and smooth, and she had more company on it: Carts and wagons, riders, other walkers went to and fro past her. At noon she stopped at an inn, larger and busier than any she'd yet seen.

The boy who set tea down in front of her had a mop of blond hair over a cheerful, harried face. "The cold pie's good," he said before she could ask. "It's rabbit and mushroom. Otherwise, there's squash soup. But don't ask for ham—I think it's off a boar that wasn't cut right. It's awful."

Moon didn't know whether to laugh or gape. "The pie, then, please. I don't mean to sound like a fool, but where am I?"

"Little Hark," he replied. "But don't let that raise your hopes. Great Hark is a week away to the west, on foot. You bound for it?"

"I don't know. I suppose I am. I'm looking for someone."

"In Great Hark? Huh. Well, you can find an ant in an anthill, too, if you're not particular which one."

"It's that big?" Moon asked.

He nodded sympathetically. "Unless you're looking for the king or the queen."

"No. A woman—oldish, with hair a little more white than black, and a round pink face. Shorter than I am. Plump." It was hard to describe Alder Owl; she was too familiar. "She would have had an eggplant-colored cloak. She's a witch."

The boy's face changed slowly. "Is she the bossy-for-your-own-good sort? With a wicker pack? Treats spots on your face with witch hazel and horseradish?"

"That sounds like her... What else do you use for spots?"

"I don't know, but the horseradish works pretty well. She stopped here, if that's her. It was months ago, though."

"Yes," said Moon. "It was."

"She was headed for Great Hark, so you're on the right road. Good luck on it."

When he came back with the rabbit pie, he said, "You'll come to Burnton High Plain next—that's a two-day walk. After that you'll be done with the grasslands pretty quick. Then you'll be lucky if you see the sun 'til you're within holler of Great Hark."

Moon swallowed a little too much pie at once. "I will? Why?"

"Well, you'll be in the Seawood, won't you?"

"Will I?"

"You don't know much geography," he said sadly.

"I know I've never heard that the Seawood was so thick the sun wouldn't shine in it. Have you ever been there?"

"No. But everyone who has says it's true. And being here, I get to hear what travelers tell."

Moon opened her mouth to say that she'd heard more nonsense told in the common rooms of inns than the wide world had space for, when a woman's voice trumpeted from the kitchen. "Starling! Do you work here, or are you taking a room tonight?"

The blond boy grinned. "Good luck, anyway," he said to Moon, and loped back to the kitchen.

Moon ate her lunch and paid for it with a coin stamped with the prince's face. She scowled at it when she set it on the table. It's all your fault, she told it. Then she hoisted her pack and headed for the door.

"It's started to drip," the blond boy called after her. "It'll be pouring rain on you in an hour."

"I'll get wet, then," she said. "But thanks anyway."

The trail was cold, but at least she was on it. The news drove her forward.

The boy was right about the weather. The rain was carried on gusts from every direction, that found their way under her cloak and inside her hood and in every seam of her boots. By the time she'd doggedly climbed the ridge above Little Hark, she was wet and cold all through, and dreaming of tight roofs, large fires, and clean, dry nightgowns. The view from the top of the trail scattered her visions.

She'd expected another valley. This was not a bowl, but a plate, full of long, sand-colored undulating grass, and she stood at the rim of it. Moon squinted through the rain ahead and to either side, looking for a far edge, but the grass went on out of sight, unbroken by anything but the small rises and falls of the land. She suspected that clear weather wouldn't have shown her the end of it, either.

177

That evening she made camp in the midst of the ocean of grass, since there wasn't anyplace else. There was no firewood. She'd thought of that before she walked down into the plain, but all the wood she could have gathered to take with her was soaked. So she propped up a lean-to of oiled canvas against the worst of the rain, gathered a pile of the shining-wet grass, and set to work. She kept an eye on the sun, as well; at the right moment she took up Alder Owl's drum and played it, huddling under the canvas to keep it from the wet. It had nothing to say.

In half an hour she had a fat braided wreath of straw. She laid it in a circle of bare ground she'd cleared, and got from her pack her tinderbox and three apples, wrinkled and sweet with winter storage. They were the last food she had from home.

"All is taken from thee," Moon said, setting the apples inside the straw wreath and laying more wet grass over them in a little cone. "I have taken, food and footing, breath and warming, balm for thirsting. This I will exchange thee, with my love and every honor, if thou'lt give again thy succor." With that, she struck a spark in the cone of grass.

For a moment, she thought the exchange was not accepted. She'd asked all the elements, instead of only fire, and fire had taken offense. Then a little blue flame licked along a stalk, and a second. In a few minutes she was nursing a tiny, comforting blaze, contained by the wreath of straw and fueled all night with Alder Owl's apples.

She sat for a long time, hunched under the oiled canvas lean-to, wrapped in her cloak with the little fire between her feet. She was going to Great Hark, because she thought that Alder Owl would have done so. But she might not have. Alder Owl might have gone south from here, into Cystegond. Or north, into the cold upthrust fangs of the Bones of Earth. She could have gone anywhere, and Moon wouldn't know. She'd asked—but she hadn't insisted she be told or taken along, hadn't tried to follow. She'd only said goodbye. Now she would never find the way.

"What am I doing here?" Moon whispered. There was no answer except the constant rushing sound of the grass in the wind, saying hush, hush, hush. Eventually she was warm enough to sleep.

The next morning the sun came back, watery and tentative. By its light she got her first real look at the great ocean of golden-brown she

178

was shouldering through. Behind her she saw the ridge beyond which Little Hark lay. Ahead of her there was nothing but grass.

It was a long day, with only that to look at. So she made herself look for more. She saw the new green shoots of grass at the feet of the old stalks, their leaves still rolled tight around one another like the embrace of lovers. A thistle spread its rosette of fierce leaves to claim the soil, but hadn't yet grown tall. And she saw the prints of horses' hooves, and dung, and once a wide, beaten-down swath across her path like the bed of a creek cut in grass, the earth muddy and chopped with hoofprints. As she walked, the sun climbed the sky and steamed the rain out of her cloak.

By evening she reached the town of Burnton High Plain. Yes, the landlord at the hostelry told her, another day's walk would bring her under the branches of the Seawood. Then she should go carefully, because it was full of robbers and ghosts and wild animals.

"Well," Moon said, "Robbers wouldn't take the trouble to stop me, and I don't think I've any quarrel with the dead. So I'll concentrate on the wild animals. But thank you very much for the warning."

"Not a good place, the Seawood," the landlord added.

Moon thought that people who lived in the middle of an eternity of grass probably would be afraid of a forest. But she only said, "I'm searching for someone who might have passed this way months ago. Her name is Alder Owl, and she was going to look for the prince."

After Moon described her, the landlord pursed his lips. "That's familiar. I think she might have come through, heading west. But as you say, it was months, and I don't think I've seen her since."

I've never heard so much discouraging encouragement, Moon thought drearily, and turned to her dinner.

The next afternoon she reached the Seawood. Everything changed: the smells, the color of the light, the temperature of the air. In spite of the landlord's warning, Moon couldn't quite deny the lift of her heart, the feeling of glad relief. The secretive scent of pine loam rose around her as she walked, and the dark boughs were full of the commotion of birds. She heard water nearby; she followed the sound to a running beck and the spring that fed it. The water was cold and crisply acidic from the pines; she filled her bottle at it and washed her face.

She stood a moment longer by the water. Then she hunched the pack off her back and dug inside it until she found the little linen bag that held her valuables. She shook out a silver shawl pin in the shape of a leaping frog. She'd worn it on festival days, with her green scarf. It was a present from Alder Owl—but then, everything was. She dropped it into the spring.

Was that right? Yes, the frog was water's beast, never mind that it breathed air half the time. And silver was water's metal, even though it was mined from the earth and shaped with fire, and turned black as quickly in water as in air. How could magic be based on understanding the true nature of things if it ignored so much?

A bubble rose to the surface and broke loudly, and Moon laughed. "You're welcome, and same to you," she said, and set off again.

The Seawood gave her a century's worth of fallen needles, flat and dry, to bed down on, and plenty of dry wood for her fire. It was cold under its roof of boughs, but there were remedies for cold. She kept her fire well built up, for that, and against any meat-eaters too weak from winter to seek out the horses of Burnton High Plain.

Another day's travel, and another. If she were to climb one of the tallest pines to its top, would the Seawood look like the plain of grass: undulating, almost endless? On the third day, when the few blades of sun that reached the forest floor were slanting and long, a wind rose. Moon listened to the old trunks above her creaking, the boughs swishing like brooms in angry hands, and decided to make camp.

In the Seawood the last edge of sunset was never visible. By then, beneath the trees, it was dark. So Moon built her fire and set water to boil before she took Alder Owl's drum from her pack.

The trees roared above, but at their feet Moon felt only a furious breeze. She hunched her cloak around her and struck the drum.

It made no noise; but from above she heard a clap and thunder of sound, and felt a rush of air across her face. She leaped backward. The drum slid from her hands.

A pale shape sat on a low branch beyond her fire. The light fell irregularly on its huge yellow eyes, the high tufts that crowned its head, its pale breast. An owl.

"Oo," it said, louder than the hammering wind. "Oo-whoot."

Watching it all the while, Moon leaned forward, reaching for the drum.

The owl bated thunderously and stretched its beak wide. "Oo-wheed," it cried at her. "Yarrooh. Yarrooh."

180

Moon's blood fell cold from under her face. The owl stooped off its branch quick and straight as a dropped stone. Its talons closed on the lashings of the drum. The great wings beat once, twice, and the bird was gone into the rushing dark.

Moon fell to her knees, gasping for breath. The voice of the owl was still caught in her ears, echoing, echoing another voice. Weed. Yarrow. Yarrow.

Tears poured burning down her face. "Oh, my weed, my stalk of yarrow," she repeated, whispering. "Come back!" she screamed into the night. She got no answer but the wind. She pressed her empty hands to her face and cried herself to sleep.

With morning, the Seawood crowded around her as it had before, full of singing birds and softness, traitorous and unashamed. In one thing, at least, its spirit marched with hers. The light under the trees was gray, and she heard the patter of rain in the branches above. Moon stirred the cold ashes of her fire and waited for her heart to thaw. She would go on to Great Hark, and beyond if she had to. There might yet be some hope. And if there wasn't, there might at least be a reckoning.

All day the path led downward, and she walked until her thighs burned and her stomach gnawed itself from hunger. The rain came down harder, showering her ignominiously when the wind shook the branches. She meant to leave the Seawood before she slept again, if it meant walking all night. But the trees began to thin around her late in the day, and shortly after she saw a bare rise ahead of her. She mounted it and looked down.

The valley was full of low mist, eddying slowly in the rain. Rising out of it was the largest town Moon had ever seen. It was walled in stone and gated with oak and iron, and roofed in prosperous slate and tile. Pennons flew from every wall tower, their colors darkened with rain and stolen away by the gray light. At the heart of the town was a tall, white, red-roofed building, cornered with round towers like the wall.

The boy was right about this, too. She could never find news of one person in such a place, unless that person was the king or the queen. Moon drooped under a fresh lashing of rain.

But why not? Alder Owl had set off to find the prince. Why wouldn't she have gone to the palace and stated her business, and searched on from there? And why shouldn't Moon do the same?

She flapped a sheet of water off her cloak and plunged down the trail. She had another hour's walk before she would reach the gates, and she wanted to be inside by sundown.

The wall loomed over her at last, oppressively high, dark and shining with rain. She found the huge double gates open, and the press of wagons and horses and pedestrians in and out of them daunting. No one seemed to take any notice when she joined the stream and passed through, and though she looked and looked, she couldn't see anyone who appeared to be any more official than anyone else. Everyone, in fact, looked busy and important. So this is city life, Moon thought, and stepped out of the flow of traffic for a better look around.

Without her bird's eye view, she knew she wouldn't find the palace except by chance. So she asked directions of a woman and a man unloading a cart full of baled hay.

They looked at her and blinked, as if they were too weary to think; they were at least as wet as Moon was, and seemed to have less hope of finding what they were looking for. Their expressions of surprise were so similar that Moon wondered if they were blood relations, and indeed, their eyes were much alike, green-gray as sage. The man wore a dusty brown jacket worn through at one elbow; the woman had a long, tattered black shawl pulled up over her white hair.

"Round the wall that way," said the man at last, "until you come to a broad street all laid with brick. Follow that uphill until you see it."

"Thank you." Moon eyed the hay cart, which was nearly full. Work was ointment for the heart. Alder Owl had said so. "Would you like some help? I could get in the cart and throw bales down."

"Oh, no," said the woman. "It's all right."

Moon shook her head. "You sound like my neighbors. With them, it would be fifteen minutes before we argued each other to a standstill. I'm going to start throwing hay instead." At that, she scrambled into the cart and hoisted a bale. When she turned to pass it to the man and woman, she found them looking at each other, before the man came to take the hay from her.

It was hot, wet, prickly work, but it didn't take long. When the cart was empty, they exchanged thanks and Moon set off again for the palace. On the way, she watched the sun's eye close behind the line of the hills.

The brick-paved street ran in long curves like an old riverbed. She couldn't see the palace until she'd tramped up the last turning and found the high white walls before her, and another gate. This one was carved and painted with a flock of rising birds, and closed.

Two men stood at the gate, one on each side. They were young and tall and broad-shouldered, and Moon recognized them as being of a type that made village girls stammer. They stood very straight, and wore green capes and coats with what Moon thought was an excessive quantity of gold trim. She stepped up to the nearest.

"Pardon me," she said, "I'd like to speak to the king and queen."

The guard blinked even more thoroughly than the couple with the hay cart had. With good reason, Moon realized; now she was not only travel-stained and sodden, but dusted with hay as well. She sighed, which seemed to increase the young man's confusion.

"I'll start nearer the beginning," she told him. "I came looking for my teacher, who set off at the end of last autumn to look for the prince. Do you remember a witch, named Alder Owl, from a village two weeks east of here? I think she might have come to the palace to see the king and queen about it."

The guard smiled. Moon thought she wouldn't feel too scornful of a girl who stammered in his presence. "I suppose I could have a message taken to Their Majesties," he said at last. "Someone in the palace may have met your teacher. Hi, Rush!" he called to the guard on the other side of the gate. "This woman is looking for her teacher, a witch who set out to find the prince. Who would she ask, then?"

Rush sauntered over, his cape swinging. He raised his eyebrows at Moon. "Every witch in Hark End has gone hunting the prince at one time or another. How would anyone remember one out of the lot?"

Moon drew herself up very straight, and found she was nearly as tall as he was. She raised only one eyebrow, which she'd always found effective with Fell. "I'm sorry your memory isn't all you might like it to be. Would it help if I pointed out that this witch remains unaccounted for?"

"There aren't any of those. They all came back, cap in hand and dung on their shoes, saying, 'Beg pardon, Lord,' and 'Perishing sorry, Lady.' You could buy and sell the gaggle of them with the brass on my scabbard."

"You," Moon told him sternly, "are of very little use."

183

"More use than anyone who's sought him so far. If they'd only set my unit to it..."

She looked into his hard young face. "You loved him, didn't you?"

His mouth pinched closed, and the hurt in his eyes made him seem for a moment as young as Fell. It held a glass up to her own pain. "Everyone did. He was—is the land's own heart."

"My teacher is like that to me. Please, may I speak with someone?"

The polite guard was looking from one to the other of them, alarmed. Rush turned to him and frowned. "Take her to—merry heavens, I don't know. Try the steward. He fancies he knows everything."

And so the Gate of Birds opened to Moon Very Thin. She followed the polite guard across a paved courtyard held in the wide, high arms of the palace, colonnaded all around and carved with the likenesses of animals and flowers. On every column a torch burned in its iron bracket, hissing in the rain, and lit the courtyard like a stage. It was very beautiful, if a little grim.

The guard waved her through a small iron-clad door into a neat parlor. A fire was lit in the brick hearth and showed her the rugs and hangings, the panelled walls blackened with age. The guard tugged an embroidered pull near the door and turned to her.

"I should get back to the gate. Just tell the steward, Lord Leyan, what you know about your teacher. If there's help for you here, he'll see that you get it."

When he'd gone, she gathered her damp cloak about her and wondered if she ought to sit. Then she heard footsteps, and a door she hadn't noticed opened in the panelling.

A very tall, straight-backed man came through it. His hair was white and thick and brushed his shoulders, where it met a velvet coat faced in crewelled satin. He didn't seem to find the sight of her startling, which Moon took as a good sign.

"How may I help you?" he asked.

"Lord Leyan?"

He nodded.

"My name is Moon Very Thin. I've come from the east in search of my teacher, the witch Alder Owl, who set out last autumn to find the prince. I think now...I won't find her. But I have to try." To her horror, she felt tears rising in her eyes.

184

Lord Leyan crossed the room in a long stride and grasped her hands. "My dear, don't cry. I remember your teacher. She was an alarming woman, but that gave us all hope. She has not returned to you, either, then?"

Moon swallowed and shook her head.

"You've traveled a long way. You shall have a bath and a meal and a change of clothes, and I will see if anyone can tell you more about your teacher."

Before Moon was quite certain how it had been managed, she was standing in a handsome dark room with a velvet-hung bed and a fire bigger than the one in the parlor, and a woman with a red face and fly-away hair was pouring cans of water into a bathtub shaped and painted like a swan.

"That's the silliest thing I've ever seen," said Moon in wonder.

The red-faced woman grinned suddenly. "You know, it is. And it may be the lords and ladies think so, too, and are afraid to say."

"One of them must have paid for it once."

"That's so. Well, no one's born with taste. Have your bath, and I'll bring you a change of clothes in a little."

"You needn't do that. I have clean ones in my pack."

"Yes, but have they got lace on them, and a 'broidery flower for every seam? If not, you'd best let me bring these, for word is you eat with the King and Queen."

"I do?" Moon blurted, horrified. "Why?"

"Lord Leyan went to them, and they said send you in. Don't pop your eyes at me, there's no help for it."

Moon scrubbed until she was pink all over, and smelling of violet soap. She washed her hair three times, and trimmed her short nails, and looked in despair at her reflection in the mirror. She didn't think she'd put anyone off dinner, but there was no question that the only thing that stood there was Moon Very Thin, tall and brown and forthright.

"Here, now," said the red-faced woman at the door. "I thought this would look nice, and you wouldn't even quite feel a fool in it. What do you say?"

Draped over her arms she had a plain, high-necked dress of amber linen, and an overgown of russet velvet. The hem and deep collar were embroidered in gold with the platter-heads of yarrow flowers. Moon stared at that, and looked quickly up at the red-faced woman. There was nothing out of the way in her expression.

"It's—it's fine. It's rather much, but..."

"But it's the least much that's still enough for dining in the hall. Let's get you dressed."

The woman helped her into it, pulling swaths of lavender-scented fabric over her head. Then she combed out Moon's hair, braided it, and fastened it with a gold pin.

"Good," the red-faced woman said. "You look like you, but dressed up, which is as it should be. I'll show you to the hall."

Moon took a last look at her reflection. She didn't think she looked at all like herself. Dazed, she followed her guide out of the room.

She knew when they'd almost reached their destination. A fragrance rolled out of the hall that reminded Moon she'd missed three meals. At the door, the red-faced woman stopped her.

"You'll do, I think. Still—tell no lies, though you may be told them. Look anyone in the eye, though they might want it otherwise. And take everything offered you with your right hand. It can't hurt." With that the red-faced woman turned and disappeared down the maze of the corridor.

Moon straightened her shoulders and, her stomach pinched with hunger and nerves, stepped into the hall.

She gaped. She couldn't help it, though she'd promised herself she wouldn't. The hall was as high as two rooms, and long and broad as a field of wheat. It had two yawning fireplaces big enough to tether an ox in. Banners hung from every beam, sewn over with beasts and birds and things she couldn't name. There weren't enough candles in all Hark End to light it top to bottom, nor enough wood in the Seawood to heat it, so like the great courtyard it was beautiful and grim.

The tables were set in a U, the high table between the two arms. To her dazzled eye, it seemed every place was taken. It was bad enough to dine with the king and queen. Why hadn't she realized that it would be the court, as well?

At the high table, the king rose smiling. "Our guest!" he called. "Come, there's a place for you beside my lady and me."

Moon felt her face burning as she walked to the high table. The court watched her go; but there were no whispers, no hands raised to shield moving lips. She was grateful, but it was odd.

Her chair was indeed set beside those of the king and queen. The king was white haired and broad-shouldered, with an open, smiling face and big hands. The queen's hair was white and gold, and her eyes were wide and gray as storms. She smiled, too, but as if the gesture were a sorrow she was loath to share.

"Lord Leyan told us your story," said the queen. "I remember your teacher. Had you been with her long?"

"All my life," Moon replied. Dishes came to roost before her, so she could serve herself: roast meat, salads, breads, compotes, vegetables, sauces, wedges of cheese. She could limit herself to a bite of everything, and still leave the hall achingly full. She kept her left hand clamped between her knees for fear of forgetting and taking something with it. Every dish was good, but not quite as good as she'd thought it looked.

"Then you are a witch as well?" the king asked.

"I don't know. I've been taught by a witch, and learned witches' knowledge. But she taught me gardening and carpentry, too."

"You hope to find her?"

Moon looked at him, and weighed the question seriously for the first time since the Seawood. "I hope I may learn she's been transformed, and that I can change her back. But I think I met her, last night in the wood, and I find it's hard to hope."

"But you want to go on?" the queen pressed her. "What will you do?"

"The only thing I can think of to do is what she set out for: I mean to find your son."

Moon couldn't think why the queen would pale at that.

"Oh, my dear, don't," the king said. "Our son is lost, your teacher is lost—what profit can there be in throwing yourself after them? Rest here, then go home and live. Our son is gone."

It was a fine, rich hall, and he was a fair, kingly man. But it was all dimmed, as if a layer of soot lay over the palace and its occupants.

"What did he look like, the prince?"

The king frowned. It was the queen who drew a locket out of the bodice of her gown, lifted its chain over her head and passed it to Moon. It held, not the costly miniature she'd expected, but a sketch in soft pencil, swiftly done. It was the first informal thing she could recall seeing in the palace.

187

"He wouldn't sit still to be painted," the queen said wistfully. "One of his friends likes to draw. He gave me that after...after my son was gone."

He had been reading, perhaps, when his friend snatched that quiet moment to catch his likeness. The high forehead was propped on a long-fingered hand; the eyes were directed downward, and the eyelids hid them. The nose was straight, and the mouth was long and grave. The hair was barely suggested; light or dark, it fell unruly around the supporting hand. Even setting aside the kindly eye of friendship that had informed the pencil, Moon gave the village girls leave to be silly over this one. She closed the locket and gave it back.

"You can't know what's happened to him. How can you let him go, without knowing?"

"There are many things in the world I will never know," the king said sharply.

"I met a man at the gate who still mourns the prince. He called him the heart of the land. Nothing can live without its heart."

The queen drew a breath and turned her face to her plate, but said nothing.

"Enough," said the king. "If you must search, then you must. But I'll have peace at my table. Here, child, will you pledge it with me?"

Over Moon's right hand, lying on the white cloth, he laid his own, and held his wine cup out to her.

She sat frozen, staring at the chased silver and her own reflection in it. Then she raised her eyes to his and said, "No."

There was a shattering quiet in the hall.

"You will not drink?"

"I will not...pledge you peace. There isn't any here, however much anyone may try to hide it. I'm sorry." That, she knew when she'd said it, was true. "Excuse me," she added, and drew her hand out from under the king's, which was large, but soft. "I'm going to bed. I mean to leave early tomorrow."

She rose and walked back down the length of the room, lapped in a different kind of silence.

A servant found her in the corridor and led her to her chamber. There she found her old clothes clean and dry and folded, the fire tended, the bed turned down. The red-faced woman wasn't there. She took off her finery, laid it out smooth on a chair, and put her old nightgown on. Then she went to the glass to unpin and brush her hair.

The pin was in her hand, and she was reaching to set it down, when she saw what it was. A little leaping frog. But now it was gold.

It was hers. The kicking legs and goggle eyes, every irregularity—it was her pin. She dashed to the door and flung it open. "Hello?" she called. "Oh, bother!" She stepped back into the room and searched, and finally found the bell pull disguised as a bit of tapestry.

After a few minutes, a girl with black hair and bright eyes came to the door. "Yes, ma'am?"

"The woman who helped me, who drew my bath and brought me clothes. Is she still here?"

The girl looked distressed. "I'm sorry, ma'am. I don't know who waited on you. What did she look like?"

"About my height. With a red face and wild, wispy hair."

The girl stared, and said, "Ma'am—are you sure? That doesn't sound like anyone here."

Moon dropped heavily into the nearest chair. "Why am I not surprised? Thank you very much. I didn't mean to disturb you."

The girl nodded and closed the door behind her. Moon put out the candles, climbed into bed, and lay awake for an uncommonly long time.

In a gray, wet dawn, she dressed and shouldered her pack and by the simple expedient of going down every time she came to a staircase, found a door that led outside. It was a little postern, opening on a kitchen garden and a wash yard fenced in stone. At the side of the path, a man squatted by a wooden hand cart, mending a wheel.

"Here, missy!" he called out, his voice like a spade thrust into gravel. "Hold this axle up, won't you?"

Moon sighed. She wanted to go. She wanted to be moving, because moving would be almost like getting something done. And she wanted to be out of this beautiful place that had lost its heart. She stepped over a spreading clump of rhubarb, knelt, and hoisted the axle.

Whatever had damaged the wheel had made the axle split; the long splinter of wood bit into Moon's right hand. She cried out and snatched that hand away. Blood ran out of the cut on her palm and fell among the rhubarb stems, a few drops. Then it ceased to flow.

Moon looked up, frightened, to the man with the wheel.

189

It was the man from the hay wagon, white-haired, his eyes as green and gray as sage. He had a ruddy, somber face. Red-faced, like the woman who'd—

The woman who'd helped her last night had been the one from the hay cart. Why hadn't she seen it? But she remembered it now, and the woman's green eyes, and even a fragment of hay caught in the wild hair. Moon sprang up.

The old man caught her hand. "Rhubarb purges, and rhubarb means advice. Turn you back around. Your business is in there." He pointed a red, rough finger at the palace, at the top of the near corner tower. Then he stood, dusted off his trousers, strolled down the path and was gone.

Moon opened her mouth, which she hadn't been able to do until then. She could still feel his hand, warm and calloused. She looked down. In the palm he'd held was a sprig of hyssop and a wisp of broom, and a spiralling stem of convolvulus.

Moon bolted back through the postern door and up the first twisting flight of stairs she found, until she ran out of steps. Then she cast furiously about. Which way was that wretched tower? She got her bearings by looking out the corridor windows. It would be that door, she thought. She tried it; it resisted.

He could have kept his posy and given me a key, she thought furiously. Then: But he did.

She plucked up the convolvulus, poked it into the keyhole, and said, "Turn away, turn astray, backwards from the turn of day. What iron turned to lock away, herb will turn the other way." Metal grated against metal, and the latch yielded under her hand.

A young man's room, frozen in time. A jerkin of quilted, painted leather dropped on a chair; a case of books, their bindings standing in bright ranks; a wooden flute and a pair of leather gloves lying on an inlaid cedar chest; an unmade bed, the coverlet slid sideways and half pooled on the floor.

More, a room frozen in a tableau of atrocity and accusation. For Moon could feel it, the thing that had been done here, that was still being done because the room had sat undisturbed. Nightshade and thornapple, skullcap, henbane, and fern grown bleached and stunted under stone. Moon recognized their scents and their twisted strength

190

around her, the power of the work they'd made and the shame that kept them secret.

There was a dust of crushed leaf and flower over the door lintel, on the sill of every window, lined like seams in the folds of the bed hangings. Her fingers clenched on the herbs in her hand as rage sprouted up in her and spread.

With broom and hyssop she dashed the dust from the lintel, the windows, the hangings. "Merry or doleful, the last or the first," she chanted as she swung her weapons, spitting each word in fury, "fly and be hunted, or stay and be cursed!"

"What are you doing?" said a voice from the door, and Moon spun and raised her posy like a dagger.

The king stood there, his coat awry, his hair uncombed. His face was white as a corpse's, and his eyes were wide as a man's who sees the gallows, and knows the noose is his.

"You did this," Moon breathed; and louder, "You gave him to the King of Stones with your own hand."

"I had to," he whispered. "He made a beggar of me. My son was the forfeit."

"You locked him under the earth. And let my teacher go to her...to her death to pay your forfeit."

"It was his life or mine!"

"Does your lady wife know what you did?"

"His lady wife helped him to do it," said the queen, stepping forward from the shadows of the hall. She stood tall and her face was quiet, as if she welcomed the noose. "Because he was her love and the other, only her son. Because she feared to lose a queen's power. Because she was a fool, and weak. Then she kept the secret, because her heart was black and broken, and she thought no worse could be done than had been done already."

Moon turned to the king. "Tell me," she commanded.

"I was hunting alone," said the king in a trembling voice. "I roused a boar. I...had a young man's pride and an old man's arm, and the boar was too much for me. I lay bleeding and in pain, and the sight nearly gone from my eyes, when I heard footsteps. I called out for help.

"'You are dying,' he told me, and I denied it, weeping. 'I don't want to die,' I said, over and over. I promised him anything, if he would save my life." The king's voice failed, and stopped.

191

"Where?" said Moon. "Where did this happen?"

"In the wood under Elder Scarp. Near the waterfall that feeds the stream called the Laughing Girl."

"Point me the way," she ordered.

The sky was hazed white, and the air was hot and still. Moon dashed sweat from her forehead as she walked. She could have demanded a horse, but she had walked the rest of the journey, and this seemed such a little way compared to that. She hoped it would be cooler under the trees.

It wasn't; and the gnats were worse around her face, and the biting flies. Moon swung at them steadily as she clambered over the stones. It seemed a long time before she heard the waterfall, then saw it. She cast about for the clearing, and wondered, were there many? Or only one, and it so small that she could walk past it and never know? The falling water thrummed steadily, like a drum, like a heartbeat.

In a shaft of sun, she saw a bit of creamy white—a flower head, round and flat as a platter, dwarfed with early blooming. She looked up and found that she stood on the edge of a clearing, and was not alone.

He wore armor, dull gray plates worked with fantastic embossing, trimmed in glossy black. He had a gray cloak fastened over that, thrown back off his shoulders, but with the hood up and pulled well forward. Moon could see nothing of his face.

"In the common way of things," he said, in a quiet, carrying voice, "I seek out those I wish to see. I am not used to uninvited guests."

The armor was made of slate and obsidian, because he was the King of Stones.

She couldn't speak. She could command the king of Hark End, but this was a king whose rule did not light on him by an accident of blood or by the acclaim of any mortal thing. This was an embodied power, a still force of awe and terror.

"I've come for a man and his soul," she whispered. "They were wrongly taken."

"I take nothing wrongly. Are you sure?"

She felt heat in her face, then cold at the thought of what she'd said: that she'd accused him. "No," she admitted, the word cracking with her fear. "But that they were wrongly given, I know. He was not theirs to give."

192

"You speak of the prince of Hark End. They were his parents. Would you let anyone say you could not give away what you had made?"

Moon's lips parted on a word; then she stared in horror. Her mind churned over the logic, followed his question back to its root.

He spoke her thoughts aloud. "You have attended at the death of a child, stilled in the womb to save the mother's life. How is this different?"

"It is different!" she cried. "He was a grown man, and what he was was shaped by what he did, what he chose."

"He had his mother's laugh, his grandfather's nose. His father taught him to ride. What part of him was not made by someone else? Tell me, and we will see if I should give that part back."

Moon clutched her fingers over her lips, as if by that she could force herself to think it all through before she spoke. "His father taught him to ride," she repeated. "If the horse refuses to cross a ford, what makes the father use his spurs, and the son dismount and lead it? He has his mother's laugh—but what makes her laugh at one thing, and him at another?"

"What, indeed?" asked the King of Stones. "Well, for argument's sake I'll say his mind is in doubt, and his heart. What of his body?"

"Bodies grow with eating and exercise," Moon replied. This was ground she felt sure of. "Do you think the king and the queen did those for him?"

The King of Stones threw back his cowled head and laughed, a cold ringing sound. It restored Moon to sensible terror. She stepped back, and found herself against a tree trunk.

"And his soul?" said the King of Stones at last.

"That didn't belong to his mother and father," Moon said, barely audible even to her own ears. "If it belonged to anyone but himself, I think you did not win it from Her."

Silence lay for long moments in the clearing. Then he said, "I am well tutored. Yet there was a bargain made, and a work done, and both sides knew what they pledged and what it meant. Under law, the contract was kept."

"That's not true. Out of fear the king promised you anything, but he never meant the life of his son!"

193

"Then he could have refused me that, and died. He said 'Anything,' and meant it, unto the life of his son, his wife, and all his kingdom."

He had fought her to a standstill with words. But, words used up and useless, she still felt a core of anger in her for what had been done, outrage against a thing she knew, beyond words, was wrong.

So she said aloud, "It's wrong. It was a contract that was wrong to make, let alone to keep. I know it."

"What is it," said the King of Stones, "that says so?"

"My judgment says so. My head." Moon swallowed. "My heart."

"Ah. What do I know of your judgment? Is it good?"

She scrubbed her fingers over her face. He had spoken lightly, but Moon knew the question wasn't light at all. She had to speak the truth; she had to decide what the truth was. "It's not perfect," she answered reluctantly. "But yes, I think it's as good as most people's."

"Do you trust it enough to allow it to be tested?"

Moon lifted her head and stared at him in alarm. "What?"

"I will test your judgment. If I find it good, I will let you free the prince of Hark End. If not, I will keep him, and you will take your anger, your outrage, and the knowledge of your failure home to nurture like children all the rest of your life."

"Is that prophecy?" Moon asked hoarsely.

"You may prove it so, if you like. Will you take my test?"

She drew a great, trembling breath. "Yes."

"Come closer, then." With that, he pushed back his hood.

There was no stone helm beneath, or monster head. There was a white-skinned man's face, all bone and sinew and no softness, and long black hair rucked from the hood. The sockets of his eyes were shadowed black, though the light that fell in the clearing should have lit all of his face. Moon looked at him and was more frightened than she would have been by any deformity, for she knew then that none of this—armor, face, eyes—had anything to do with his true shape.

"Before we begin," he said in that soft, cool voice. "There is yet a life you have not asked me for, one I thought you'd beg of me first of all."

Moon's heart plunged, and she closed her eyes. "Alder Owl."

"You cannot win her back. There was no treachery there. She, at least, I took fairly, for she greeted me by name and said I was well met."

"No!" Moon cried.

194

"She was sick beyond curing, even when she left you. But she asked me to give her wings for one night, so that you would know. I granted it gladly."

She thought she had cried all she could for Alder Owl. But this was the last death, the death of her little foolish hope, and she mourned that and Alder Owl at once with falling, silent tears.

"My test for you, then." He stretched out his hands, his mailed fingers curled over whatever lay in each palm. "You have only to choose," he said. He opened his fingers to reveal two rings, one silver, one gold.

She looked from the rings to his face again, and her expression must have told him something.

"You are a witch," said the King of Stones, gently mocking. "You read symbols and make them, and craft them into nets to catch truth in. This is the meat of your training, to read the true nature of a thing. Here are symbols—choose between them. Pick the truer. Pick the better."

He pressed forward first one hand, then the other. "Silver, or gold? Left or right? Night or day, moon—" she heard him mock her again, "—or sun, water or fire, waning or waxing, female or male. Have I forgotten any?"

Moon wiped the tears from her cheeks and frowned down at the rings. They were plain, polished circles of metal, not really meant for finger rings at all. Circles, complete in themselves, unmarred by scratch or tarnish.

Silver, or gold. Mined from the earth, forged in fire, cooled in water, pierced with air. Gold was rarer, silver was harder, but both were pure metals. Should she choose rareness? Hardness? The lighter color? But the flash of either was bright. The color of the moon? But she'd seen the moon, low in the sky, yellow as a peach. And the light from the moon was reflected light from the sun, whose color was yellow although in the sky it was burning white, and whose metal was gold. There was nothing to choose between them.

The blood rushed into her face, and the gauntleted hands and their two rings swam in her vision. It was true. She'd always thought so.

Her eyes sprang up to the face of the King of Stones. "It's a false choice. They're equal."

As she said the words, her heart gave a single terrified leap. She was wrong. She was defeated, and a fool. The King of Stones' fingers closed again over the rings.

"Down that trail to a granite stone, and then between two hazel trees," he said. "You'll find him there."

She was alone in the clearing.

Moon stumbled down the trail, dazed with relief and the release of tension. She found the stone, and the two young hazel trees, slender and leafed out in fragile green, and passed between them.

She plunged immediately into full sunlight and strangeness. Another clearing, carpeted with deep grass and the stars of spring flowers, surrounded by blossoming trees—but trees in blossom didn't also stand heavy with fruit, like a vain child wearing all its trinkets at once. She saw apples, cherries, and pears under their drifts of pale blossom, ripe and without blemish. At the other side of the clearing there was a shelf of stone thrust up out of the grass. On it, as if sleeping, lay a young man, exquisitely dressed.

Golden hair, she thought. That's why it was drawn in so lightly. Like amber, or honey. The fair face was very like the sketch she remembered, as was the scholar's hand palm up on the stone beside it. She stepped forward.

Beside the stone, the black branches of a tree lifted, moved away from their neighbors, and the trunk—Not a tree. A stag stepped into the clearing, scattering the apple blossoms with the great span of his antlers. He was black as charcoal, and his antler points were shining black, twelve of them or more. His eyes were large and red.

He snorted and lowered his head, so that she saw him through a forest of polished black dagger points. He tore at the turf with one cloven foot.

I passed his test! she cried to herself. Hadn't she won? Why this? You'll find him there, the King of Stones had said. Then her anger sprang up as she remembered what else he'd said: I will let you free the prince of Hark End.

What under the wide sky was she supposed to do? Strike the stag dead with her bare hand? Frighten it away with a frown? Turn it into—

She gave a little cry at the thought, and the stag was startled into charging. She leaped behind the slender trunk of a cherry tree. Cloth tore as the stag yanked free of her cloak.

196

The figure on the shelf of stone hadn't moved. She watched it, knowing her eyes ought to be on the stag, watching for the rise and fall of breath. "Oh, what a stupid trick!" she said to the air, and shouted at the stag, "Flower and leaf and stalk to thee, I conjure back what ought to be. Human frame and human mind banish those of hart or hind." Which, when she thought about it, was a silly thing to say, since it certainly wasn't a hind.

He lay prone in the grass, naked, honey hair every which way. His eyes were closed, but his brows pinched together, as if he was fighting his way back from sleep. One sunbrowned long hand curled and straightened. His eyes snapped open, focused on nothing; the fingers curled again; and finally he looked at them, as if he had to force himself to do it, afraid of what he might see. Moon heard the sharp drawing of his breath. On the shelf of stone there was nothing at all.

A movement across the clearing caught Moon's eye and she looked up. Among the trees stood the King of Stones in his gray armor. Sunshine glinted off it and into his unsmiling face, and pierced the shadows of his eye sockets. His eyes, she saw, were green as sage.

The prince had levered himself up onto his elbows. Moon saw the tremors in his arms and across his back. She swept her torn cloak from her shoulders and draped it over him. "Can you speak?" she asked him. She glanced up again. There was no one in the clearing but the two of them.

"I don't—yes," he said, like a whispering crow, and laughed thinly. He held out one spread and shaking hand. "Tell me. You don't see a hoof, do you?"

"No, but you used to have four of them. You're not nearly so impressive in this shape."

He laughed again, from closer to his chest this time. "You haven't seen me hung all over with satin and beads like a dancing elephant."

"Well, thank goodness for that. Can you stand up? Lean on me if you want to, but we should be gone from here."

He clutched her shoulder—the long scholar's fingers were very strong—and struggled to his feet, then drew her cloak more tightly around himself. "Which way?"

Passage through the woods was hard for her, because she knew how hard it was for him, barefoot, disoriented, yanked out of place and time. After one especially hard stumble, he sagged against a tree. "I hope this passes. I can see flashes of this wood in my memory, but as if my eyes were off on either side of my head."

"Memory fades," she said. "Don't worry."

He looked up at her quickly, pain in his face. "Does it?" He shook his head. "I'm sorry—did you tell me your name?"

"No. It's Moon Very Thin."

He asked gravely, "Are you waxing or waning?"

"It depends from moment to moment."

"That makes sense. Will you call me Robin?"

"If you want me to."

"I do, please. I find I'm awfully taken with having a name again."

At last the trees opened out, and in a fold of the green hillside they found a farmstead. A man stood in the farmhouse door watching them come. When they were close enough to make out his balding head and wool coat, he stirred from the door; took three faltering steps into his garden; and shouted and ran toward them. A tall, round woman appeared at the door, twisting her apron. Then she, too, began to run.

The man stopped just short of them, open-mouthed, his face a study in hope, and fear that hope will be yanked away. "Your Highness?"

Robin nodded.

The round woman had come up beside the man. Tears coursed down her face. She said calmly, "Teazle, don't keep 'em standing in the yard. Look like they've been dragged backwards through the blackthorn, both of them, and probably hungry as cats." But she stepped forward and touched one tentative hand to the prince's cheek. "You're back," she whispered.

"I'm back."

They were fed hugely, and Robin was decently clothed in linen and leather belonging to Teazle's eldest son. "We should be going," the prince said at last, regretfully.

"Of course," Teazle agreed. "Oh, they'll be that glad to see you at the palace."

Moon saw the shadow of pain pass quickly over Robin's face again.

They tramped through the new ferns, the setting sun at their backs. "I'd as soon . . ." Robin faltered and began again. "I'd as soon not reach the palace tonight. Do you mind?"

Moon searched his face. "Would you rather be alone?"

198

"No! I've been alone for—how long? A year? That's enough. Unless you don't want to stay out overnight."

"It would be silly to stop now, just when I'm getting good at it," Moon said cheerfully.

They made camp under the lee of a hill near a creek, as the sky darkened and the stars came out like frost. They didn't need to cook, but Moon built a fire anyway. She was aware of his gaze; she knew when he was watching, and wondered that she felt it so. When it was full dark and Robin lay staring into the flames, Moon said, "You know, then?"

"How I was...? Yes. Just before...there was a moment when I knew what had been done, and who'd done it." He laced his brown fingers over his mouth and was silent for a while; then he said, "Would it be better if I didn't go back?"

"You'd do that?"

"If it would be better."

"What would you do instead?"

He sighed. "Go off somewhere and grow apples."

"Well, it wouldn't be better," Moon said desperately. "You have to go back. I don't know what you'll find when you get there, though. I called down curse and banishment on your mother and father, and I don't really know what they'll do about it."

He looked up, the fire bright in his eyes. "You did that? To the king and queen of Hark End?"

"Do you think they didn't deserve it?"

"I wish they didn't deserve it." He closed his eyes and dropped his chin onto his folded hands.

"I think you are the heart of the land," Moon said in surprise.

His eyes flew open again. "Who said that?"

"A guard at the front palace gate. He'll probably fall on his knees when he sees you."

"Great grief and ashes," said the prince. "Maybe I can sneak in the back way."

They parted the next day in sight of the walls of Great Hark. "You can't leave me to do this alone," Robin protested.

"How would I help? I know less about it than you do, even if you are a year out of date."

"A lot happens in a year," he said softly.

199

"And a lot doesn't. You'll be all right. Remember that everyone loves you and needs you. Think about them and you won't worry about you."

"Are you speaking from experience?"

"A little." Moon swallowed the lump in her throat. "But I'm a country witch and my place is in the country. Two weeks to the east by foot, just across the Blacksmith River. If you ever make a King's Progress, stop by for tea."

She turned and strode away before he could say or do anything silly, or she could.

Moon wondered, in the next weeks, how the journey could have seemed so strange. If the Seawood was full of ghosts, none of them belonged to her. The plain of grass was impressive, but just grass, and hot work to cross. In Little Hark she stopped for the night, and the blond boy remembered her.

"Did you find your teacher?" he asked.

"No. She died. But I needed to know that. It wasn't for nothing."

He already knew the prince had come back; everyone knew it, as if the knowledge had blown across the kingdom like milkweed fluff. She didn't mention it.

She came home and began to set things to rights. It didn't take long. The garden wouldn't be much this year, but it would be sufficient; it was full of volunteers from last year's fallen seed. She threw herself into work; it was balm for the heart. She kept her mind on her neighbors' needs, to keep it off her own. And now she knew that her theory was right, that earth and air and fire and water were all a part of each other, all connected, like silver and gold. Like joy and pain.

"You're grown," Tansy Broadwater said to her, but speculatively, as if she meant something other than height, that might not be an unalloyed joy.

The year climbed to Midsummer and sumptuous life. Moon went to the village for the Midsummer's Eve dance and watched the horseplay for an hour before she found herself tramping back up the hill. She felt remarkably old. On Midsummer's Day she put on her apron and went out to dig the weeds from between the flagstones.

She felt the rhythm in the earth before she heard it. Hoofbeats, coming up the hill. She got to her feet.

The horse was chestnut and the rider was honey-haired. He drew rein at the gate and slipped down from the saddle, and looked at her with a question in his eyes. She wasn't quite sure what it was, but she knew it was a question.

She found her voice. "King's Progress?"

"Not a bit." He sounded just as she'd remembered, whenever she hadn't had the sense to make enough noise to drown the memory out. "May I have some tea anyway?"

Her hands were cold, and knotted in her apron. "Mint?"

"That would be nice." He tethered his horse to the fence and came in through the gate.

"How have things turned out?" She breathed deeply and cursed her mouth for being so dry.

"Badly, in the part that couldn't help but be. My parents chose exile. I miss them—or I miss them as they were once. Everything else is doing pretty well. It's always been a nice, sensible kingdom." Now that he was closer, Moon could see his throat move when he swallowed, see his thumb turn and turn at a ring on his middle finger.

"Moon," he said suddenly, softly, as if it were the first word he'd spoken. He plucked something out of the inside of his doublet and held it out to her. "This is for you." He added quickly, in a lighter tone, "You'd be amazed how hard it is to find when you want it. I thought I'd better pick it while I could and give it to you pressed and dried, or I'd be here empty-handed after all."

She stared at the the straight green stem, the cluster of inky-blue flowers still full of color, the sweet ghost of vanilla scent. Her fingers closed hard on her apron. "It's heliotrope," she managed to say.

"Yes, I know."

"Do...do you know what it means?"

"Yes."

"It means 'devotion.'"

"I know," Robin said. He looked into her eyes, as he had since he'd said her name, but something faltered slightly in his face. "A little pressed and dried, but yours, if you'll have it."

"I'm a country witch," Moon said with more force than she'd planned. "I don't mean to stop being one."

Robin smiled a little, an odd sad smile. "I didn't say you ought to. But the flower is yours whether you want it or not. And I wish you'd take it, because my arm's getting tired."

201

"Oh!" Moon flung her hands out of her apron. "Oh! Isn't there a plant in this whole wretched garden that means 'I love you, too?' Bother!"

She hurtled into his arms, and he closed them tight around her.

Once upon a time there ruled in the Kingdom of Hark End a king who was young and fair, good and wise, and responsible for the breeding of no fewer than six new varieties of apple. Once upon the same time there was a queen in Hark End who understood the riddle of the rings of silver and gold: that all things are joined together without beginning or end, and that there can be no understanding until all things divided are joined. They didn't live happily ever after, for nothing lives forever; but they lived as long as was right, then passed together into the land where trees bear blossom and fruit both at once, and where the flowers of spring never fade.

.

Made in the USA
Las Vegas, NV
10 October 2023

78887124R00125